Diviner's Nemesis II -Retribution-

Maggie Shaw

Diviner's Nemesis II -Retribution

Maggie Shaw

eregendal.com

First published in the United Kingdom in 2020
eregendal.com, Rosehill Road, Crewe, Cheshire CW2 8AR
Printed in the United Kingdom by Lulu.com

ISBN 978-1-9996071-4-2 (paperback)

Contents

INTRODUCTION
and
ACKNOWLEDGEMENTS

Diviner's Nemesis is a story of revenge, set against a backdrop of occultism and the paranormal in late 1970s London. After newlywed Liz Graham accepts the Chair of the psychic society P.S.I. she faces a conflict between love and conscience as her husband, archaeologist Alec Graham tries to bring his arch enemy Jonathan Keast to justice. Keast is equally determined to take back the society he had founded 21 years before. Will Liz overcome the evil forces ranged against her before they can destroy her? This sequel explores prescience, faith, betrayal, forgiveness and redemption as it follows the clash of two male egos through the experiences of the woman they sacrifice to their rivalry.

The story of Liz Kirkland was originally written in a series of five episodes in the 1970s. Parts 1 and 2 are contained in *Diviner's Nemesis 1: Avenger.* Parts 3, 4 and 5 are contained in this sequel, *Diviner's Nemesis 2: Retribution.* The evolution of the story over time has been influenced by the wisdom and advice of many people, most significantly Bob Thomson. I would also like to thank Helen Lamb and Roy Butler for their assistance with the manuscript. Any faults in the work are my own alone.

The motto, *The further we get from the earth, the closer we get to insanity* (page 201) was a favourite saying of the West Cumberland actor Bill Gidley. The Biblical passages quoted are from the New Revised Standard Version and the King James Version of the Holy Bible. The Tarot sequences are based on the system set out in the book *The Tarot Speaks* by Richard Gardner (Rigel Press Ltd 1971).

Prologue

Card 1: The Magician

a skilled artisan

trickery, deceit

Prologue

Dr Alec Graham was working in his book-lined study when the call he had been expecting came through from his driver Theo.

'Sandy Angus is back from Basle,' Theo confirmed: 'I followed 'im from Victoria to Downey Road. 'E went into number 15. Sam's keeping tabs in case 'e comes out again.'

'I'll come straight over. Meet you outside number 21.'

Alec put away the potsherd symbols he had been classifying for a colleague, and slipped on a heavy overcoat against the cold, cloudy late December day. He looked into the lounge on his way out to tell his wife Liz he had been called away on business. She was lying asleep on the sofa beneath a handful of magazines, her black hair cascading over the arm, her heart-shaped face gently lit by the coloured lights on the tall Christmas tree nearby. Rather than disturb her, he left a message with the housekeeper in case Liz awoke later and wondered where he was. He sped off in his black Lincoln Continental sedan, hoping to get to the address before Sandy Angus had flown again.

Downey Road was a hybrid street with modern tall apartment blocks at one end and Victorian weathered-brick terraces at the other. Theo had parked his maroon Honda Civic hatchback outside number 10 to watch number 15, his curly head pressed against the seat to make himself less visible. Beside him in the passenger seat sat his sandy-haired colleague, Sam. Alec opened the nearside rear door and slid onto the back seat.

The house they were watching was grimy and soot-streaked with unwashed curtains behind dusty windows and a peeling brown front door. It was not the sort of house a man like Sandy Angus would choose to live in while his wealthier friends had a bedroom to spare. Alec suspected either a decoy or a trap.

'Has anyone entered or left the house since you phoned?' he

asked.

They shook their heads in reply.

He nodded. 'Sam, check the back of the house. Keep an eye on things there. I'll watch the front from the Lincoln until I'm sure it's safe to go in. Theo, cover me.'

Nothing moved for half an hour after they had repositioned. Alec began to fear his quarry had long since given them the slip. He checked his revolver, concealed it in the pocket of his grey velvet suit, wrapped a scarf loosely around his bearded face, and strolled across the street to the dilapidated house. At first his forceful knock raised no answer. Then he heard the shuffle of elderly feet. An impoverished arthritic old man opened the door to him.

'You took a long time getting here, Dr Graham! You'd better come in,' the man said abruptly in a south London accent, competing against his squealing hearing aid.

'How did you know I was coming?' Alec demanded, signalling to Theo behind his back to follow him inside.

The old man tried to adjust his hearing aid and took it out in disgust. Without comment he turned his back on the open front door. He stiffly led the way along the tiled hall and up the narrow wooden stairs. Alec followed cautiously, reassured that Theo would be right behind him. As he reached the top of the stairs, the front door slammed. Startled, he turned to upbraid Theo but found no-one below. A cough made him look back up. The old man pushed open the back-bedroom door. Alec stepped warily inside and came face to face with Jonathan Keast.

The wealthy businessman was like a surreal imposition in the bare dusty room, so out of keeping with his surroundings that he was the last person Alec had expected to see there despite the elaborate nature of the trap. Keast had been standing by the cracked window, his bearded chin resting on his right hand as he watched Sam hiding in the overgrown back garden. Between him and the door stood the only piece of furniture, a dusty broken treadle sewing machine, on top of which lay a large manila envelope.

Keast gestured to Alec to come in further. He complied and shut the door behind him for protection, his hand on the butt of the revolver in his pocket, his footsteps resounding hollowly on the bare floorboards.

'Use your gun if you wish, Dr Graham, but I assure you that if you do, you will not leave this house alive.'

'Don't you intend that anyway, Mr Keast?'

Alec thought twice about his uncertain position and with a contemptuous glower at his adversary turned back for the door.

'Wait, Dr Graham. I suggest you learn why I arranged for us to meet here before you leave. After all, you wouldn't want your wife to know what really happened when your father died.'

'She already knows the truth, as you learnt when you kidnapped her.'

'Only your version of the truth. It is easy enough to place the blame on a dead drug addict who can no longer answer for himself.'

'To her he can, Mr Keast; and she knows quite well where the blame lies: not on the poor helpless drug addict but the man who sold him the drugs. Is this name-calling the only reason you lured me here? I would have thought trading family insults a dangerous game to play, considering how your affluent wife committed suicide some nineteen years ago; and your meteoric rise from obscurity to power is scattered with corpses, none of which can quite be linked back to you.'

'The unsubstantiated allegations of a government man! Did you tell your wife about that too - the trips to Chile, the Middle East, Glasgow and Crete at such significant times with your team of licensed executioners?'

Keast's grasp of the facts from the little Liz had told him four months before under duress, alarmed Alec though he took care to conceal his reaction and its implied admission. Keast was getting too dangerous, but still his leverage in political circles was enough to prevent Alec's brother Philip getting the permission to remove him and end his doubtful influence in European business circles and British affairs. The only way to obtain that permission was to gain convincing proof of Keast's depravity, or otherwise to catch him red-handed in the crossfire. But once again, even with the evidence obtained from members of the psychic society P.S.I. since Liz had deposed him, Keast had still managed to keep at least one step away from any criminal proof.

Dangerous men require dangerous methods, Alec thought, and resolved to bait a trap himself to gather the evidence to destroy Keast. He started with a natural defence.

'Government what, Mr Keast? I don't know what you're talking about! I am an archaeologist, specialising in symbolism, and considered by many to be an authority in my field. I get dozens of invitations to visit universities and museums all over the world. If these visits are occasionally at significant times, that is purely coincidental.'

Keast studied his face for several seconds after he had spoken, his expression disbelieving. At length he said, 'Isn't it unfortunate, then, Dr Graham, that I have proof of your involvement in the torching of a factory in Santiago, and a pool hall in Glasgow. The envelope beside you contains copies of some of my evidence: photographs, with the witnessed testimony of the photographer who has since died in a bar brawl in Hong Kong.'

'How convenient for you. You always did have a way with cameras.'

Alec picked up the envelope from the sewing machine and studied its contents. One of the six photographs inside was particularly incriminating, a view of Alec standing to the left of some factory gates at night, his bearded face lit by the flames as the works' name panel flamed with the blazing building. Again, Alec bluffed a lack of concern, to find out whether Keast had any more evidence. He tore the envelope with its contents in half and dropped them on the dusty floor.

'Ten percent of nothing, for another spectator. Mr Keast, why are you trying to blackmail me? What is it you want, that you will not mention until you have found some leverage against me?'

'I already have the leverage, Dr Graham: I trade silence for silence. Choose not to testify against Douglas Angus, and I shall choose not to incriminate you where it would do the most damage.'

'What, you plead for the surviving Angus twin?' Alec was astonished that Keast should think the assassin that valuable.

'In the circumstances, it's a solution I find preferable to his: disembowelling you to stop you testifying against him permanently. He is waiting outside the door for your decision.'

Alec nodded thoughtfully and placed a psychic wall around his mind as Liz had taught him, to conceal his intention to deceive as he prepared the trap which he hoped would place both Keast and Sandy Angus in his grasp.

'I am willing to barter, Mr Keast. However, I would expect a far more important guarantee than that alone for the price of my silence.'

Keast had felt the psychic barrier go up and sensed at once that Alec intended deceit. He played along to bluff him in return.

'Excellent, Dr Graham: I knew you would be a man who responds to reason. What is your price?'

'You leave my wife alone.'

Keast studied Alec's expression, at a loss to understand what sort of duplicity he was attempting in giving his enemy such a challenge. It suggested that his attitude towards his wife was one of pure possession with no element of love. Keast recalled some gossip he had heard about a young salesman Alec had recently transferred to Graplax, a company about to be linked with P.S.I. He decided to test Alec's jealousy with a taunt. Finding the requested guarantee easy to make for one who was selective about the pledges he kept, he shook his hand.

'Certainly, Dr Graham. I believe I forgot to congratulate you on your marriage at the time. Such an amenable young woman, I found; especially the last time I met her. When was it? Ah, yes, in P.S.I.'s theatre the day Rolf Krueger and Sandy Angus died. But you look puzzled. Surely Liz didn't forget to tell you about our little rendezvous.'

Alec glowered at him in contempt and turned to go. Keast laughed at his back and called out to Angus to let him pass.

Alec left Downey Road and drove home with Sam and Theo following on behind. Before he could proceed any further, he knew he had to contact his brother Philip about the developments and their implications.

The two cars arrived back at Briarbank less than three hours after Alec had left, without Liz noticing their absence. She woke up on the lounge sofa when Alec slammed the front door, and went into the hall to greet him with a kiss. Despite the heaviness of sleep in her eyes, she still looked model-perfect in her maroon velvet Sabatina dress.

'Chasing next door's cat again?' she asked. It was his usual reason for slamming the front door.

As he returned her kiss, he remembered Keast's parting statement. Feelings of betrayal coursed through him. So, she had not told him about meeting Keast that last time, had she? Then, he rationalised, he need not tell her about the trap he had laid for Keast or feel any guilt about setting her up as the bait.

'Yes, dear,' he lied, knowing she trusted him too much to pry.

She sensed his estrangement but sleepily presumed the cat had won again and returned to her magazines in the lounge while he retired to the study, not to sulk as she thought but to contact Philip by phone.

Chapter 1

Card 10: The Wheel of Fortune

Taking chances, winning or losing; compulsive unlucky gambling

Shortly after 9 a.m. on the first Friday in February, Harry Simms called at Liz Graham's office on the fourth floor of P.S.I.'s headquarters in Neptune House, hoping to see her despite having no appointment. The short, stout balding man breezed in before her secretary Terry could announce him. Liz had been gazing out of the central window behind her broad desk, her eyes watching the rush hour traffic on Tottenham Court Road but her mind elsewhere. Caught out, she made a pretence of fumbling with the cords of the venetian blinds and sat down at her desk. He sat opposite her, regarding her with concern on his kindly face.

'What have you got for me today, Uncle Harry?' she asked, trying to look interested.

He handed her a bulky bound book, a hand-written grimoire compiled by an unknown author, which looked about a hundred and fifty years old and was in a worn, faded condition. Her interest became real. She studied several pages, finding she could decipher the nigh-illegible brown ink script which had thwarted others.

'I picked it up last night, at an auction out of town; thought you might be interested. Not cheap, even though it is a transcribed copy rather than the original, but no takers so for what it is it was a snip. If you don't want it, say so: I'll easily find another buyer.'

'No, I'm interested. How much?'

He hazarded three hundred pounds expecting her to haggle, a game she enjoyed playing with him now that the cost no longer mattered to her. To his surprise, she accepted his first price and took out her cheque book. Certain something was wrong, he stayed longer to find out what it might be, chatting in the hope she would open up to him.

'Guy and Fran send their regards. They're very grateful you've put your own name and position to *The Way I See It* articles. It's given their magazine *Helicon* a great boost in the respectability ratings. With luck they may even give up *The Iron Fist* to concentrate on *Helicon*; but that might just be my wishful thinking. Are you sure you can cope with three pages a month, on top of your work here? You do look as though you've been overdoing things.'

'There have been problems,' Liz admitted. She continued more brightly, 'But not with the articles: what a good excuse they give me to lock myself in Alec's study and daydream all weekend. And Fran's told me the income is almost overtaking expenditure now, so there's a chance we'll all start getting paid soon; on a co-operative basis, of course, which'll mean I'll still get now't.'

Harry laughed with her, though he knew she was using humour to stop him enquiring further into her personal life. He gave her a fatherly look over the top of his glasses.

'And are things going better here still?'

'Oh, yes. The society has recovered from the upheaval in August and the departure of all the drug addicts after I ousted Jon Keast. Our membership drive soon brought in more people to replace them - you'll have seen our adverts around, I'm sure. Admittedly, there are a few dissenters who seem to resent the way I came into office. They resist my leadership because my way is different to Keast's way; but their voice is larger than their numbers. It's as if they're watching out for themselves because they still expect him to walk in one morning instead of me.'

'Surely that can't happen, not after all the evidence you gave the police about his drug ring here? He and his cronies must be kicking their heels in jail by now.'

'So they should be, Uncle Harry, except that it's never got anywhere near a court. Alec's furious about it, but somehow none of the strings he pulls seems to connect'.'

'That's a great pity. But life can be like that: perhaps it's a lesson your husband still has to learn.'

Harry paused as he spotted a disc of black printed yellow card half inside a newspaper on the top of Liz's high-piled in-tray. 'What is that? Is it a pentagram?'

'Sort of.' Liz picked up the disk and pointed out some of its features. 'This one looks malevolent from the way the symbols are broken. That's unusual: they're normally drawn for protection, like pentacles and Solomon's Knot. Terry found it on my car when we got to work this morning. I wonder if your grimoire has something about it.'

She leafed through the worn and faded book, shaking her head. Much of the text described the ranks of demons commanded by the king of hell, Purzson. A paragraph near the end of the book caught her attention.

'Ah, here it is: a precise description of this pentagram; and yes, it is malefic: see, here? What a coincidence I got them both today.'

The intercom buzzed. Terry informed her the P.S.I. Italia delegate Arnaldo Lucia had arrived. Harry stood up and pocketed his cheque with a smile.

'That's the rest of my tax bill taken care of. You're my favourite customer, Mrs Graham: I hope you have a wonderful time at Bethany's tonight.' He crossed to the door but turned back to add, 'And when you do decide it's time to tell someone about your problems, come round, won't you? Father Jay and I can't help you until you want to be helped.'

She nodded awkwardly, at a loss for an answer. He gave her a polite nod in reply and left. She picked up the newspaper from her in-tray and tried to control her troubled thoughts by concentrating on its front-page headlines: a gas explosion where the Angus twins used to live in northwest London, and Sir Kenneth Bywater's speech condemning back-door nationalisation. When her emotions had subsided again, she prepared her desk by throwing all the papers into her top drawer and taking out the P.S.I. Italia file.

Terry showed in the slim olive-skinned Italian delegate Arnaldo Lucia. He was an elegant ageless man in a stylish dark brown suit who was a little too proud of his appearance for Liz to feel at ease with him. They exchanged a formal handshake in greeting across the desk and sat.

'Good morning, Arnaldo. What brings you over here so suddenly?'

'The pressure is on us again, Liz. Certain factions in my country are not satisfied; yet our financial position is already poor with our lower investment returns because of our uncertain economy.'

'I thought we'd talked this out over the phone, two days ago.'

'P.S.I. Italia is not happy with your solution. Our members say we should liaise with P.S.I. France and Switzerland about it.'

'Hermann Muller was convinced that with careful thought you could find a solution without such substantial backing from Berne, if you'd only follow the plan I put forward two weeks ago.'

'Alas, my members disagree: look and see.'

Arnaldo produced a pile of documents which he quickly scattered across Liz's desk to illustrate seven points supporting his case. She realised he was using the sales technique of distracting her with lots of differently based statistics on separate sheets of paper to hide the fact that he had brought no additional ideas to the table. She tried to butt in three times without success and could only stop him by gathering all his papers together again.

'Arnaldo, why are you wasting our time? I'm sure we both have better things to do than this. If you want miracles to solve your problems, ask God. If you want P.S.I. Switzerland's help, convince Hermann Muller; if you want P.S.I. France, convince Claude Auvergne. I will not order them to assist you - I don't have that authority. Even the Annual Conference hardly has that authority.'

'That is true, Liz, but your recommendation would go a long way to assist us.'

'You already have my recommendation, and it doesn't seem to have assisted you at all! You seem determined to get your own way, and nothing less will do. But the assistance of others is a concession, not a right; and if you can't find the courage to face your problems with faith, how can you expect others to find the courage to help you? Faith is the one alternative you haven't tried yet. God made this universe, you know: God can work miracles in men too.'

'And so you come back to theism! Liz, not everyone believes in your God: each of us has our own view of God, and for many God is non-existent. You cannot ask members to walk on water when half of them are practical atheists. Even ten of your delegates fall far short of the belief your policies assume is there.'

Liz hesitated as the temptation to resign flashed through her thoughts. She set it aside and replied, 'I cannot deny that some people disagree with my views, and my policies must reflect my views so they will naturally disagree with those too. They were part of the majority that elected me into office. If you have the majority now, elect me out. I'll happily step down as soon as P.S.I. elects a new chairman into office. But beware you don't give Jon Keast an opening to return. You were Italia's vice-delegate in his time so you will fully understand what that could mean.'

Lucia dropped his head and lit up a cigarette to stall for thinking time. When he looked up again to exhale some smoke, her accusing face was still turned to him expecting his reply.

'You know very well I do not want that, Liz. You are more than just a friendlier face across this desk. You were the one who expelled his infernal drug racket and all the violence it entailed. But in one thing Mr Keast was wise. Under him we expanded gently: first into this country, then into that country; but you throw all that aside saying, "No, we shall take over the world".'

'Someone has misinformed you, Arnaldo: I am no Napoleon. We can't follow Keast's plans because August's upheaval set P.S.I. back by years. We need to actively recruit more members, to market more products and produce more new products, because our finances are no longer shored up by his roguery. We need new outlets; we need new branches. We have to grow; or we'll be forced to cash in and run on our assets, and bankrupt ourselves within ten years.'

'So you say. But that is not what our accountant Mr Kingsley says. He says things will even out soon enough.'

Arnaldo stubbed out his half-smoked cigarette, took his papers from her hands and stood up, his expression hardening.

'So, you deny me the assistance P.S.I. Italia needs, the assistance I have requested three times, and which you could give if you chose.' He put the papers back in his briefcase, his face looking as though she had deliberately delivered him a personal affront. 'Then, Madam, I shall call a formal emergency conference of delegates to consider the issue. And I shall personally make sure a vote of no confidence is brought against you when it ends!'

He marched out with a flourish. Liz stared at his back. Although she knew he was only using emotive tactics to manipulate her, shestill felt unsettled by his threats.

As soon as Arnaldo had cleared the doorway, new member of P.S.I. and M.P. Max Vincent sidled in. Liz wondered in dismay what Max wanted this time. In the five months since he had joined the politician had made his impression on her as a bombastic boor. He settled in front of the window, standing with his feet apart and his ample chest extended, ready to deliver a speech.

'I was thinking,' he began with an opening which always made her face fall: 'It seems to me we're not doing enough about this youth problem. In fact, from what I've been told, we're doing nothing at all about it in practical terms; and I've been discussing it with the British delegate Josephine Simon, so I know what I'm talking about. So what are you going to do about it, huh?'

Liz leaned on her desk, tempted to be rude but knowing that would only make him worse. Instead, she tried to out-manoeuvre him. 'I'm surprised you ask, Max: you can't have heard about the new P.S.I. discussion group some of the young members are organising, in the theatre every Wednesday evening. One or two of us older hands will be there too, to answer any questions they may have and pass on any good ideas they come up with. And depending on how things go, we'll also be giving them a page in the magazine, instead of throwing them an issue on youth every two years.'

'Yes, I had heard about that; but that doesn't help when they come up to me and say "what about the drugs issue?" And the number who have been asking me about the campaign! When's the campaign going to start? Who will be leading this year's campaign? And from you? Nothing! It doesn't even look as if we'll be having a campaign this year.'

Liz sensed Max was throwing in a joker to confuse her rather than raising a genuine issue. She cautiously enquired, 'What sort of campaign?'

'What sort? Heavens! Don't you even know that? No wonder some of the delegates are calling for an emergency debate. I suppose you don't even consider that necessary.'

'An emergency debate is only necessary if a quorum of delegates wants one. If an issue is not being sorted out by normal means or is too large for any individual or branch to decide upon, then an extraordinary meeting is called for, whether emergency or routine; and if people are worried, it is especially important to hold one. Don't try to accuse me of denying anyone their democratic rights in this society, for that is patently untrue.'

'Of course I'm not saying that,' Max amiably returned: 'It's just that when there's an issue at stake I like to see something gets done about it; and I want to make sure something gets done about this very soon.'

'Very laudable, Mr Vincent. I'm sure the young people will be delighted to welcome you to their Discussion Group in the theatre downstairs this Wednesday night, so that you can see for yourself just what is going on now, and resolve these issues you've raised.'

'Alas, Mrs Graham, I shall be at the House again that evening. But I shall make sure I keep informed.'

Max bade her good day and strolled out. After he had gone Liz reflected for a few moments on the mounting pressures being placed on her from all directions. Self-pity tempted her to fear she was breaking under the strain, but she rallied her spirits with the thought that her Higher Power would only permit her to face as much stress as she could handle.

Bethany's arrival an hour later came as a welcome change from her poor attempts to concentrate on her work, as did the fresh pot of coffee Terry sent in with her. Her friend for many years, Bethany had long copper-coloured hair and was wearing a designer-cut dark green wool suit. She breezed in with her mouth in gear before her eyes had engaged.

'Morning, Madam Chair. How's things? Got some rather important news for you about a wax effigy someone... Christ, Liz, you look awful. What's up?'

'Just pretending to be an emotional football again,' Liz said, referring to a time ten years before when Bethany had rightly accused her of being as much.

'As long as no-one's scored a goal with you this time. Seriously though, Liz, isn't it time you left him? He's destroying you, you know, bit by bit. Marriage vows don't say anything about staying put till you're destroyed.'

'Maybe not, Bethany, but I couldn't leave him. I couldn't even threaten it - what if he thought I meant it?'

'Fine. So you do still love him - then give up your position here. Everything was hunky-dory before you told him we'd seen a car called PS 1, so presumably it can all be hunky-dory again if you stop being a footloose career-orientated working wife by going home for good and giving him lots of babies instead.'

Liz smiled wryly at Bethany's polarised analysis of her situation and gently shook her head. 'No, that's not the problem; and no, I don't want to leave here either: this is where I belong.' She stood up to look out across the grey streets of the capital, and explained, 'Here I have the opportunity to put my ideals into practice. It's the work of a lifetime, and I want to give my life to it.'

'Then you'll have to be quick: you'll die of starvation by Easter!'

Bethany joined her at the window.

'Liz, I'm a member of your club only by default, not design, so stop preaching to me. At the conference six months ago, you spoke about a house divided. Isn't that what's happening to you now? If you don't want to tell me about it or you can't tell me, fair enough: I'll get over it. But you won't get over it, not if you keep it all bottled up inside.' Bethany's scolding tone relented, and her usual bright manner returned. 'And now, if you'll drive me there, I'll take you to lunch at this great little restaurant I've just discovered a couple of miles away; table already booked, even the parking space reserved.'

Liz accepted the invitation with a nod and an appreciative smile. Bethany's practical help and the unexpected calm in the battle's midst, came like a day of sunshine in the long winter. She put on her blue Sabatina coat and picked up her handbag. Bethany followed her out of the office, tipping Terry a wink as they passed.

1 : 2

The bistro was crowded, but even at the height of the lunch hour rush its friendly staff still managed a personal touch. Liz responded well to the relaxed atmosphere, making Bethany hesitate to raise business during their meal for fear of spoiling her appetite: it was a long time since she had seen Liz eat so heartily. Only when they had both finally conceded defeat to their portions of gateau did Bethany venture off their sociable tone.

She opened her voluminous handbag and took out a crude three-inch doll which she dropped onto the white tablecloth with an expression of extreme distaste. The ugly manikin had been handmade from wood, feathers and black cloth, and its head had been painted on back to front. Liz reached for it with great interest, having recently read an article about voodoo dolls. As soon as her hand touched the effigy, she went pale and clutched the table for support. The doll fell to the floor. Bethany caught Liz before she fell too and urgently called for a waiter to bring water. Her flustering attracted the attention of the people around them, much to Liz's embarrassment once her mind focused again. She said to those nearby that she must have been overdoing things and waited until she was no longer the centre of attention before she returned the conversation to the doll.

'It was another premonition, Beth.'

'Don't you have enough problems already, without premonitions of more?'

Liz nodded reflectively. 'Where did you find it?'

'In the glove box of your car.'

'What? You didn't tell me? You just let me drive across London with a thing like that in the car?' Her raised voice attracted the attention of those nearby again.

'I couldn't help it! I only found it by accident when you asked me to get out a hankie. This fine specimen is the fourth little nasty to turn up so far. That's why Terry asked me to keep an eye on you while you're out and about today. And she's worried you might still be carrying the first one around with you - a malevolent pentagram, I think she said.'

Liz nodded and produced the yellow and black disc of card from her handbag, together with the grimoire. 'There's no real cause for concern, Beth. These are man-made: God's protection will be more than enough to counteract any malice focused in them.'

'But you almost flipped just now, and you barely touched that doll!'

'That was something different. These things only work if the maker's willpower to curse is stronger than the victim's peace of mind. If it makes you feel better, there's a standard method of self-protection you can try. Concentrate deeply and say the incantation *ca-ro-me* slowly ten times and know without a shadow of a doubt that the curse will go with the words and vanish on the wind when you've finished. But beware, if you don't have complete conviction, you're only indulging in wishful thinking and the curse will remain, because the magician's willpower has proved to be stronger than your own. Go on, have a go with this voodoo doll.'

Her knowing manner riled Bethany enough to take up the challenge to spite her. Far from sustaining the conviction though, Bethany burst out laughing halfway through and had to give up.

'And that's why there aren't many wizards around these days - too much cynicism,' Liz declared smugly. 'You say this doll is the fourth threat. What else has turned up?'

'A regular little battery of nasties, apparently. Yesterday evening Pete Corrie found a Runic curse pinned to a copy of your photograph in an article you'd written for the P.S.I. magazine. And this morning Terry found a wax effigy melting on her radiator, studded with fingernail parings in your shade of maroon nail varnish. Heaven knows what will turn up next - beheaded cockerels and assorted entrails, I suspect.'

'That's unlikely. Only childish perverts with a taste for gore go in for sacrificial witchcraft these days. This is something much more subtle. I'll ask Charles Lafayette to get the P.S.I. Britain clairvoyants to read them. The only problem is getting these things over to Neptune House without me taking them, and without muddying their psychic traces even more.'

'Don't ask and stop hinting,' Bethany said in a resigned voice: 'I'll take them back with me in a taxi.'

Half an hour later they met up again in Charles' office on the second floor of Neptune House. The lean, gentle Frenchman greeted them warmly and ushered them in to sit with him at his desk.

'You are here about some menacing artefacts, I believe, ladies.'

Liz nodded. Bethany opened a paper bag and emptied out the four evocations of the evil eye for Charles to inspect. He looked at the sorry collection; the wax effigy, the malefic pentacle, the voodoo doll and the Runic curse; and laughed softly to reassure them both, knowing that such supernatural threats were only effective when they raised panic or alarm in the intended victim.

'These? These would not harm you,' he said.

'Really? Then why did Liz have a premonition when she touched the voodoo doll? And don't say we imagined it: Liz entertained a whole restaurant-full of witnesses.'

'That is a separate psychic phenomenon. These things tell us someone is trying to scare you, Liz. If you had a premonition of misfortune while handling one of them, the maker must intend personally to do more than frighten.'

'That's what I fear, Charles. Could you ask someone to check them, please? I'm not sure if I'm seeing straight at present. And I have to go over to P.S.I. Chelsea this afternoon, to see Pete Corrie about some press specs.'

'Certainly, Liz. Give Pete my regards. And try not to worry. That would only give your adversary a better chance to win.'

Pete Corrie was waiting for Liz at the reception of the Peace and Sincerity Institute in Chelsea when she arrived with Bethany still in tow. Pete had become the manager of the printing house in Douglas Angus' stead after the landslide election placing Liz in office. He took them up to his panelled first-floor office. The atmosphere in the room was business-like and calm. Pete sat confidently at the far side of the broad desk, his shirt sleeves rolled up and his jacket hanging forgotten on the coat rack. He opened the conversation with his distinctive mannerism of stretching his arms behind his neck and bringing his clasped hands over his head onto the desk.

'Before we get down to business, Liz; did you hear about my find here last night?'

'Bethany told me this lunchtime.'

'Terry thought that in the circumstances the news would be better broken by a friend,' Bethany said. 'Mr Lafayette seems to think it's all just someone's sick idea of a joke.'

'It could be, but I'm not so sure. Rumours take time getting to us here at P.S.I. Chelsea, and I don't like what I'm hearing now. It's far more than a curse on a snapshot, Liz: someone is trying to undermine your position; and who else would that be than Jon Keast?'

His suggestion astounded Bethany. She saw Liz falter and quickly scoffed at the idea to rally her friend's spirits. 'Rumour-mongering, perhaps, Mr Corrie; but silly little dolls too? Hardly Mr Keast's style - kidnapping at gunpoint is more in his line.'

'The unexpected is always his line when he is crossed, Miss Broome. How else could he have survived here as long as he did?'

'No, Pete; I know that Jon Keast hasn't gone for good, but I don't see him in this - his presence would have coloured my premonition.' Liz continued more brightly in an abrupt change of subject: 'While we're on the subject of powerful men, you will be interested to hear that in response to our enquiry about computerised typesetting machines, the great Sir Kenneth Bywater has invited me to lunch on Wednesday.'

'The man himself!' Pete remarked, amused rather than impressed. 'You are honoured indeed, considering our order, even if we place it all with Concordia, will be worth peanuts against their monthly turnover. Presumably I am not invited, and the hard sell comes after the cosy chat in the directors' dining room.'

'Correct, Pete. What a disappointment when he discovers I don't drink! My intentions are to stall any decision until your team has a chance to check their claims. It would help me to know what I'll be talking about, so I'd like you to show me what you use at present and explain what you need to replace it. I'd also like to take your list of specifications with me, to keep the Concordia sales team on the right lines.'

'No problem: I can take you down and around right now if you want...'

The telephone interrupted him with a call for Liz from Neptune House. She stood up to take the receiver from him. Her confident manner swiftly dissolved.

'Hello, Charles. What have you found?'

'Nothing that would be better for being heard sooner,' he warned. 'We started with the voodoo doll because of its significance for you. Mary Sebastian checked it first as she was the only consistent clairvoyant we could find at such short notice; but Bill Wilson came in a short time ago and seconded what Mary said. The main indications so far, are that the doll seems to have been made by a member: Mary says a man but Bill is unsure. Whoever it is, the person knew enough about psychic matters to confuse the aura. We can only suspect the rest, but we will work on it further. It would appear that if you do not capitulate in some way, you may be capitulated; so to speak.'

'Do you mean, a traitor in the ranks wants to kill me?' Liz asked in disbelief to clarify his imagery.

'I would not state it that strongly myself; but yes, if you do not compromise, even that could be on the cards.'

Liz paled in dismay and dropped the receiver into its cradle, cutting off the call.

1 : 3

Liz arrived back at her Tudor-style detached home Briarbank shortly before five. She parked her white Oldsmobile outside the front door beside a lime green Marcos sports car which was blocking the driveway to her garage. As she let herself in, Alec came out into the hall to comment about how early she was. She fondly returned his light kiss on the cheek.

'P.S.I. Britain forecasted a bit of trouble for me, so Charles Lafayette sent me home early. Whose is the green sports job in the drive?'

'Greg Vincent, one of my sales team from Birmingham. You've probably heard me mention the name before. Come and meet him.'

Greg Vincent was sitting in an armchair in the lounge, looking very much at home as he sipped a cup of tea. He was a handsome, aloof young man in his late twenties, with a bright but mocking smile. His aura suggested to Liz that he was a good salesman with a latent psychic talent who was still relatively immature for the circles in which he moved. She sat down on the sofa to make conversation.

'If you're from Birmingham, you must be one of the Graplax reps, Greg.'

'For my sins, yes: I've just transferred there, to start an export campaign. I'm stopping off in London for a couple of days to pay a few calls on the family before I go across to the continent.'

'We were just discussing the international situation when you came in,' Alec said casually.

Liz sensed the salesman's unvoiced contradiction of her husband's statement.

'Really? And what are your conclusions?' she enquired to draw them, shielding her spirit to foil Greg's automatic but untrained psychic attempts to assess her.

'Alec believes this is a time for everyone to work together to overcome the state of flux in the European economic situation,' he replied, effortlessly side-stepping her attempt to call their bluff. 'I maintain that in a short while EEC measures will ease the problems and economic life will return to a more balanced norm.'

Liz hardly took in what he said for the turmoil in her head at hearing him refer to Alec by his first name. When he looked for a response, she hastily turned his last words back on him. 'The EEC? That fine amalgamation of countries is still conducting a subtle but very vicious economic war.'

'Nonsense, Liz! You really shouldn't comment on financial matters - you know it's not your metier,' Alec scoffed in a patronising tone she did not appreciate.

'I was only teasing. After the day I've had at work, I'm all too ready to tilt at shadows.'

'You work?' Greg remarked, but his surprise was false: Liz felt certain he already knew about her job at P.S.I. and suspected from the familiar surname that she was being set up.

'Liz is the chairwoman of an international organisation working for greater understanding of psychic matters,' Alec replied for her, giving her a reassuring smile.

'A pressure group? For fortune tellers?' Greg scoffed.

'Not quite. I find some of your plastic products a little absurd too,' Liz coldly returned.

'Don't mock too much, Greg,' Alec warned, much to her surprise: 'This fortune tellers' pressure group is well-established in fourteen countries in Europe and the Middle East, and it runs a successful publishing house in London too. And despite a considerable upheaval last year, it's about to embark on a programme of expansion.'

'Really? Then your society has quite a lot in common with Graplax, and our recovery plans,' Greg remarked, revealing to Liz why Alec had just supported her.

'Indeed, Greg,' Alec said: 'And quite a few of its members are influential people in their own right: it has well-placed contacts in the government and commerce of every country where it has a base.'

'Then we have the benefit of your organisation's influence to assist Graplax in its recovery programme?' Greg eagerly asked Liz. He had been warned to expect her suddenly sour expression and stony face.

'Liz doesn't quite see things that way, do you, Liz?'

'You know very well why I do not. I don't think we need to go into all that again.'

'For Greg's benefit.'

She looked thoughtfully at her husband and resolved to give him such a surprise that he would not try such a trick on her again. With a brittle smile she forcefully replied, 'The Psychic Society is a non-profit-making organisation working to promote greater understanding of psychic issues and to educate people involved in psychic matters. We publish literature on psychic issues and we train psychics like you, Greg, to develop their talents to the greatest effect. Graplax, on the other hand, is just one small part of Alec's father's industrial empire, and a pretty sick part by all accounts. Could a person honestly do justice to either interest selling both mysticism and plastic? P.S.I.'s strength dissipates easily enough already without carrying the weight of an unsteady industry on its shoulders too.'

'Surely the increased revenue P.S.I. would receive in commission would help your society to expand further faster,' Greg suggested.

'If commercial interests were pulling the strings, P.S.I. could no longer be unbiased. It is important for the society to reach as wide an audience as possible, and to do that it must remain impartial.'

'Then, er, how can you stay unbiased when you are married to Alec?'

'Don't try Liz on that one!' Alec laughed.

'With difficulty,' she retorted, cutting his humour dead.

Greg sensed from her tone and Alec's expression that he would be wise to make his apologies and leave them to continue their argument without him around to use as their foil. He diplomatically said his parents would be expecting him home for dinner soon and escaped their battleground before Alec went too far for him.

Liz took the opportunity of Greg's departure to park her car in the open garage, though Sam or Theo would automatically have done it for her, and snatched a few moments alone to clear her thoughts before she faced the impending continuation of the morning's argument. She re-entered the house by the kitchen door and found the housekeeper Mrs B preparing vegetables for dinner at the sink while Theo worked repairing a timer at the breakfast table. On impulse, Liz asked them for their views about Greg

Vincent.

'So you've met Dr Graham's friend, then,' Mrs B commented, directing her expression of disapproval towards the sink.

''E comes from Essex originally, but 'e lives in Solihull now. 'Is dad's a member of your lot: Max Vincent, that new MP.'

Liz sighed to hear the confirmation that the surname had not been coincidental and that the salesman had known far more about her than he had indicated. She thanked them both and hurried back to face her husband armed with the new ammunition.

Alec had planned to use silence to intimidate his wife. When he saw her resolute expression as she entered the lounge, he recognised he would have to speak at once or give her the advantage.

'Why did you humiliate me in front of my guest?'

She poured herself a cup of lukewarm tea and sat on the sofa, her cold calm appearance not betraying the whirlpool of negative emotions within. Once settled she answered, 'Because you were using the situation to force me to say yes to your proposal, because you know I will never choose to accept it while you stay as you are.'

'Why do you refuse to listen to reason? You haven't yet sacked your secretary, even though we both know she could betray you to Keast at any time. So I suggest this one little thing to protect your position, but you refuse it point blank. Why, even Greg sees why Graplax and P.S.I. should join forces. But do you?'

'Greg doesn't know all the facts: you won't tell him, and you won't let me; so his suggestion is unfounded. Except, of course, that his father is a member of P.S.I. and has also been having a go at me today. Or is that a coincidence too, as you would have me believe.'

'Of course that was no coincidence. Greg's suggestion has much more foundation than you realise. Why do you constantly refuse to put my offer of a link with Graplax to the P.S.I. delegates to consider? Are you frightened a merger would weaken your own power and position? Yet the longer you deliberately ignore the offer, the easier it will be for men like Max Vincent to get the members to throw you out, when he tells them you blocked an arrangement which could bring only benefit to both sides.'

His admission about Max Vincent, with all its implications of betrayal, took Liz aback. She turned on him, suddenly spitting fire.

'Alec, can't we have even one evening without all this?'

Her unguarded response played into his hand. He remonstrated with a patronising gibe to make her feel the one at fault.

'Liz, what is the matter with you? This last month has been like living with a scorpion.'

'Sure, and to me the past three months have been like living with a high-pressure salesman. Won't you ever give up telling me you're right and I'm wrong?'

'Of course I'm right: any fool could see the logic in my argument; but do you? I must have married an imbecile.'

She gazed at him in startled affront. 'Thank you for those few kind words, my dearest dear. Now, if you have finished and can excuse me, I shall go shower and change for our dinner date.'

She stalked out and went upstairs, tense and troubled.

The therapeutic properties of the shower helped restore Liz's emotional equilibrium. She began to rue their latest heated exchange. Knowing her angry response to Alec's inconsiderate pressure had only made him worse, she sought a way to make up with him. When she turned off the shower, she heard him moving about in the bedroom. She quickly towelled herself dry in her bathrobe and peeped cheekily round the bathroom door.

'I know, Alec: let's pretend it's Lima all over again and you're about to catch out the know-it-all Sampsons from the next suite. I'll wear that red dress again, and do my version of that awful dance Greta Sampson did after dinner.'

'If it would make you feel better,' Alec conceded magnanimously, restraining himself from the temptation to order her to hurry up.

He turned aside to check his appearance in the wardrobe mirror, satisfied that the slightly broader tie and the matching powder blue handkerchief in the top pocket of his charcoal grey suit, achieved the formal artistic air he wanted to create. He was so preoccupied with his image that Liz sneaked up on him unnoticed. She swung back the wardrobe door, wrapped her half-naked body around his and kissed his lips with passion.

He flinched. Then he deliberately turned his face aside, putting her away from him with an expression of disdain. She stepped back, horrified to discover how unacceptable he found her advances, and hastily covered her body with her bathrobe before she offended him further. Deeply hurt, she silently dressed in a slate grey velvet frock and mechanically arranged her long black hair. She made up her dismayed face with uninspired artistry, wishing she did not have to go out with him after such a rebuff.

They arrived at Ainhurst on time and received a warm welcome from Bethany's parents Stanley and Jenny Broome. Sculptor Stanley classed Alec as one of his few intellectual equals, and Jenny had always liked Liz for being a reliable and caring friend to their daughter. They ushered them into the austere hall where Bethany was standing with her latest boyfriend, Hugh. Bethany's new admirer was a smart, conservatively dressed young man, the antithesis of everything her former much-missed rogue of a lover Mike had been.

While Jenny completed the introductions, Bethany gathered coats and deposited them on a nearby couch. Stanley had originally placed the couch in the hall so that visitors could sit and contemplate one of his early sculptures standing on the far side of the parquet floor. Bethany saw Liz switch on a broad false smile as Hugh shook her hand during the introductions and knew at once that something was wrong. Though her main aim that evening was to ensure Hugh impressed her parents as a suitable suitor with excellent career prospects, she also resolved to find out once and for all what was upsetting Liz.

The dinner went well despite Jenny's nervous steerage as hostess. When Stanley and Alec tried to dominate the conversation with esoterics, Hugh politely turned away and strove to impress Jenny with his interest in homely matters and his work in investment banking. Jenny sensed that though Hugh was infatuated with her daughter, Bethany was only leading him on, and diplomatically tried to warn him without saying as much. Bethany kept glancing at Liz through the meal, concerned about her unnatural quietness. Then she saw Liz thirstily watching Alec's wine glass as he raised it from the table to his lips, and knew that whatever was wrong was very serious indeed.

After the meal, Bethany offered to wash up and press-ganged Liz into helping her. In the kitchen, the two friends resumed their twenty-year-long conversation and a natural smile returned to Liz's face. Bethany deftly interspersed little personal enquiries through their chatter, which Liz avoided answering with the trusting innocence of one who did not realise she was being quizzed. All Bethany gleaned was that Alec had begun to act as everyone except Liz had always expected of him, but that Liz was desperately trying to pretend he was not. As Liz hung up the damp tea towel and turned towards the hall, Bethany caught her hand to hold her back.

'Liz, I know something's wrong, and if you don't want to talk about it, I'll understand. But you did prove to me a few months back that a problem shared is a problem halved, and I would really like to return that favour if I can.'

Liz patted her hand in gratitude, her eyes glistening. 'I know, Beth; and thanks for saying that. But there are some things one doesn't talk about outside the home.'

'Fine: then I'll call round tomorrow and see you at Briarbank instead.'

The look of fear which passed over Liz's face alarmed her. She grasped her shoulders to implore her to say what was wrong.

'Liz, I don't care if you've made a vow of silence to the Archangel Gabriel! If you don't tell someone soon, you'll make yourself ill.'

'It's not the silence,' Liz admitted softly: 'it's the indecision that's the killer.'

She pulled away from Bethany, unable to say more. Bethany let her go and followed her back to the lounge to re-join the others. At the end of the evening, Bethany watched her leave with Alec and knew from her face he was taking her back to an emotional jail. She resolved to ask their priest Father Jay to help her free Liz from her prison of silence, and turned back to smile at Hugh, not realising that she was using him as much as Alec had always used Liz.

1 : 4

Liz and Alec hardly spoke during the journey back to Briarbank. Tension crackled in the air as the limousine drew up on the shingle drive. They stalked stiffly from the car into the well-lit house. Liz hung her coat on the stand and tried to slip off upstairs to bed, but Alec stopped her and ordered her into the lounge. He poured himself a whiskey. When she saw his courtesy did not extend to her, she opened a bottle of soft ginger ale and poured it into a wine glass with a shaking hand.

'You know I take a dim view of you discussing our business with other people, Liz.'

She chose not to answer his unfounded accusation, which riled him more.

'I thought I'd made it quite plain; our marriage is off limits to everyone else. No more drumming up support from all and sundry for your ridiculous stance against my perfectly rational business proposition. You like to talk about the responsibilities of your work - it's about time you thought of your responsibilities to me.'

'I don't try to change you, Alec, so stop trying to change me. No amount of pressure will force me to alter my decision and say yes. And if you're going to start quoting the responsibilities of marriage, what about our commitment for a family? Or am I meant to manage that without you too?'

'You little slut! I should throw you out right now!'

'You may not need to - there's only so much a person can take. I dread our times alone together these days because I know exactly what's going to happen.'

'But what can you do about it? - sleep in another room? - eat at different times? - go out when I come home?'

'Of course not: that would only prove what a prison our marriage could be. If you refuse to cease this infernal pressure, you leave me only two courses of action, either to resign from P.S.I. or...'

'Leave P.S.I.? And let all your dear new friends travel the wrong way again? Oh, no: you couldn't do that!'

'Or leave you.'

'Oh, you wouldn't do that either!' He laughed scornfully. 'How would you get by? You wouldn't have all your fine clothes or your jewellery any more, or a beautiful home and a chauffeur-driven car. It would be back to a poky bedsitter with a beast of a landlord and shared vegetarian meals with student neighbours because you can't afford meat, and sweat-shop hours for promises at the Print Workshop. No, you can't afford to walk out on me!'

Liz set down her glass before its contents betrayed her agitation.

'Do you really believe that, Alec? That whatever I might earn, I would never rise out of that existence without you? Because if you do, you don't know me very well.'

'Don't you understand, woman? Your prestigious position with P.S.I. is only yours because you are married to me. Walk out of here, and you can safely walk out of your career there too. What will Keast fear from you once you are no longer protected by my wealth, my experience, and my social standing?'

'What utter rubbish, Alec! You're so wrapped up in your status and your pride. Why on earth did you marry me?'

'Why? I was foolish enough to believe from your performance that you could supply everything my life lacked. But you refuse to give enough of yourself.'

'You accuse me of refusing to give? Alec, I have bent over backwards to change myself in every way you asked, whenever it didn't compromise my beliefs. No, I know why you married me - it was just as Jon Keast said: to get financial control of your father's estate so that you can buy that mansion you're after in Cheshire and play Lord of the Manor. I was the perfect choice, wasn't I: how I would fool your mother Goldie, how I would impress Philip, how I would make the perfect lady at your side; how I would let you get your hands on the money!'

She stood up to clasp his arms and implored, 'Alec, I have never wanted you for your bank balance. I've always wanted you for you. I love you...'

He threw her off in disgust. 'What is love, more than a fancy word for lust and greed. Your demonstrativeness sickens me, but I live with it. So you live with it too!'

Liz paled and stepped back in dismay. Suddenly she saw a different explanation for Greg Vincent's presence when she had arrived home early from work.

'You mean, this is all just another charade? No, Alec, I can't live with that. If you don't love me, I have no reason to stay.'

She took off her earrings, her bracelet, her brooch and her engagement ring, her small mementos of happier occasions with him, and placed them in a little pile on the coffee table. All she kept on was her wedding ring and the crucifix she had worn since she had come of age.

'Take back your jewellery: I have no need to pawn it,' she said, and picked up her handbag to go.

He saw her resolute face and realised he must have miscalculated: he had not expected her to walk out on him when it was so late in the evening.

'Liz, don't be such a fool!' he protested, grasping hold of her. 'There is no need to be so dramatic just because we disagree about a couple of matters. Sit down while I get Mrs B to make us some supper and we can talk this out properly.'

'It isn't just because we disagree, Alec: it's because you're destroying me,' she whispered, choking back her tears.

She wrenched herself free and fled from him, determined to escape at last from the hell he was creating around her. Heedless of his astonished calls for her to come back, she ran to the garage and started up the white Oldsmobile. As she drove out onto the shingle drive, he stood in front of the car to stop her, his arms raised. She ignored him and pressed harder on the accelerator. The limousine leapt forward, spraying shingle across the drive. He dived aside onto the lawn to get out of her way and helplessly watched her car turn out of the drive onto the road.

1 : 5

The Manse doorbell rang. Father Jay left Bethany where they had been chatting in the lounge and went to answer the front door. He was a tall, lean man with a long well-worn face and a loosely tied long ponytail. As Bethany had warned him, Liz Graham was standing outside in the porch light, hunched and tearful. He welcomed her with a warm smile and ushered her into the kitchen, anticipating a time for confidences.

'What's happened, Lisbeth?'

She struggled to speak but could only cry in response to his sympathy. He settled her down at the kitchen table with a box of paper handkerchiefs and a mug of tea, and waited for her to bring her emotions under some control.

'I'm sorry, Father Jay: I didn't mean to be like this,' she said at length. 'I've left Alec.'

The priest made a sympathetic comment. He had ministered to

a congregation long enough to have learnt that husbands and wives often left each other for good, only to be happily back together again before a week was out; though this did not make the sorrow between times any the less acute.

'What happened?'

'It was the last straw. So I walked out; drove off.' She struggled to hold back her tears on making such an admission.

'This had been brewing for some time, hasn't it?'

She nodded awkwardly and sipped her tea.

'Then why didn't you come to see me sooner, Lisbeth?'

She shrugged her shoulders. 'At first it wasn't too bad - I just laughed it all off. But now he's completely changed, since January. It's like living with a high-pressure salesman. And we haven't made love once this year. I did wonder if it was all some sort of blackmail, to make me say yes to his confounded proposal, but now I'm not so sure.'

'You think there is someone else?'

'I don't know what to think.' She told him about Alec and Greg, and Alec's relentless pressure on her to link P.S.I. with Graplax which had finally pushed her too far. Father Jay listened, holding her in prayer as he waited for the right words to speak into her situation. When she ran out of words he gently replied.

'Lisbeth, could it be your emotions are blinding your vision a little? You say Alec doesn't love you. I think he does. Might he not be finding it harder to prove that to you now when you are a capable woman of the world in your own right as well as by him?'

'No, it's not as simple as that. I told you once, after I'd got engaged to Alec, that I'd given up the bad boys for good. Then I found out how ruthless Alec can be, last August. I accepted that because I believed he loved me. But now his emotional blackmail is destroying me. He must think nothing of me: the restrained affection he parades in public is just a charade. When we argue he drops his mask; and then all you see are the pound signs underneath.'

'Have you thought about why he hides behind his pride and his wealth, even from you? He must feel very insecure if he acts like that all the time.'

'Oh, he doesn't hide it, he flaunts it. When I finally let on I saw through him he was furious. He doesn't want a wife: he just wants another expensive possession to show off to his friends, to go with his big house and his Stanley Broome sculpture, while he cashes in his father's estate to buy a mansion he doesn't need either. But I answer back more than his other possessions. When I won P.S.I. from his rival Jon Keast, he saw what a mistake he'd made about me: I'm not just his sweet little showpiece to model a Sabatina wardrobe and display a small fortune in jewellery. I'm a real person in my own right.'

'If that is the case, don't you think you might have acted too?'

Liz thought about his question before answering him. He saw a conventional facade steal back into her manner, and with it that insidious play-acting which was such an integral part of life in the circles where she had come back to live.

'I don't think I acted too. Not that I'm any the less to blame for this than Alec. I think my fault has been in giving too much.' Her superficial tone of voice belied her words, saddening Father Jay.

'I know that in your own way you give more than you take, Lisbeth; but are you remembering here to forgive? How much chance are you giving; and how honest are you really being to yourself? You knew that help is here; yet for two months you've played the martyr and told no-one about your problems. Is that not also a form of pride? Why was it that Harry Simms and Bethany both told me of their concern about you before you thought to come here? Why have you only turned up now?'

'I made a promise to Alec before we got married, not to discuss our private life outside. I didn't want to break that promise.'

'Ah.' Father Jay paused and then said, 'I know how hurt you feel, but I can offer little more than words of consolation unless you let me help you see a truer picture. When I married you and Alec, I wondered whether your love for each other would be strong enough to bridge the gulf of beliefs between you; but you both looked so proud and happy together that I thought my prayers for your future as a couple would be answered.'

He broke off to pour himself more tea, and continued, 'None of us thought at your wedding in June that in August you would win all you did. The psychic matters I tend to face are on the divine plane, where your society stays very firmly in the mundane levels; but even so, I can see that our Lord has given you a place of great opportunity for taking part in the Divine Plan. Naturally the devil seeks to discourage you - he wouldn't be the devil if he didn't.'

Her facial expression told him his words had hit home. He tried to reinforce his point.

'The devil tempts you away from God's purpose, Lisbeth: he is using his followers to ensnare you in a web of intrigue and despair to make you give up your work. Your silence has helped him. Keep faith in God, to keep the evil one at bay. Ask God for divine help with this heavy burden. He will ease its weight from your shoulders if you ask him to.'

'Of course,' she whispered, reading more into his words than he had intended.

'If you like I could speak to your husband on your behalf?'

A look of panic crossed her face. 'Please, no, Father Jay - then he'll know for certain I've been talking about him behind his back,' she pleaded with a fear he knew was no act.

'But if I don't speak to him your marriage is finished, isn't it? You won't go back to him of your own accord or try again. So there's nothing to be lost.'

She hesitated and then said, 'Uncle Harry told me once that marriage is a simple contract between two people to try to love each other, and God is love so He won't be cruel enough to force those two people to go on living with each other when their lives together are hell.'

'You swore before God to try. I don't doubt that you have

tried, but are you now? If you still love him, you wouldn't stop till you were certain every possible avenue open to you had failed.'

'I don't want to go back to that hell, Father Jay.'

There was a crash in the lounge. Liz spun round towards the door in alarm, fearing Alec had already traced her there.

'Calm yourself: that'll be Bethany getting bored. She came around to warn me you might turn up and I left her in the lounge,' Father Jay reassured. 'It's your choice, Lisbeth, whether I see him or no; but I do assure you that at this stage you have nothing more to lose.'

'All right then, if you must. But Alec will have to do a lot of changing before I consider going back.'

Father Jay let that one ride and ushered Bethany into the kitchen. She sat down beside Liz with a cheerful greeting and gave her a big hug.

'A bit late in the day, but you finally made it here, Liz. What happened?'

'Alec and I had another row. This time I walked out.'

'Quite right too! You should have done it several weeks ago. Would you like a place to stay?'

Liz nodded. 'If you can find a spare toothbrush.'

'And some face wipes – your mascara's given you cheek stripes.'

Liz left with Bethany soon after. Father Jay watched them go, relieved that Liz would be staying in a safe place that night. As soon as the limousine had driven away, he phoned Briarbank. Alec asked him to call round despite it being nearly midnight.

Alec received the priest in his lounge. His manner was strained and diffident as he tried to hide his bewilderment at the unexpected turn of events. He offered a drink, which Father Jay politely refused. As they sat down, the priest noticed the little pile of gold jewellery Liz had left on the coffee table. It told him she did not plan to come back.

'Your wife has just been to see me.'

'Running to you with her tales, was she?' Alec demanded, but realised how insensitive he sounded and apologised, 'Forgive me, Father Jeremy. My wife and I had a serious argument tonight. She walked out on me, and when I tried to stop her leaving, she almost ran me over in the drive.'

'Really? Could she have been under a little pressure to act like that?'

'We have all been under pressure, Father Jeremy. My mistake appears to have been in asking her for some assistance which it is not impossible for her to give, and then reminding her of my request. She took exception to my mentioning the matter again and started hurling insults at me. When I suggested she should be satisfied with what she has, she took off all her jewellery, threw it down on the table and marched out.'

His mute expression of wounded indignation did not deceive Father Jay. The priest saw that behind his hurt pride, Alec still loved his wife more than he loved anything else, but was so self-situated he was astonished to find such a weakness in himself now that she had gone. Father Jay suspected that Alec had not appreciated how badly his nagging had affected his wife, nor how his insensitivity to her needs was damaging their marriage.

'She'll be back, of course,' Alec continued: 'As soon as she gets bored with her friend Bethany's company or needs a change of clothes.'

'I'm not so sure. She thinks you don't love her anymore.'

Alec picked up a photograph of Liz from the marble mantelpiece, turning his back on Father Jay to conceal the turmoil of his thoughts. He had discovered when he had least expected it that his love for his wife was as strong as his desire to avenge his brother Kevin's death and equal to his hatred of Jonathan Keast. Only the belief that Liz would be his again after he had destroyed Keast, enabled him to continue following his plan for vengeance.

'But she has to come back,' he insisted.

'Then you'll have to prove you still love her - you'll need to find her and ask her to come home.'

'You don't know what you're asking of me, Father Kingston.'

'I have a far better idea than you realise, Dr Graham. To love need be no weakness: to block love is always destructive.'

Alec's hands clenched the photograph, his back still to the priest. Father Jay's compassion went out to this emotionally fettered man.

'Alec, try to look further back than these last few months. Remember the moment you asked Lisbeth to marry you - try to recall what you were hoping for then from your marriage. It's not too late yet to achieve that; but if you don't find the courage to reach out, it could be very soon.'

Alec still did not turn, even to watch the priest leave. Oblivious to all else, he set the photograph of Liz down in front of him and gripped the marble mantelpiece, concentrating on the stone's cold bite against his hands in his determination to overcome the emotional agony of his conflict between love and revenge.

1 : 6

'I have decided to take a more active part in P.S.I.' Bethany announced.

Liz was so astonished she almost did an emergency stop. It was early the following Monday morning and she was driving them both into town in the white Oldsmobile.

'Good. What's made you decide that?'

'Then I'd have every right to tell people like that awful Max Vincent where to go.'

Despite Bethany's flippancy, Liz could tell her intentions were serious and was glad her friend was taking more interest in the society.

At the office in Neptune House, Liz found herself more decisive about her work, having made a decision about her problems at home. She powered through the backlog that had accumulated. Terry saw the difference in her with relief. The blonde secretary, beautiful but for her heavy make-up and smart in a dark brown trouser suit, commented about the improvement in Liz when she brought in some fresh coffee.

'Thanks, Terry' Liz said with a rare smile. 'Please could you make me an appointment to see Mrs Nora Kirkland of Kirkland and Co. as soon as possible.' She explained to Bethany, 'I must break the news to my parents sometime, so I may as well get Mum to find me a place to live.'

Bethany laughed with her, but knew that Liz was trying hard not to let her personal sorrow affect her professionalism at work. A far-away look stole back into Liz's eyes when she stopped for a few moments' break. Bethany snapped her fingers in front of her face to startle her out of her reverie.

'Stop regretting what you've done, Liz: you're far better off now you've left.'

'Am I? I've only ever been really happy with him. I feel so alone now - the only person I've ever loved more than life itself, just picked me up and threw me away.'

Terry turned back in the doorway. 'You're not alone, Liz,' she said, her deep voice conveying an intensity Liz was too preoccupied to notice. 'Jon Keast once told me you're the loneliest person I'd ever meet, because you love the loneliest man he'd ever met; but I know that's only so if you want it that way. You're surrounded by friends here; and though many of us can't fully understand your vision, every one of us would support you if you need someone.'

Suddenly the office seemed claustrophobic. Liz thanked Terry for her expression of support, and said she needed to get away from her desk for a few minutes before she got back down to her work.

As usual when she felt the need for time out, Liz returned to the building's basement theatre. Its aura of existing outside time always calmed her troubled mind and help her redirect her thoughts from the transient to the eternal. She sat pensively on a seat in the front row of the auditorium and stared across the empty stage at the white backdrop, allowing her spirit to drift in the ethos.

Bethany paced slowly down the steps, remembering the last time she had been there, when the theatre was crowded with members in uproar because Liz had been knifed at the August AGM and lay wounded on the stage. She crossed to centre stage, recalling Liz's extempore speech moments before that scene and tried to imagine how she must have felt as she delivered her momentous off-the-cuff address to a packed auditorium of people, many of whom had not been on her side.

'*The evil that men do lives after them; the good is oft interred with their bones,*' Bethany declaimed thoughtfully: '*So let it be with Caesar.*'

The left stage door swung open. She looked back as Charles strolled in. He acknowledged her with a friendly nod and turned to Liz. Bethany crossed to her side, adding up the clues in the interruption to a sum of trouble and bad news.

'My apologies for disturbing your meditation, Liz: Teresa told me I should find you here. Is everything all right?'

'Everything is fine, Charles. Why do you ask?' she said, her voice distant and at peace.

'I asked some more clairvoyants to assess your collection of curses. We now have four opinions, and they all say the same. Keep to your office: things do not appear too good for you outside.'

'Fine, Charles: just a few more moments here and I'll go straight back. I've enough work to keep me there to the back end of next week.'

'What about the appointment Terry's making for you to see your mother?'

'Once made, I cannot break one of those!'

'Liz, this is no joking matter!' Charles scolded. 'A similar thing happened to your predecessor shortly before you deposed him. The clairvoyants are all of the same opinion: if you venture out of your office, things won't go as you plan.'

'Yes, Charles: I do understand your warning; but there really is no need to worry. Do you realise how small all this is beside eternity? These are eternal forces fighting around us, using us as their temporal weapons. No worry will save us from that, only faith in the side we choose to support.'

Liz crossed to centre stage and gazed up across the empty tiers of seats. Unknown to her, up in the glass-walled projection room at the back of the theatre, an unexpected audience was tuning in as the sound technician Tim showed the discussion group organiser Toni Sullivan how to operate the audio-visual systems for the evening debate next day. Liz turned back to face Charles and Bethany across the bare stage.

'In this place I promised to lead P.S.I. to the best of my ability and in the strength of my Higher Power. Here now I remember that dedication and I am renewed by it. Do you think the Deceiver won't kick back? He lost a small part of his empire to God here - of course he'll try to win it back. But I handed my life over to God again today, so I can face whatever happens in His strength. I take note of your warning, of course, Charles, and I'll take every precaution, but I will not let it unsettle me. By God, the devil will not have his way!'

'So be it!' Charles snapped and marched out, his posture a little more rigid than it had been when he had come it.

'Liz, wasn't that a little harsh?' Bethany said as the door swung shut behind him.

Liz shook her head and was about to answer when the auditorium speakers came to life.

'Mrs Graham, Reception has just called,' Tim announced from the projection room: 'Your husband is waiting to see you at the main entrance.'

Liz acknowledged the message with a wave and turned to leave the theatre. Bethany caught her arm to hold her back.

'Don't be silly, Liz! It's just like Alec to turn up before you're over it - he'll know you miss him so you're bound to go back. Let me see him for you and tell him where to go.'

'No, Beth: if Alec has been considerate enough to visit my office in person, courtesy requires me to meet him in person.'

She pulled free and walked on up the aisle steps to the central auditorium doors.

'Then I'm coming with you!' Bethany insisted, chasing after her.

Liz turned to face her with a reflective smile as she caught up at the door. 'Thanks, Beth, but please try to remember I do still love Alec very much. If he asks me to go home and promises to change, I'll go straight back.'

'If you do, you're mad! But I quite understand.'

Toni Sullivan was standing in the hallway waiting at the lift bank as they arrived. The young jeans-clad student member gave the chairwoman a nervous but encouraging smile.

'I'm terribly sorry, Mrs Graham,' she began in her distinctive hurried staccato, 'but we overheard you in the theatre, what you were saying, while we were trying out the video and things, in the sound box for tomorrow night.'

'What did I say?' Liz asked uncertainly.

'About the devil, trying to stop you. It made us think. One or two people are saying you're not good enough for P.S.I.; but if they knew what you're going through for us, they wouldn't be so critical. None of us realised.'

'Perhaps, Toni, it would be better to leave them uninformed,' Liz replied, while behind her the lift doors slid open. She could imagine how people like Max Vincent and Arnaldo Lucia would receive Toni's defence of her.

'If that's what you want,' Toni agreed, blushing. She paused as they stepped into the lift, and continued, 'Anyhow, those of us who heard you, we want you to know we admire you very much, and we're behind you all the way, whatever others may say. And we'd very much like you to take one of the chairs in next week's discussion. The theme's *No Longer Alone*, about spiritual friends.'

Liz was about to refuse but realised how it would sound to her young supporter and laughed at herself. 'Very happy to take part; though I'm no expert on spirit guides.'

'You're with the best one - how else could Tim have stopped using and be working with us now?' Toni said; 'And you won't be alone - we've already invited Charles and Mary to talk about the more spooky side.'

'A star-studded cast - I shall look forward to it.'

The lift halted at the ground floor and the doors slid open. Liz shook Toni's hand. 'Thanks very much for your encouragement. I shan't forget it.'

She stepped out of the lift into the rear part of the reception hall with Bethany behind her. Toni followed them both, curious to see what the chairwoman's estranged husband looked like.

Alec was waiting in the foyer, standing near the reception desk. The desk was staffed by a man Liz did not recognise. This was contrary to office procedure, which required that she meet any new receptionist before they took up post. Also in the foyer was a well-dressed middle-aged woman, sitting on one of the waiting area seats and leafing through a well-thumbed magazine.

Alec turned to greet his wife, his smile strained, his aura devoid of emotional feedback. 'Hello, dear,' he said without inflection.

'Good morning,' she replied politely. She was conscious that someone in the foyer was caught up in a powerful inner conflict, and walked across to join Alec at the desk expecting the turmoil to be radiating from him; but he was without emotion, his feelings shut off behind a wall of self-control.

'Is there a place where we can talk in private?' he asked.

She knew she would feel defenceless alone with him. Guardedly she replied, 'There is nothing that can't be said here.'

The lift doors opened again. Terry hurried out carrying two coats and handbags on her arm and spoke before she realised what was happening.

'There you are, Liz. Your mother said she'll see you in her lunch hour as she's very busy; so you should leave right away... Oh, gosh: I'm sorry.' Her face gaped at Liz and Alec as she halted beside Bethany and automatically handed her coat and bag to her.

'I would find it easier to speak my mind if we were alone, Liz.'

'I've had enough of being alone with you, Alec.'

She realised the conflict was not emanating from the middle-aged visitor, but from the strange receptionist, and tensed.

'Has it really come to that?' Alec asked. His eyes betrayed no emotion: his veneer was impenetrable.

Bethany suddenly realised the receptionist was drawing a gun from inside his jacket. 'Liz!' she screamed: 'The desk!'

Alec saw the danger and sprang across, pushing Liz to the ground. Before the receptionist could fire, Alec cracked his wrist with a karate chop and followed through with an uppercut to his jaw. The man fell back onto the chair behind the desk like a crumpled rag doll. Around them, the people present gasped with shock.

The plate glass entrance doors swung open and the clairvoyant Mary Sebastian hurried in from the street, her hennaed hair straggling wildly.

'What's happened?' she demanded, running over to help Liz pick herself up and wondering why the others had not moved.

'The receptionist,' Bethany said, astonished: 'He just tried to shoot Liz. Alec stopped him.'

Liz stood up and turned to face her husband, furious.

'If this is your idea of how to get me back, Alec, I don't find it very funny!' she spat, and pushed past him to collect her coat and bag from Terry.

'Where are you going, Liz?' he demanded, hurrying after her.

'To get a solicitor,' she said without looking back.

'Don't go, Mrs Graham!' Mary Sebastian cried: 'The warning was most explicit. You would be a fool to leave this building.'

Liz chose not to hear. She donned her coat and marched out through the rear exit of the building into the quadrangle carpark. Sickened by the scene she had just been forced to take part in, she quickly unlocked the Oldsmobile to escape, only to find her husband climbing in the passenger door.

'Get out!' she ordered.

He resisted the temptation to take on her anger. 'Not until you have heard what I have to say.'

'I've heard enough of your lies!'

'Is it a lie to tell you I'm sorry? I want you back, Liz. I missed you last night.'

'Is it easier for you to swallow your pride and apologise to me, rather than tell all your fine friends you've lost your latest status symbol?'

'I don't understand, Liz. You said you loved me. If that is so you would forgive me for that pointless argument we had last night, as I have forgiven you. I was a fool to be so thoughtless, and I apologise. Please come home. I miss you.'

'Nonsense! You'll only miss me when your friends call round and realise you're not man enough to keep your wife.'

He was struggling now not to express his anger. In a tone of reasoned hurt he asked, 'Liz, what's happened to you? You've changed.'

'That stupid pantomime you just staged is what's happened, Alec. Surely you don't think that'd fool me? It'd take a lot more than a gun trick and some acrobatics to get me sobbing gratefully in your arms. Now, get out!'

'But I had nothing to do with that.'

'Sure, and you always say I underestimate the bad in people.'

'Listen to me, Liz: I....'

'No: I've listened to you too long, Alec. So get out before I get some members to drag you out.'

His patience finally snapped. He opened the passenger door and stepped out onto the oil-stained tarmac, his manner distant, cold and dangerous.

'Very well, if that is the way you want it. You will be hearing from me, Elizabeth Kirkland.'

He slammed the passenger door and stalked off across the carpark to his waiting Lincoln. Liz started up her engine and drove out onto the busy rain-washed street.

She felt safe in the self-contained environment of the car, protected behind its smoked glass windows from the wintry downpour, the faceless people wielding umbrellas on the pavements, the slow-moving traffic stirring up the torrents in the gutters, and the unknown danger waiting for her outside. She turned on a tape of Bach toccatas and fugues to drown out the sound of the rain pounding on the roof and turned up the heater to get warm, confident in her solitude, alone and in control.

The car behind flashed its lights. After a pause it flashed urgently again, several times. At the next set of red traffic lights, Liz turned her head to look back at the car, an orange Austin Maxi hatchback, but the sheeting rain stopped her from identifying either the vehicle or its occupants.

The lights changed to green and Liz drove on. The orange car followed, still flashing. She tried switching on dipped headlights to see whether the driver behind was warning her about the poor visibility. As her fingers touched the switch, the side of her hand struck a sharp object on the dashboard. She recoiled in surprise and put the stinging pinprick to her mouth to suck out any dirt from the wound. Her skin tasted so bitter that she hastily spat into a paper handkerchief and glanced down to see what had pricked her. Before she could make out what it was, the demands of driving forced her attention back to the road.

At the next set of lights against her, she looked again and found a small wooden tablet hanging from one of the controls. The tablet was painted cream with black and red detail which picked out Egyptian hieroglyphs in what she recognised instantly to be another curse. She cautiously wrapped the tablet in paper handkerchiefs, pulled it off the dashboard and threw it into the glove box, taking care not to touch it a second time.

The lights changed. Liz drove on, ignoring the orange car behind her despite its insistent flashing, in case its two occupants were the subjects of Charles' warnings.

As she drove onto the bridge across the Thames, she was struggling to keep her glazed eyes open. Her limbs felt heavy and unresponsive. She resolved to stop for a few moments as soon as she could, and paused behind the traffic waiting to join the roundabout at the south-eastern end of the bridge. The bus in front of her moved off onto the roundabout. She inched her car forward ready to follow, her head swimming and the blood pounding in her ears.

She saw a gap in the traffic and accelerated to slip into it. As she did so, a grey mist fell across her vision, obscuring her concentration. The white Oldsmobile drifted across the three lanes, cutting in front of other vehicles. A responding chorus of protesting horns briefly roused her back into consciousness. She saw her perilous situation and tried to regain control but overcompensated. The car slewed back across the lanes, forcing a delivery van to make an emergency stop to avoid her. She automatically jumped on the brakes to stop the slewing but was too sharp. The car skidded into a spin on the oily wet road and halted at the kerb. Liz slumped forward across the steering wheel and passed out.

1 : 7

Bethany and Terry watched the out-of-control limousine from their ringside view in Terry's new orange Austin Maxi as they waited to join the roundabout. Fearing the worst, Terry parked a short way down the next exit and Bethany ran back to help her friend. The white Oldsmobile had slewed to a halt across the kerb, miraculously untouched despite the heavy traffic and atrocious weather. Behind it a lime green sports car had stopped with its engine running, and a young man was leaning in through Liz's open passenger door. Bethany called out indignantly. The young man looked up at her, slammed the door shut and fled back to his car. Helpless to stop what she presumed was an opportunist thief, she shook her fist at him as he drove off past her.

Inside the limousine, Liz groaned. Bethany cried out in relief and opened the passenger door to help her. She was lying against her seatbelt, slumped over the steering wheel. Her face was pale and her breathing shallow, but otherwise she appeared uninjured. Bethany eased her back into the seat and undid the seatbelt. When her eyes did not open, she patted her cheeks to bring her round.

Terry opened the passenger door wider and leaned in to see the situation for herself. She noticed the bundle of handkerchiefs in the open glove box and took them out.

Liz's eyes flickered open. 'Stop, Terry: danger,' she warned distantly.

'Thank God, Liz: you're all right!' Bethany cried.

Terry cautiously unwrapped the bundle of tissues and found the wooden tablet inside. Bethany looked at it in dismay.

'I think it's poisoned,' Liz said. 'It was hanging on the dash. My hand struck it when I turned on my lights. It stung so I sucked it; it was bitter, so I spat it out. Horrible.'

'Thank God you did, Liz,' Bethany returned. 'And that explains what the sneak thief in the lime green bomber was after.'

'I'd better put it in my car and take it to Charles when I get back to the office,' Terry offered. 'Don't be surprised, Liz, when he says "I told you so".'

'Watch out: a police car's spotted us,' Bethany warned, nodding back along the roundabout.

'Please don't tell them: it could only be Alec - both times, only Alec,' Liz pleaded in alarm.

'Don't worry: you've only had a mechanical breakdown,' Terry reassured with a sly smile.

She got out of the limousine as the police carparked behind with its lights flashing, and walked over to talk to the two policemen inside. While she distracted them, Bethany helped Liz move across into the passenger seat and took her place at the wheel. Bethany made some feint attempts at starting up the engine and then let it roar into life. The policemen looked up and acknowledged Bethany's wave of final success with a return wave as she drove the Oldsmobile away.

Bethany took the next exit off the roundabout, but slowed down again as soon as the police were out of sight, to give Terry time to return to her orange hatchback and catch up with them.

'So that was Terry's new car,' Liz commented, dazed still from the effects of the poison.

'Yes. We flashed you dozens of times, but you wouldn't stop.'

'I didn't know it was you. The only person I was expecting behind was Alec. Two attempts, and both times it could only be Alec.'

'That's nonsense, Liz! He's not fool enough to bump off his wife just because you walked out on him.'

'He's proud enough though - crocodile tears at a flashy funeral: terrorists win again; the desolate widower, still with his father's estate. Aye, but he could play that part well.'

'No, Liz: if you believe that you're cracked, psychic powers or no. The person I wouldn't trust is the personal secretary who still handed you your coat to send you out for an appointment, knowing you'd just been warned in no uncertain terms not to leave the office.'

'Not you too! Alec kept going on about her - he thinks she fancies me!'

'Don't be so sure that isn't mixed in with it. Wait: she's flashing her lights again - she must want us to stop.'

Bethany drew the limousine over to the kerb beside some shabby shops. Terry parked her orange hatchback in front of them and walked back to speak to her through her open window.

'That lime green bomber is following us, Bethany. It just drew in back there when it saw us stop.'

'So he didn't get what he was after. We'd better try to lose him,' Bethany said, and suggested a simple plan to give their follower the slip in the back streets.

The Oldsmobile slipped back into the traffic, and the orange hatchback followed right behind. As they drove on south, the orange car hung further and further back until at length it disappeared from sight after a sharp turn in the road. Bethany turned the limousine left off the main road and drove through the residential side streets parallel to the road for a mile before re-joining it at the next shopping centre, while Terry turned right along a broader thoroughfare which returned to the river.

With bated breath Bethany drove on south, keeping watch for the green sports car in the rear-view mirror. A few minutes later it came back into view behind them. Bethany swore. Liz turned back to see what the car looked like.

'Beth, I know that car. It's Greg Vincent's Marcos, Alec's friend and Max Vincent's son.'

'Don't worry, Liz. Even if he is responsible for everything, which I very much doubt, he's hardly likely to try anything more out in the street,' Bethany reassured. But she too felt concerned about the possible implications of the Marcos and remained tense throughout the rest of their journey south.

The Marcos followed them all the way and parked behind them outside the Kirkland and Company estate agency. Its menace meant little to Liz in the face of an interview with her mother. Bethany knew Nora Kirkland had never appreciated Liz for what she was, seeing her only as the daughter who had failed to live up to her expectations. Nora had thought Liz's marriage was the one good thing she had done in her life, and Liz feared her reaction when she heard she had failed in that too.

However, Nora surprised them both when told the news. Though her manner was still business-like and insensitive, she agreed that in a conflict between marriage and career, Liz was right to place her career first. In her professional capacity, she advised Liz to rent a property on a six-month lease before looking for more permanent accommodation and gave her a list of suitable properties to view next day.

As Liz and Bethany got back into the Oldsmobile an hour later, Bethany laughed.

'You know, Liz, when you and I were at school, I used to dream of your mother and my father being marooned together on a desert island and never bothering the rest of us again. It always seemed most fitting: only the two of them would be unhappy instead of the rest of our families. It's a shame life is never that tidy.'

Liz smiled and scanned the road as the limousine turned back onto the street. Once again, the lime green sports car moved in right behind.

'Maybe I should've fired Mum at Vincent's lime green bomber.'

'Don't worry: he definitely won't do anything now - he's far too showy to risk it. Let's get home.'

The Marcos followed them back to Westfield House but, as Bethany had predicted, its driver made no moves against them. While they locked themselves away in Bethany's apartment, the car parked up opposite the building on the road outside. For the rest of the evening, its driver sat there in wait.

1 : 8

Despite all that had happened that week, Liz kept her Wednesday lunch time appointment with Sir Kenneth Bywater. She did not want to miss the opportunity of meeting such a famous man. Terry collected her from Bethany's apartment mid-morning and drove her in the orange hatchback across south London to Sir

Kenneth's offices in Concordia House.

The sun was shining, the lime green sports car had finally gone, and they had plenty of time to get there. During the journey Liz studied Pete Corrie's list of specifications to refresh her memory of his advice when she had visited P.S.I. Chelsea the week before. She did not look up again until Terry was parking the car in an underground carpark which served Concordia House and the modern shopping centre next door. Terry led the way to the Concordia basement entrance and chatted informally with Liz as a lift took them up into the house lobby.

'Charles is still worried about you - he doesn't want you to see Sir Kenneth. Mary Sebastian has even put the wind up Pete Corrie, which is pretty hard to do.'

Liz recalled Bethany's comment about her personal secretary's trustworthiness. Would Terry have said that, Liz wondered, had she been attempting any duplicity?

At the Concordia House front desk, the receptionist directed Liz to take a lift to the top floor and handed Terry a message. The secretary read the slip of paper and paled.

'Oh no! My sister Bella's been trying to contact me about Mum. She's been taken ill again. Bella's asked me to go straight over and meet her at Mum's house in Windsor.'

'You'd better go then, Terry. I'll manage perfectly well on my own with these papers from Pete,' Liz said, aware of Terry and Bella's problems with their depressive mother.

Terry took a lift back down to the basement carpark. Liz took the next lift up to the top floor. A young secretary met her as the door slid open.

'Mrs Graham? I'm sorry, but Sir Kenneth has been delayed in town. He shouldn't be too long, if you don't mind waiting here for a few minutes until he gets back?'

She showed Liz into a spacious but deserted modern waiting room and left her there. Liz sat down to re-review Pete's specifications but soon tired of that. She strolled to the window to look out across the modern shopping centre spread out below the building. The magnificence of the urban view took less of her attention than the smallness of the cars and the people in the streets and walkways below.

The quiet hiss of a lift made her turn towards the open doorway. Max Vincent walked past the lounge, doubled back to look again, and strolled in with an automatic vote-catching smile which she automatically returned.

'Mrs Graham, what a surprise! What brings you here?'

'Window shopping for P.S.I. Chelsea. And you, Max?'

'Popped in to see a friend of mine in Sartex: export chappy, busy at the moment. What have you decided about the campaign?'

She sat down and gathered her papers, her expression reflective as she tactically replied, 'I've decided to act immediately a request for a campaign comes to me from a national delegate or vice-delegate through the usual procedural channels.'

'What, you aren't going to ballot the members so that we can make a start?' Though his tone was jovially indignant, the cunning glint in his eyes made Liz wonder whether P.S.I. was using him or he was using P.S.I.

'I won't bend the rules to suit your whims. Unless this issue is brought up more formally, I'll make it a subject for discussion at the next quarterly delegates meeting; but I think you will find everyone rather too busy with the membership drive over the next few months to find enough time and energy for a campaign as well.'

'Not till the next quarterly? But that's two months away! We need action now, to strike while the iron's hot!'

'Then persuade P.S.I. Britain's delegate Jo Simon to have a campaign here and prove to the rest of us it's worth making it an international concern.'

Another lift arrived in the corridor outside, diverting Max's attention. Elegant Arnaldo Lucia emerged, to Liz's surprise.

'Harry won't be long, Max,' he declared, and noticed Liz.

'Why, Mrs Graham, what are you doing here?'

'Mrs Graham is here on behalf of P.S.I. press,' Max answered for her. 'We were having such an interesting talk about the next campaign. Do you realise Mrs Graham doesn't intend holding a ballot to assess the true feeling of the members for two months!'

'Is this true?' Arnaldo asked Liz.

She smiled wryly, caught out by Max Vincent's sly manipulation of her words to suit himself, but was not quite outflanked. 'As true as my intention to follow procedure over this issue as with all issues. I want no hasty decisions that will have to be reversed in six months' time.'

'You mean, you want time to persuade everyone round to your point of view,' Max challenged. His continuing verbal attack made Liz wonder what had really brought him and Lucia to Concordia House that lunch time; but his psychic screen was too impenetrable for her to pick up more than a sense of indirect danger.

'As I told Arnaldo on Friday, Max; I was democratically elected and all my decisions have to be ratified by the members through their elected representatives. If you question this matter so much, call for the delegates to hold an extraordinary meeting and demand an emergency resolution.'

This time Arnaldo had an answer to her challenge. He replied, 'Is it worth the expense, Liz, of calling the fourteen delegates to meet to discuss this obscure matter of policy? P.S.I. has not the money to waste on administrative quibbles.'

'True, Arnaldo. Nor should we waste money on first class air tickets for the Italian Delegate to say in person what he has already said on the phone, yet you are here; because it is a matter of principle, and principles are more important than money. P.S.I.'s present structure was designed to ensure the interests of all members are safeguarded, not just the interests of the few who make their voices the most heard.'

'So you claim,' Max challenged; 'But the structure of P.S.I. is your design now, not the provenly successful structure devised by

Jonathan Keast, nor even the structure the members requested. Who can really say whether your way is better than any other? Just because you're the chairperson now?'

Arnaldo continued, 'Had I my way we would dispense with the position of Chairman altogether; but P.S.I. Britain has the largest vote and does not understand the problems such a figurehead naturally creates. In my branch, the co-operation of delegates in a self-regulating council is enough; but they say no, to be leaderless is to be directionless; and they get what they ask for.'

'Yes, a self-opinionated incompetent who thinks she rules by divine right!' Max mocked.

'Do you see that little between me and Jon Keast? If this charade is some plot to throw me out, gentlemen, think on. Should you succeed, you will open the door for Mr Keast to return. If that is not what you intend, make sure before you continue that he hasn't somehow arranged for you to do what he had failed to do.'

'Unfortunately, I joined P.S.I. after Mr Keast left, so I never had the chance to meet him,' Max began expansively, but Arnaldo waved him silent before he went too far.

'Liz, you have raised a possibility I had not considered. Max, I would not like to see Mr Keast back in office, nor would any of my fellow delegates. But he would undoubtedly return to what he would consider his rightful place if Mrs Graham were no longer the possessor.'

'Max!' greeted a man from the doorway, interrupting the debate before it turned too far in Liz's favour. Max leapt up to greet the man with effusive bonhomie and strolled away to the lift bank with him, throwing Arnaldo a pointed reminder that he should leave with them. Arnaldo hung back to shake Liz's hand.

'I am glad to have known you, Mrs Graham,' he warned with a courteous nod, and walked out after Max.

Liz was so astonished by his ominous comment that she followed him out to ask what he meant, but stopped in the doorway to discover Greg Vincent in the corridor, leaning against the wall opposite with folded arms, apparently on guard. Greg shot her an arrogant smile which declared his confident supremacy over her. She stepped back into the lounge in dismay and sat down by the window. He pushed himself away from the wall with an indolent grace and strolled into the lounge to drop smoothly onto a seat beside the door.

'What am I really here for?' Liz asked him apprehensively.

'A chat with Sir Ken about computers, I thought. Mind, I thought you were a fortune teller, not a computer buff.'

'I am; the P.S.I. printing house wants the computer, not me.'

'Good: then you can tell me my fortune!'

He thrust his right hand towards her. She looked at his palm with interest but faltered. A short divided life line wrote death right across the hand. Hastily she hedged, 'Palmistry is not my real metier: I cast horoscopes and read Tarot cards and have intuitive insights.'

'Really? What's your intuition about me?'

She thought how naïve he must be not to realise he was playing with fire by opening himself up to her. 'Does it worry you?' she enquired to disconcert him.

'Of course not!' he denied, a little too firmly.

She fixed her eyes on his to make her words hit home and pronounced, 'You are a little boy in a man's world, Greg Vincent: you are like coal; like a tree at the bottom of a weak cliff.'

He turned aside to break her dominating gaze and disdainfully huffed, 'Pretty pictures, that's all! Alec told me you came from the Lake District - I don't think you've left it behind.'

'If you can't be bothered to listen, I won't bother to explain,' she said, and stood up to look out of the window at the view, her back turned to him to declare the conversation closed.

'No, please do, Mrs Graham: I am listening,' he said with an eager docility that made her smile to find how easily she could manipulate him by his curiosity.

She kept her back turned to pick up his true reaction rather than be misled by his facial expression as she spoke. 'All things have their purpose in existence, Greg. To you they exist for pleasure: the whole spectrum of life is your playground.'

'And what's wrong with that?'

'I don't say that you are wrong. Just remember when you play your games, that your playground is a workplace to most other people, and to some it is a prison. If you choose to go against convention, be prepared for the consequences of your actions. For some people that is when the game comes to an abrupt end.'

'What do you mean?' he scoffed.

'You know well enough yourself, beneath that devil-may-care front. That is why you are like coal: you may seem to be as strong as the stone-hearted people around you, but you are not, for your conscience can still be ignited.'

'What do you mean?' he demanded, no longer laughing.

'Look at yourself! You couldn't even face my friends yesterday when you failed to find the poisoned tablet in my car. Like a weak tree at the bottom of a crumbling cliff, you stand in a very uncertain position; and you know it.'

'Why are you trying to warn me?'

'Because you asked me what I see. You're a scapegoat, Greg - if your superiors have any comeback from their deeds, they will not protect you: they'll let you be crushed to save themselves. It's up to you to decide whether you want to continue in such a position. But take heed - to make the wrong decision now could be fatal, for we are both dealing with ruthless men.'

Greg crossed the room to join her at the window. She turned her head and looked him straight in the eye again.

'They lied about you, Mrs Graham. How can Alec despise you so?' he asked.

'Some people can't face the truth. I'm glad you still can.'

'No, I'm still only pretending to be stone. You've made me stop to think, and what I see disturbs me; but I have no pretty pictures to explain.'

'And you're a salesman?' she mocked gently, turning back to look at the view. In an uncertain voice she asked, 'Tell me, Greg, just what is Alec's involvement in all this?'

The young secretary interrupted them, calling Liz away for her appointment with Sir Kenneth Bywater. With her back to the secretary, Liz saw through the charade and knew the invitation to lunch veiled a far more sinister meeting. She turned to grasp Greg's arm, knowing she could lose nothing more by begging his help and might possibly save herself from the fate behind the veil.

'I know you don't know me, Greg, though we have met before: humanity is our only bond,' she began, and paused to choose her words. The secretary became pressing. Liz hastily implored, 'Greg, what will you do when the words run out, and the only thing between me and death is you?'

She picked up the document wallet from P.S.I. Chelsea and followed the secretary out.

1 : 9

Sir Kenneth Bywater met Liz in his spacious wood-panelled office from which he ran his extensive business empire. He sat in a heavy leather armchair behind his broad oak desk, a tall thickset man who looked even more impressive in the flesh than he appeared in the media. His clean-shaven heavily dewlapped face and his silver grey crewcut hair gave weight to the popular impression that he was a bull of a man.

He rose majestically as Liz entered and firmly shook her hand with an apology for his lateness which she politely dismissed as of no consequence. With his fifteen-inch advantage in height, she found his presence overpowering despite herself. Beneath his courtesy she sensed a ruthlessness which contradicted the psychic sensitivity expressed in his brown bovine eyes.

'Before we lunch, I had intended to show you round the

Museum of Computer Technology which I have been setting up in a part of this site. We do still have time,' he suggested.

'I should be most interested, Sir Kenneth.'

He escorted her to the wing of Concordia House that held the collection of computers and allied technology which would shortly be opened to the public. His prize exhibit was a second-generation computer, a transistorised mainframe housed in its own extensive suite of rooms on the ground floor and maintained lovingly by a team of white-coated workers. He showed Liz into a long room lined with a row of cabinets holding large drums of magnetic tape visible through clear Perspex doors. The apparently random rotations and disengagements of the drums distracted Liz as she tried to concentrate on what Sir Kenneth was saying and gauge his intentions from his thoughts.

'This computer, Ingot 5, is so large and heavy we had to install her on the ground floor on special foundations to prevent vibrations from outside interfering with her - we couldn't even have a carpark underneath. In her day Ingot 5 was a leader in her field; but it's a fact of life that all things are superseded and have to be replaced. Today a computer of her capacity would take up far less space, require twenty fewer specialist workers, and cost considerably less. But it was only through her that my company expanded enough to be able to replace her, so it was worth the expense of being an innovative leader with her all those years ago.'

Liz made an appropriate comment to show that she was listening. She had little personal interest in computers. Though she recognised their uses, she felt concern about their dehumanising influence on those people whose love of the technology running riot through society, had made them throw away all reference to the wisdom of the past.

'You too will find considerable savings in manpower and time once you have installed your computerised type-setting equipment,' Sir Kenneth continued. 'I must say, though, it does rather surprise me that you are replacing such expensive items of equipment at this point, when your society no longer has the industrial backing it used to rely upon up to six months ago.'

Liz almost laughed at his euphemism for the drug trading which had cashiered the society. She wondered how Sir Kenneth was so well-informed about P.S.I. when as far as she knew he had taken no interest in it.

'Our aim is to make the P.S.I. printing house completely self-financing, Sir Kenneth. The new equipment will help us work more cost-effectively. But our modest order must mean little enough to your large concern. So to what do I owe the honour of meeting you here?'

'You are right to ask, Mrs Graham. It was not to help you choose some computronic equipment that I invited you for lunch.' He smiled, and admitted, 'I was curious to meet the woman who had superseded Jon Keast and replaced him as chairman of P.S.I. That was quite an achievement; and it would take a lot to sustain.'

She was taken aback to hear her host refer to her adversary with the familiarity her secretary also used. Guardedly she enquired, 'You are a friend of Mr Keast?'

'Let us say we belong to the same business club. From the outset I made it my business to know what Jon was up to with P.S.I. I've dabbled a little in the supernatural myself. In my experience, those who get on in life are often psychic, given the right set of circumstances: when the chips are down, the gift gives them the edge. Jon was using his better placed psychic members to gather confidential information which he then used in business. I considered it my duty to ensure he didn't use any classified information he gained against our nation or her allies - sometimes a man can become too greedy.'

Liz was disconcerted to hear the scale of Keast's influence through P.S.I. and wished she still had Alec to protect her from such business machinations. She cautiously asked, 'Did Mr Keast know you were watching him and P.S.I.?'

'Without doubt. He and I came to a little understanding. In

return for a friend or two of mine in P.S.I., I would not expose the identities of his government infiltrators.'

'You blackmailed him? So presumably, my arrival must have upset the fine balance you had both achieved.'

'Worse: it forced out all my men with his. Fortunately, you started a membership drive and accepted so many new people, it was easy to make up the loss. You even accepted Max Vincent, a man Jon would never have made a member. Yet despite this, despite August, and despite your age and your defective policies, my men reported that P.S.I. was starting to re-establish itself. It showed all the signs of becoming a powerful new force in society. That had to be stopped. But how, with men who could not yet be trusted, and without involving my own name this time.'

'You mean, Jon Keast was blackmailing you as well?'

'Not at all: scandal is simply bad for business. Jon Keast back in the chair at P.S.I. will be good for business. But how to get the gifted new chairman out, and get him back in, without my being involved? I recruited several people to assist me - people who thought they were working towards far different aims to mine and Jon's. They worked independently of each other but together acted to persuade you to resign. And if you continued to be obstinate, they were powerful enough to destroy you.'

Sir Kenneth glanced at his watch and gave Liz an amiable smile. She realised that he had completely dissociated her, the person he was with, from his image of her as his victim, and felt concerned to find herself sliding into the past tense in his consideration.

'Let me guess who was involved. Greg and Max Vincent, Arnaldo Lucia, the gunman in the lobby...' She faltered, realising who else she should include in the list.

Sir Kenneth smiled knowingly at her. 'You see, you weren't guessing, Mrs Graham. Your survival so far was not through luck: you really were quite gifted. Yes, your husband Dr Graham was involved too; and P.S.I.'s young accountant who gave me lots of useful figures and did some excellent rumour-mongering for me. Six people, three of whom so dislike Jon Keast they would have turned on me had they known my true intention was to put him back in power.'

A casually dressed man entered the room and joined Sir Kenneth. Liz recognised him in dismay as the strange receptionist Alec had disarmed at Neptune House. She tried to edge towards the exit to escape from the trap. Sir Kenneth shook his head at her, still smiling.

'Why must you be so obstinate, Mrs Graham? All I wanted of you was to step down as chairman of P.S.I. under whatever conditions are necessary. It was your own fault you were under such duress recently: I really did think you loved your husband more than power. It doesn't matter to me how the vacancy occurs, but I suspect that it would matter to you, and I am willing to negotiate.'

He glanced again at his watch.

'Late for a lunch engagement?' Liz asked, stalling for time.

He stared at her, his gaze going straight through her as she knew hers had gone through Greg. She hastily raised her mental defences against his attempted intimidation.

'Very shortly the fire precautions will be tested in this suite - with so much expensive and irreplaceable equipment here we have to be strict,' he said. 'You have no more time for obstinacy, Mrs Graham. You have only a few seconds to decide whether you will compromise with me, and live; or not.'

'What d'you mean, compromise?'

A bell rang vibrantly above their heads. The computer staff responded to the alarm and evacuated the suite while Sir Kenneth and Liz continued to talk.

'Don't you appreciate your position, seer? Either leave behind all your connections with P.S.I. for good and return to your husband; or never see anyone again.'

'You don't understand what you're asking, Sir Kenneth.'

'Your decision, yes or no.'

'But how can I betray P.S.I. back into Keast's hands? No, I cannot agree to that.'

The alarm changed from a continuous peal to two-second bursts which warned that the evacuation time was almost over. Liz glanced round, alerted by the changing bell, and realised she was alone in the computer suite but for Sir Kenneth and his assistant.

'Very well, Mrs Graham. You have made your decision. Now you will die by it.'

Sir Kenneth turned on his heel and marched out. Liz chased after him but was elbowed in the stomach by his assistant in the doorway. As she fell to the floor, he escaped from the suite behind Sir Kenneth with only a second to spare. The door automatically closed behind him and sealed shut.

The alarm bell stopped ringing. An eerie silence settled on the suite, disturbed only by a gentle humming from the computer. After a few seconds a cold hissing emanated from the ceiling. Liz pulled herself to her feet with the support of a control panel and looked up to see the cause of the ominous noise. Between the lighting panels in the ceiling, chrome rosettes sprayed a heavy white mist which settled on the floor and made the room temperature plummet.

Liz realised in dismay that she had been caught in the automatic fire extinguisher sequence for the suite, designed to save the equipment by suffocating any fire with carbon dioxide. Soon the gas would fill the suite and suffocate her too if she did not get out. She stifled her rising panic and tried to think through her predicament. Logic said the system would need vents to let the normal air escape as the carbon dioxide entered. She looked up at the windows and saw a row of open fanlight vents above them. They were far too small for her to escape through with the air.

She thought again and reasoned that the law would require the system designers to provide for an eventuality like her presence in the suite at that stage of the sequence: there would have to be an emergency exit for people trapped there. She searched for the exit, panting as the carbon dioxide started to take effect. The suite of rooms proved to be much larger than she had expected. The more she exerted herself, the more she gasped for air, the faster her heartbeat raced and the slower her movements became. Before long she was stumbling along the wall, gasping for breath, desperately seeking a way out but finding none.

Her hand hit a door handle. She looked up and saw a large green emergency exit sign on the panel above. To her relief the handle turned, but when she tried to push the door open, it barely moved an inch: something heavy on the other side was blocking it. She threw herself against the door with the last of her energy to push the obstruction aside but failed to shift it further. As the carbon dioxide engulfed her body, she sank to the floor. Her fingers scratched feebly down the paintwork into silence.

1 : 10

The moment the alarm bells pealed in Concordia House, Greg Vincent knew they rang for Liz Graham. He abandoned his lunch in the executive restaurant and raced down the stairs to the ground floor, avoiding the lifts in case they shut down in the fire practice. Other workers in the main building toiled on, ignoring the testing of the annexe block fire alarm system. Greg reached the entrance to the Ingot 5 computer suite as Sir Kenneth and his assistant walked away from the self-sealing doors. He pressed back into the shadows to let them pass, and then ran on down the passage away from them, searching for another way into the suite.

The alarm bell stopped ringing. Above the computer suite doors, red lights shone warning of the danger still within. Around a corner, in a short side passage, Greg found an emergency door at the bottom of a flight of three concrete steps. A heavy packing case obstructed the exit, jammed between the door and the bottom step. Through a slight gap in the doorway drifted misty streamers of carbon dioxide. A weak scratching noise down the inside of the door told him someone on the other side was pressing against the obstacle trying to get out. Fearing the worst, he tried to move the packing case up from the stairwell but could not get a good enough hold to lever it out.

Footsteps sounded along the main passage. Greg called out for help. A security guard came to his aid, saw the problem and swiftly helped him roll the heavy packing case away up the steps into the passage. The emergency door swung open. Out fell a limp hand.

'Mrs Graham!' Greg cried. He caught her wrist and pulled her unconscious body out of the billowing cloud of gas. Behind her, the emergency door fell shut, sealing in the carbon dioxide.

Greg carried Liz into the passage and placed her on the floor, seeing her blue lips and still chest and fearing he was too late. The security guard knelt down beside her and pumped five sharp breaths into her mouth to refill her lungs with air. He then checked her throat for a pulse.

'It's weak, but it is still there. You'd better get a doctor,' he said, and breathed into her mouth again to try to revive her.

Greg hesitated. The last thing he wanted to do was alert Sir Kenneth through his staff to the fact that he had helped Bywater's victim escape her fate. He saw a healthier colour return to Liz's face as her chest moved again of its own accord, and feared the guard might be sending him away so that he could finish the job.

'I don't know my way around here - I'm just a visitor.'

'Go, man! I can't leave her in case she goes into shock.'

The all clear sounded, briefly distracting the guard's attention. As he turned back, Greg punched him across the jaw and knocked him out. Greg bundled Liz up in his arms and ran off with her before the guard could come around and protest.

He carried her out of Concordia House by the nearest fire exit, emerging on the vehicular ramp to the carpark beneath the building. Though Liz weighed little in his arms he was tiring by the time he reached his green two-seater Marcos. He strapped her into the passenger seat, belted himself in at the wheel, and rapidly sped off with the windows down, trying not to draw more than the normal attention to himself.

He drove for several miles across the suburbs southwest of Concordia House, concerned that someone might follow him and not wanting his duplicity to be too obvious. When he felt confident enough to risk stopping, he parked up in a residential side street. Liz's eyes flickered open. She coughed deeply several times until the reflex exhausted her. Weakly she tried to touch her aching head with her left hand but had no strength: her arm dropped limply to her side and her head fell back against the seat.

'I'm sorry, Greg,' she croaked in a dry voice, giving him a wan smile. 'Thank you, for saving my life.'

'You have a Concordia House security guard to thank too, and all he got for his trouble was a bruised jaw!' Greg replied. Suddenly the full implications of his impulsive action came to him. He reeled with the impact of what he had thrown away so readily to play the knight in shining armour. 'What do I do now?' he whispered, almost to himself.

'Phone P.S.I. Talk to Charles or Pete,' Liz answered distantly, not realising his question was rhetorical. She faded back into semi-consciousness again.

Greg carried out her suggestion for want of a better alternative and called Neptune House on his car phone. Charles took the call and would have taken it to be a hoax but for his department's recent warnings to Liz. He realised Greg felt shocked by events and quickly got the basic details from him before asking him to bring Liz across town to Neptune House.

While he waited for them to arrive, Charles phoned for a doctor to attend and called Pete at P.S.I. Chelsea to tell him what had happened. By chance the editor of *Helicon* and *The Iron Fist,* Guy Simms was with Pete, negotiating to buy P.S.I.'s old typesetting equipment for the Print Workshop when it was no longer needed. A blond, tie-dye clad Adonis, Guy leapt up to follow the lead, and Pete quickly followed to make sure any story he picked up did not go too far.

They arrived at Neptune House to find Charles waiting in the foyer. Behind them Terry came in through the rear entrance doors. Charles turned on her with uncharacteristic anger.

'Miss Carter, why aren't you with Mrs Graham?'

'Don't you start! I've already been on one wild goose chase,' she retorted. 'There was an urgent message waiting for me when Liz and I checked in at Concordia House, to go over to Windsor as my mother was ill. Liz said she could manage fine without me, so off I drove like a lunatic, only to find Mother looking the picture of health when I got there. So I rang my sister Bella to ask what the hell she's playing at leaving me a message like that. She said it was nothing to do with her: she's been asleep all morning after a late night at work.'

'A trap?' Pete suggested to Charles.

He nodded and turned towards the main doors as a young man hurried in announcing that he was a doctor.

Terry blanched. 'Oh, my God! What's happened to Liz?'

'So far as I can tell,' Guy answered, referring to his notes, 'Liz was trapped deliberately in a CO_2 blanket fire extinguisher test, rescued by a security officer and someone called Greg Vincent, who no longer has it in for her and is now driving her over here in his bright green sports car; and the P.S.I. printing house is probably not about to replace its typesetting system after all.'

'You aren't thinking of printing any of this, are you?' Pete warned: 'Think again, or you definitely won't get a deal from P.S.I. Chelsea.'

Guy shrugged his shoulders and put his notepad away.

On the road outside, Greg's Marcos drove past signalling to turn down the next side street and into the Neptune House carpark.

'That's the lime green bomber that followed Liz across town yesterday,' Terry said.

Greg carried Liz into the building through the rear entrance, refusing any help from her colleagues. Charles thanked the doctor for coming and led the way to the first aid room on the second floor. As they took the lift Greg gave a brief report of Liz's condition and described what had happened. His version of events for the doctor's benefit was noticeably different to the story he had told Charles: Sir Kenneth Bywater's intent became an unfortunate accident; and Greg's rescue of Liz and hasty departure from Concordia house became a mistaken journey back across town thinking she had recovered after first aid. The story changed yet again while he waited with Charles, Pete and Guy outside the first aid room for the doctor to complete his examination of Liz in Terry's presence.

'We can manage from here, M. Vincent: Liz is quite safe now,' Charles reassured, uncertain what to do about the uneasy visitor.

'But she is not safe, not even here; and I won't leave her until I am sure she is. Oh, how right she was when she said we're up against ruthless men!' Greg cried.

'You're claiming now it was a plot?' Pete demanded.

'With Bywater as the ringleader,' Greg confirmed. 'His plan was virtually infallible. For every step that might go wrong he had planned another step to correct it. And his last step would have succeeded if Mrs Graham hadn't made me realise this one wasn't a game after all. And his players weren't pawns - they included my father Max Vincent, your Italian delegate Arnaldo Lucia, Mrs Graham's husband Dr Graham, and your accountant Martin Kingsley. I was just the errand boy. And all of us, indirectly, were working for some businessman called Keast.'

Charles and Pete exchanged expressions of dismayed alarm. Charles lifted the nearest phone receiver to call Martin Kingsley but failed to locate him.

Pete glowered intimidatingly at Greg. 'How do we know we can trust you even now?'

'Don't ask me, ask Liz.'

The doctor emerged from the treatment room. He told them

that though Liz appeared to be recovering after her ordeal, she should spend some time under observation in a cardiac ward. He gave Greg a sympathetic smile and added, 'And she asked to speak to you.'

Greg entered the small darkened treatment room. On a couch below the fanlight window Liz lay pale in the dim artificial light. Terry was standing at the foot of the couch, her cold manner warning Greg that his presence was an intrusion. He ignored her and sat down on the hard chair at Liz's side. Her eyes flickered open. He looked down at her with an expression of remorse and hope. She touched his right forearm with her left hand.

'I must thank you again, Greg, for saving my life. I know what a sacrifice it will prove to be to you,' she whispered, and weakly clasped his right wrist. She remembered all too well how less than three hours ago he had thrust his right palm towards her, demanding to have his fortune told. The decision which would shorten his life had been made: that lunch-time he had set off on a new course from which there would be no turning back.

'Let me stay around for a while, Mrs Graham: let me keep an eye on you. You've turned my life back to front and inside out - I don't know what to do or where else to go.'

She patted his hand to reassure him. 'This is no place for boys, Greg, but if this is where you want to be, then stay.'

Her head dropped aside on the pillow as she fell back asleep.

1 : 11

A week had passed before Liz felt strong enough to return to Briarbank to collect her belongings. She took Bethany with her for support, and Greg accompanied them in his self-appointed role as Liz's protector. As the Oldsmobile followed the Marcos onto the shingle drive of the large Tudor-style house, Liz saw with relief the open garage doors which told her Alec's Lincoln was away. She asked Greg to wait outside in his car while she and Bethany called at the house.

The front door opened. Alec's mother Goldie came out to meet them, dressed for the winter in a red woollen suit with a navy and white blouse and the usual yard of pearls wound twice round her neck. A quieter reflective sorrow had replaced her usual exuberant manner. She frowned to see Liz falter in dismay and extended her hand to encourage her.

'This is still your home, Liz,' she said, sensing the isolation Liz felt. Hoping she might still salvage something of the marriage, she invited, 'Come in and have coffee with me.'

Liz entered and sat down with Bethany in the lounge but declined the coffee. 'I have to go uptown after I've picked up my things here: I start back at work this afternoon.'

'Yes, Alec tells me you almost die in an accident. You feel better now?'

'I'll feel better back in harness.'

'But why do you not tell me about all your troubles, Liz? There are phones in Greece as well as London.'

'What could I have said, Goldie? That Alec and I have made a mistake?'

'This marriage is no mistake - you are well-suited for each other. But Alec is not the only one to make mistakes. You bend yourself in every way to fit into his life; but do you not see you bend yourself for him too much? As long ago as last August I tell you not to spend your life trying not to upset Alec - a big fiery row can do him so much good!'

'You know I never could stand an argument,' Liz said lamely. She wished Goldie would abandon her foreign affectation and use more verbal tenses besides the present; but caught herself in the absurd resentment and knew she was rather bridling at Goldie's well-meaning concern which she could not dismiss as mere interference.

'You are still young, Liz: you still have time to learn. I know you still love Alec. Try to believe Alec still loves you - I know he does, though he thinks he does not. He is too proud to admit that he cannot trample over you just as he cannot trample over me. Trust God to help him see and make everything better again.'

'It can be very hard to hold on to God when your world is collapsing about you. My horoscope is marked with the fatalistic signs of the Grand Cross of ill-fortune and the Grand Trine of good. I can't fight against such powerful cosmic influences. Spiritual principalities wage war around me - I'm helpless in their wake.'

'What nonsense is this, Liz? God is stronger than fate - God makes fate; fate does not make God. If you must use divination to guide you through this darkness, turn to your Tarocchi cards, not the stars. Better, go to your Father Jay who pleads for you - his guidance cannot lie.'

A car turned into the drive. Liz started up from her seat like a frightened bird, recognising the sound of Alec's Lincoln. Goldie's lips tightened with a flash of anger at her alarm.

'Believe in yourself, Liz! This is still your home; you are still my daughter. However black this parting seems, it is only brief. God has joined you to Alec - neither of you can break that bond, so do not ignore it, however much your sorrow may tempt you...'

She broke off, realising Liz was too interested in what was happening outside to hear her. Alec had garaged his car and walked across the drive to have words with Greg. The young man left his car to meet him halfway. They stood arguing in the middle of the front garden.

'You would be unwise to have that boy on your conscience.'

Liz was so preoccupied that she misunderstood what Goldie meant. 'His death will be of his own choosing, not mine,' she tartly replied, shocking Bethany out of her bystander role.

'Hold on, Liz: am I hearing right? Have you become so much like Mr Keast, you can write off the young man who loved you enough to save your life at the risk of his own, and condemn him to death without even batting an eye?'

Liz faltered to realise her slip in mentioning Greg's impending death in front of Bethany. She said with a shiver, 'We are all condemned to death, Bethany, and most of us die in the manner of our own choosing.'

'Do not be hard on your friend, Bethany. It is not easy, to know that a man is about to die, yet be helpless to prevent it. Or to know that some disaster is about to happen, yet be unable to stop it.'

Liz shivered again and stood. 'I must pack.'

She ran out of the lounge and up the stairs to hide in the bedroom before Alec entered the hall. Bethany watched her flight and turned to look at Goldie.

'She needs you as her friend now, Bethany; nothing else. I know you will not let her do anything rash.'

'Huh! I'm hardly the one to keep Liz on the straight and narrow. But it goes without saying that I will try.'

From the hall came the sound of the front door opening. Goldie stood up to greet Alec as he came in.

'Liz is here to collect some of her things. Bethany is in the lounge with me, waiting for her to come down.'

'Tell Liz I'll be in the study if she wants to see me,' he tiredly replied. He shut the study door behind him. Shortly afterward his muffled voice could be heard through the door as he harangued someone on the phone.

Liz carried her hastily packed case down to the hall and left it by the stairs. She paused at the study door to listen, needing to enter to get some of her papers. Alec replaced the receiver and dialled another number. She ventured in, hoping his second call would be as long as his first, but the minute she closed the door he cut off the call and replaced the receiver. She crossed awkwardly to the bookcase, praying he would not turn on her. Even across the room she could feel his eyes burning into her back.

'Just came for some books and my passport. I have to fly out to P.S.I. Italia at the end of the week.' Her embarrassment was making her justify herself again.

'Then you will need these too.'

He retrieved her bank stationery from the top drawer of the desk and placed her passport with them on his pale green blotter. She thanked him and moved closer to pick up the papers. As she reached across the desk, he caught her wrist and held her hand captive above the little pile.

'I will not give you the satisfaction of a divorce, Liz.'

'Nor will I ask you for one, Alec - to me it really is for life.' She looked nervously up into his eyes and saw his hurt pride mimicking her bruised emotions. 'Don't worry, I won't pester you with calls.'

'Perhaps we should have done as you once suggested, had an affair and be done with it.' His words were devoid of expression.

She resisted the temptation to remind him he would not have inherited his father's estate that way; but her voice hardened. 'We didn't, though, did we; so now we're picking up the pieces.'

He released her hand as though rewarding her for passing some unmentioned test. She took out the Oldsmobile's keys and dropped them in front of him. 'I think you'll be wanting these.'

He pushed the car-keys across to join her pile of belongings. 'No: after all you two have been through, the Olds should be yours,' he said with calculated magnanimity, having equipped the car with a tracking device.

She thanked him awkwardly. After a short silence she said, 'I've got a place to live. I'm renting a house near my parents - it's called Chalgarth. Mother found it for me. Bethany's agreed to stay there with me a while, to help me settle in.'

'Good. I shall be moving away sometime soon. That place in Cheshire I was bidding for, Leigh Manor: It's just been confirmed I've got it. The place will not be the same without you - that was to be the setting for my choicest stone. For a while, Liz, I really believed in you. But the faith you demand is too much.'

He picked up a small jewellery box and opened it to take out a small gold medallion and chain. 'You may as well have this - I have no use for it. It was to have been a birthday present. Shall I fasten it for you?'

She nodded and put her books down beside her passport to move closer. He slipped the chain over her head and straightened the medallion without thinking. She longed to hold him in her arms once more and wondered whether their present closeness might be his arrogant way of inviting a reconciliation without admitting that he was the one to weaken. She risked touching his hand. When he did not recoil, she touched his bearded cheek and placed her hand behind his neck. Trembling, she drew his head across to kiss his lips. The gentle kiss of reconciliation she had intended became intensified by the passion she had subjugated for so long.

Once again he flinched. Once again he put her away from him. She stepped back in distress and grasped the medallion to tear it from her neck, but saw it and stopped. The symbol she held was a hand-crafted representation of the Tarot image of God as the divine Fool. Her bitterness subsided at once, but with nothing more to lose she knew she had to find out why Alec was treating her with so much disdain and yet with so much love.

'What have I done? What is it you find wrong with me?'

'Don't you know? I know everything about you; yet still you refuse to tell me. Why did you never admit to me that Jonathan Keast went back to Neptune House to say goodbye to you?'

'Who told you that? Oh, Sir Kenneth Bywater, I presume, when he persuaded you to place even more pressure on me. Did you know that because of him you too have been working for Mr Keast?'

She backed off in tears, struggling to stop herself from saying more as she hastily gathered up her papers to leave.

'Is that what you're reduced to now - slandering my friends because you have no answers for me?'

She fled sobbing from the study. Bethany and Goldie tried to intercept her in the hall but she pushed past them and ran outside.

Bethany picked up her case and hurried out after her while Goldie blocked the hall to prevent Alec following them. Angered by her interference, Alec ordered Goldie aside. She refused to move.

'No, Alec; that is enough damage for one day. You will regret it. I know.'

1 : 12

Toni Sullivan brought the debate to a close, pleased with the success of P.S.I.'s Wednesday night discussion group's second meeting. As the auditorium lights came up, sound engineer Tim signalled his congratulations to her from the projection room. She acknowledged him with a wave and thanked her speakers, Charles, Mary and Liz.

The audience of thirty drifted towards the theatre exits. Charles apologised for having to leave promptly and followed the crowd. On his way out he passed Bethany and Terry descending the auditorium steps with Greg behind them. His head turned briefly to fix a look of concern on Greg. Liz noticed, and followed his gaze, paling to perceive the young man was haloed by the psychic shroud of death.

'So you see it too, Liz,' remarked Mary Sebastian, who had been distracted by Greg all evening.

'I saw it a week ago, in his hand. I've just been waiting for it to happen.' Liz replied. She was aware too that Toni was watching them all in bewilderment.

'You won't prevent it.'

'I can try.'

Mary snorted and hurried off. Terry, Greg and Bethany gathered round Liz with congratulations, preventing her from following her. Toni watched Mary leave the theatre and interrupted them to ask Liz what was wrong. Liz attempted to use her question as a way to avoid a late-night invitation.

'I don't think I'll go out on this surprise you three are planning, after all. It's been a long day and I feel rather drained.'

'You can't back out now, Liz: Terry's already booked it,' Bethany protested.

'I thought you said you'd just hit on the idea tonight.'

'Where we're going. I can't leave things to chance, even if you do,' Terry said with an arch smile.

'Then Greg, you'd better go home, and let us have our hen party in peace,' Liz said.

'It won't be the first hen party I've gate crashed. I won't get in your way,' Greg promised lightly.

'No, Greg. I want you to go home.'

'Liz, you can't do that: you'll leave yourself unprotected,' Bethany warned.

'Quite: I'm staying with you,' Greg said.

'Greg, I order you to go home,' Liz commanded.

'Something's gonna happen, isn't it,' Toni gasped.

'All the more reason for me to stay with you, Liz,' Greg insisted.

'Fair enough. That is your decision,' Liz declared, as if washing her hands of the consequences. Bethany recalled her comment earlier that day at Briarbank about Greg's death.

An announcement over the public address system asked Liz to go up to the sound box. She acknowledged the message with a wave to the projection room in response, apologised to the others and left the theatre. When she arrived in Tim's domain, she found Martin Kingsley with him, the young accountant who had betrayed her and P.S.I. to Sir Kenneth Bywater.

In the past Martin had seemed an arrogant young professional; but now he hung his head in shame for fear of meeting anyone's eye. Liz saw the change and wondered whether his humility came from genuine remorse or just a ploy for reinstatement.

'You wish to speak to me, Martin?'

'I do,' he admitted, and paused a moment to choose his words.

'I want to apologise, Mrs Graham, except apologies aren't enough, I know. I never meant to get involved in Sir Kenneth's racket; and I wouldn't have, but for the way Max and Arnaldo goaded me on. But it was all my fault I fell for it all.' He paused again, too embarrassed by the foolishness of his actions to go on.

'How did it all begin?' Liz coaxed, sensing his difficulty.

'It was about three weeks ago. Max and Greg took me to a nightclub. I'd met Max through P.S.I. I knew he was trying to turn people against you, so I went along with him so that I could show him he was wrong. That night they introduced me to Sir Kenneth and his younger daughter Cassie. Despite my best intentions, I drank far too much for my own good. Next day Sir Kenneth confronted me with evidence that someone had found me with Cassie in a rather compromising situation. He threatened to get me dismissed from here, and all sorts; unless I volunteered to help him. I had too bad a hangover to refuse. When I realised later just what it would involve, I tried to back out of it. But Sir Kenneth already had the key to my obedience - he threatened to lose me my job again, and I became his grovelling servant once more.'

Martin's confession did not surprise Liz, but she wondered how full it had been.

'What information did you give Bywater?'

'Outlines of P.S.I.'s present financial position, projected expenditure, that sort of thing. I've given Jo Simon and Bethany Broome the complete list and copies of all the documents involved, to help them complete P.S.I. Britain's investigation.'

'Jo showed me the papers you gave her this afternoon. Your freehandedness was rather unfortunate for P.S.I. and probably still is, isn't it?'

She watched Martin as he ruefully agreed with her, his head hanging lower. His remorse seemed genuine, and she sensed he had learnt enough from the incident not to commit such a betrayal again. Her point made, she added with a gentle smile, 'As if anyone could work out our plans from the number of paperclips we think we'll use! Forget it, Martin: it's all over and done with now. You fell into a trap set by a cunning and evil man, just as I did. Take the good out of it by heeding the moral of the tale, but leave behind the rest. It's time to start again.'

Astonished by her pardon, he stuttered, 'Tim said you'd understand - but I didn't think anyone could! And I can't forget my mistake. And Greg said; I should ask if... Mrs Graham, it looks like I'll lose my job here anyway, and that's precisely what I was trying to avoid. I love working for P.S.I. Please, would you let me stay on despite what I've done? I promise you it will never happen again.'

'That's not my decision to make, Martin; even though I don't think you'll make the same mistake again either. But I'll certainly recommend the delegates keep you on; and they do usually follow my lead. And let me give you this piece of advice for the future: promise nothing if you can, in case something prevents you from keeping it and forces you to break your word.'

'For the future, maybe, Mrs Graham; but for today, how else can I prove my sincerity now, except by pledging my future undying loyalty?'

'Tim is your witness, Martin. Be warned, before long I may well need your support.'

She gave him an encouraging smile and left him to re-join Bethany and Greg for Terry's mystery night out.

1 : 13

To their surprise, Terry took them to Plover's, a West End 'taste of the forties' retro night-club which was just becoming the fashionable place to be seen at in London. They hurried in through the brightly lit canopied entrance, escaping from the pouring rain outside. As they checked their damp coats into the cloakroom, proprietor Barclay Plover entered the foyer to welcome them personally.

'Miss Carter, what a long time it's been since you graced us with your presence,' he greeted Terry. He turned to Liz and said, 'I believe you must be Mrs Elizabeth Graham, the accomplished new Chairwoman of P.S.I. I met your predecessor several times. It's an especial pleasure to welcome a lady whose remarkable talents are matched by such beauty.'

'Liz, never trust Barclay,' Terry warned light-heartedly: 'Just because he owns the best night-club in London, he thinks he owns half the women too.'

'But Teresa, what do I want with half the women in London when I have your adorable sister?' he returned. 'I am pleased to tell you a cancellation means you can have table two on the dance floor after all, instead of the balcony table which was all I could offer you yesterday.'

Liz shot Terry a suspicious look, which Barclay broke as he stepped forward to usher their party through the swing doors into the club. They entered a compact balconied dance hall furnished in rich maroons and creams, with lights shining brightly on the small uncrowded dance floor and burning low above the surrounding tables. A curved stage showcased a versatile seven-piece jazz band playing American dance music popular in the forties. In the shadowy margins, waiters plied between the crowded tables and the bar under the ornate balustrade of the balcony stairs. Barclay took the party to a table on the edge of the dance floor, waved a waiter over to take their order and wished them a pleasant evening.

'That's the first time Barclay's ever taken me to my table himself,' Terry remarked once he had gone.

'Must have been love at first sight, Liz: did you notice how I never even got a look in?' Bethany joked.

'Nonsense!' Liz returned. 'I'm glad we're not on the balcony: this table's much more in the centre of things. Is that Patrick Mower over there?'

Her question sparked off some light-hearted famous face spotting at their table, while the infectious music set their feet tapping. At Terry's suggestion Greg invited Bethany up for a dance; she accepted by giving him her left hand. Liz watched them on the dance floor but then noticed beyond them on a more secluded balcony table, a man's half-hidden silhouette which she thought was familiar.

Greg guided Bethany twice round the dance floor with skilled but lifeless ease before returning her to their table and leading Liz out on to the dance floor instead. Liz proved to be an unpractised partner and repeatedly trod on his toes. As she apologised to him, she noticed his attention was drawn to the same balcony table.

'Something of interest, Greg?'

'I'm not sure.'

'Is that why you're so glum tonight beneath the smile?'

'No - I just keep thinking what a fool I used to be.'

'We're all fools at times - I can't stop making a fool of myself!'

Alec's medallion burned against her neck, making her recall Goldie's advice not to have Greg on her conscience. She quietly suggested they stopped dancing before she broke all his toes and walked with him back to the table.

'Where did you two learn to dance?' Terry teased as they sat.

'Liz knows the steps - the new dance comes from both partners trying to take the lead,' Bethany said. 'We were the only girls at our school for young ladies who didn't mind being the men in dance class. It took me three years of private tuition to break the habit. Liz didn't bother.'

The dance floor cleared for the resident singer Isabella Santon, a tall slender beauty of twenty-seven with long black hair and a full-length close-fitting black sequinned gown. Her deep rich contralto voice took effortless command of her audience: all but Greg seemed to hang on her every note. After her second song, a waiter brought her a glass of water and spoke in her ear, making her turn to look in Terry's direction. She used her third song to move from table to table as she sang, timing her progress to reach

Terry's table during the song's instrumental break.

'Someone's been asking after your girlfriends, T.C.' she hissed, an overwhelming vision of beauty who looked hard as granite underneath.

'Find out who it is, Bella, and come and tell us,' Terry replied.

The singer nodded and moved on to the next table and the next verse.

'Is that your sister?' Greg asked in surprise.

Terry nodded. 'Some people have all the luck! I look like the back end of a bus and can't sing a note. Santon's her stage name - she's Isabel Carter at home, or our Bella, or I.C.'

The song ended in an improvised rallentando, and Bella moved back to the band amid enthusiastic applause. She exchanged a few words with a waiter while sipping her glass of water, and then nodded to the saxophonist to start the next song.

Another waiter paused by table two and offered Liz a folded note on his tray. She opened the slip of paper to find the unsigned hand-written message, *Mrs Graham, come to the main entrance at once.* Wordlessly, she handed the paper to Greg and stood up to obey the instruction.

'No, don't go!' he ordered. 'This is Sir Kenneth's writing - I'll deal with it myself.'

'That's what they hope, Greg. Please, let me handle it - if you go you will die,' Liz warned.

Bethany stood up too, alarmed because she knew Liz would not lie about such a premonition, and volunteered to take the place of them both. The head waiter saw the commotion and hurried over to ask them what was wrong. Greg assured him that nothing was amiss, asked him to keep an eye on the ladies while he was away for a few minutes, and hurried off through the swing doors out into the foyer.

Bella finished the set with an up-tempo number and retired backstage at the start of the dance interval, leaving the floor through a stage door concealed below the balcony staircase. Terry poured herself another glass of wine from her half bottle, disappointed that her sister had not come straight over to her table at the end of the set. Bethany turned to speak to Liz but found her preoccupied, concerned about Greg's lengthening absence. Fed up with them both, Bethany sipped her fruit juice cocktail and wondered how she could join the couples jiving on the dance floor now that her only available dance partner had disappeared.

Hands touched Bethany's left shoulder and Liz's right. They spun round to find Bella seated elegantly between them in Greg's place. To cover her surprise, Liz complimented the singer on her performance. Bella thanked her in a deep silky voice with a nonchalance implying compliments were only her due, and complained, 'It isn't for the lighting tonight! Christ, it's hot on stage. I don't know what Barclay's done with the spots: they're all wrong!'

'Who was asking after us, Bella?' Terry enquired.

'That couple over there on the balcony, by the plastic jungle arrangement - recognise them? Oh, you can't see them from here! Is that why Barclay's fiddled with the lights, I wonder!' Bella said, and refreshed herself with half of Terry's glass of wine.

'Hey, go easy - you've still got another set,' Terry warned.

'Do you know who they are?' Liz pressed, sensing that Bella enjoyed teasing her sister too much to tell her what she wanted to know straight off.

The singer shot Liz a withering look and scornfully returned, 'It's not your husband, Mrs Graham, if that's what you're worried about. Just some guy called Philip King who's with one of the local tarts, and some private dick called Sam Buxton who walked out shortly before your tough went for a drive and hasn't come back.'

Liz blanched to discover who had been observing her evening there from the balcony. Speculative visions of angry scenes with a jealous Alec tumbled through her mind.

'What precisely did Mr King want to know?' Bethany asked, puzzled that Liz's brother-in-law and Alec's manservant should have asked who they were when the two men would have recognised everyone in Liz's party.

'He wanted to confirm Mrs Graham is the Elizabeth Chairman of P.S.I. Mrs Graham, and who the rest of you are. The waiter checked with Barclay and told him yes, Mrs Graham is, and with her is the sculptor Stanley Broome's daughter, our T.C. and a tough. Then cos one of you's my sister, the waiter told me.' Bella gave a suggestive leer. 'What's been going on?'

'Mr King is my husband's brother. Alec must have sent him here to spy on me - we've just separated,' Liz answered, disliking her inference.

'Good for you - you're much better off single. And I should congratulate you too for ousting Jon Keast. Now, there is a bad one - he made a fool of you, T.C. just like he made a fool of every woman he brought here.'

'Bella!' Terry protested indignantly.

Bella laughed and finished her glass of wine in one mouthful. 'What's up, T.C. Is darling Bella not tactful enough, you old liar?' she taunted. She stood up. 'Ah, well: I must away for part two.'

She slipped away with a wave and went backstage to change costumes for her next set.

'Quite a sister you've got there, Terry,' Bethany remarked.

'If she didn't have such a big mouth. Where the hell's Greg gone? He ought to know about King and the private eye.'

'Perhaps he already does, to have insisted on taking my place,' Liz said. 'If you'll both excuse me, I'll just go and have a word with my brother-in-law.'

'No, send him a message to come down here!' Bethany said.

Liz smiled and shook her head. 'And lose what little advantage Bella gave us?'

She walked away between the tables as though heading for the powder room, but doubled back out of Philip's sight and took the service stairs up to the balcony. Blond, debonair Philip did not notice her until she was only a few feet from him. With a

94

conspiratorial smile he invited her to sit down in the seat between him and his escort, a besequinned brunette amazon he introduced as Alison. He eyed Liz's more bohemian powder blue dress with amusement.

'Alec will be very upset with me for acknowledging you, of course, Liz,' he continued: 'You really have got him going now, you know. Some champagne?'

'Not today, thank you, Philip,' Liz frostily replied, displeased that he had tempted her to drink alcohol when he knew the reasons she had fought to stay sober for more than seven years. 'What are you doing here? Other than sending one of Alec's henchmen out to deal with a defaulting boyfriend of his who only fell from grace because he saved my life?'

'My, aren't we bitter tonight!' Philip teased. He turned on his persuasive charm. 'Liz, I have far more experience than that Vincent boy could ever have; and Alison is much too well paid to complain if I leave with you instead. I know you must be starving by now, and you know I've always had an eye for you.'

'You disgust me, Philip! To betray your brother's trust - what a vile snake in the grass you turn out to be! I can't stop you filling his ears with lies, perhaps, but I can at least tell you the truth. Alec and I are married for life. That is my belief. If I go with anyone else I will knowingly commit a cardinal sin; and I can assure you, you are not worth going to hell for.'

He laughed amiably at her indignation.

'Oh, Liz, go home. All sorts of nasty things are happening outside tonight. If you do go home, we will protect you from them; if you don't, we won't be able to. We were not pleased with Sir Kenneth for tricking us into helping Jonathan Keast.'

His unexpected advice forced Liz to revise her opinion of him yet again.

'I can't go home, Philip; not yet: I'm too hurt. But it does help to know Alec sent you to plead for him, however badly you've gone about it. How did you know I'd be here?'

'Your friend Bethany told Mother this morning that Terry was taking you clubbing tonight; I suspect to reassure Mother you aren't pining away alone at home.'

'But there are a hundred clubs in London.'

'Liz, Alec knows everything about Teresa Carter - he made it his business to know, because she was Keast's lover as well as his secretary, and probably she still is. Her choice of club was obvious - why, he even told me which coat she'd wear!'

Liz stood up indignantly. 'You are trying to discredit Miss Carter again,' she objected with a loyalty that was wavering more than her confident tone implied.

'It doesn't matter to me whether you believe me or not. But it might matter to you and Alec.'

Liz wished she had never agreed to go on this disastrous night out on the town and wondered how she could escape.

'I'll see you around,' she told Philip and turned to slip away.

He stood up and stopped her.

'Liz, if the time ever comes when you find yourself right out on a limb with no-one to help you, give me a ring, no strings attached. Maybe your luck will change.'

She nodded with glistening eyes and hurried off. A few minutes later she reappeared at table two, brave-faced again. Bethany and Terry scolded her for being away so long and quizzed her about what Philip had said. She fobbed them off with vague answers given in an informative way which Bethany saw through without comment, sensing the device was for Terry rather than herself.

Bella returned to centre stage amid enthusiastic applause, a vision of chic in silver sequins. While she was singing the bright opening number of her second set, Terry remarked to Bethany that Greg had been away a long time. Bethany innocently rose from the table to look for him, leaving Terry alone with Liz. After the song had ended, Terry spoke to her in a low voice.

'I know I'm worth nothing in comparison with you, Liz. You

are like a goddess, and I feel like some small worthless bird. But even a bird can sing a song of adoration, and even goddesses sometimes cry.'

'You have drunk too much, Miss Carter,' Liz rebuked. 'Your goddess is only made of plaster: she will smash when you knock her off your pedestal. Or is that what your lover wants you to do?'

'What do you mean?' Terry protested, pulling back from her rejection with frightened eyes.

'You know very well! Keast failed to get rid of me through Bywater, so he's having another go through you.'

'You must be joking, Liz! I haven't seen Jon since you threw him out last August. Do you think if I wanted him back, I'd help you settle in so well? I'm sorry if my admiration upsets you. I assure you it will not intrude on our professional relationship again. But don't accuse me of betrayal when my only fault was to think of you as my hero.'

Her protest threw Liz into a quandary: she sprang up to escape her presence and her own indecision about what she should do about her.

'Please excuse me, Terry - I must go take some air to clear my head,' she said, and hurried off out into the foyer.

1 : 14

Greg had left the Plover's club room to find the foyer almost empty. At the open door, a man in a dark suit smoked a cigarette as he gazed out at the dark rain-washed street.

'You asked for Mrs Graham?' Greg challenged.

The man turned, revealing himself to be Bywater's right-hand man.

'Ferris!' Greg thrust the note at him. 'Why this? Why now?'

Ferris sneered as he pinched out his cigarette and threw the butt into the street. 'You'll do just as well.' He slid a Luger out of his jacket pocket.

Greg turned back to escape into the crowded club room, but found his way blocked by Sam Buxton. He saw he was trapped and raised his hands in submission.

'To your car,' Ferris ordered.

Greg obeyed, walking out into the wet night with Ferris behind him, the concealed gun pressed into his ribs. Out in the street some drunks barged past them, pushing Ferris aside as Greg appeared to search for his car keys at the door of his lime green Marcos. Greg took the chance to flee but ran straight into Sam's left hook. Stunned, he stumbled and fell back against the bonnet. Ferris wrested his car keys from his right hand and got into the driving seat. Sam bundled Greg into the passenger seat and strapped him in.

Greg came around a few moments later to find Ferris driving him through the West End. The car turned into a narrow alley off the main thoroughfare and drew up in a yard at the back of a theatre, beside a quarter-open stage door. A sleek black Bentley stood in the dark shadows cast by the tall buildings crowding round the yard. Sir Kenneth stepped out to meet the sports car. Behind him waited his driver, a bearded bohemian with porcine eyes.

'I told you he'd be here, Travers,' Sir Kenneth said as Ferris got out of the driver's side.

Travers opened the passenger door and pulled out the captive. He turned on Bywater in fury.

'That's not her, you double-crossing bastard!' he swore, and pulled out a Colt Python. Before Bywater could react, a bullet smashed through the centre of his forehead. He dropped to the wet ground like a bull felled by the slaughterer.

'My God!' Ferris cried and pulled out his Luger to retaliate.

As Ferris fired, Travers pulled Greg across his body to shield himself and fired back. Ferris staggered and fell dead with a bullet through his heart. Travers released Greg who dropped too, having taken Ferris' bullet in his chest.

Travers knew he had little time to act after the deafening cracks of the shots in the enclosed yard. He swiftly wiped the fingerprints from his gun and placed it in Greg's right hand. Then he fled the scene, diving through the stage door into the maze of the theatre beyond.

As he disappeared, Greg came to from the shock of taking the bullet. At first, he was aware only of an agony of pain radiating from his chest. He tried to cup his hands over the entry wound but found the fingers of his right hand tangled round the gun and his left arm covered in blood.

Panic swept over him as his body fought a losing battle to compensate for his injuries. He saw his car and stumbled into the driving seat, his confused thoughts racing between the desire to escape and the need for medical help. With difficulty he started the engine and turned the steering wheel to drive the car out of the yard. The pains in his chest stabbed like knives with every movement he made, and his eyes glazed as unconsciousness threatened to overcome him again in waves of tempting oblivion. He shivered with cold and sensed in numb acceptance that this time he would not survive. With nothing left to hope for, he turned the car towards Plover's and Liz, doubting he would get that far.

For one last time he raced through the rain-drenched London streets, struggling to avoid the other vehicles along his path. Somehow the need to see Liz one more time kept him going. With squealing tyres, his sports car raced out of the darkness and skidded to a halt outside the club.

Liz and Bethany were standing just inside the foyer when his car appeared. As Liz ran out to meet him, the driver's door fell open. Greg swung out his legs and tried to stand with the support of the windscreen frame, but staggered onto the pavement. He stepped towards the shelter of the awning and collapsed to the ground, his fall too heavy for Liz to soften his landing. He lay there, ashen faced, gazing up at her with glazed eyes. She saw the bloodstains on his jacket and his shirt and knelt beside him to cradle his head in her lap. Tears glistened on her cheeks. He gave her a weak smile and tried to speak, but choked and coughed up blood.

'Sir Kenneth is dead,' he struggled to whisper: 'They will say I did it... and you won't be able to prove... Oh, Liz! I only went because I love you. I didn't think it would happen to me.'

He choked more severely. She turned his head to one side on her lap to help him breathe. Frothy scarlet blood spilled out of his mouth and over her powder-blue dress. He rallied slightly and clutched her hand in fear.

'It's very dark where I'm going to.'

'Ask God's forgiveness and take His hand: then you'll find His light is there to show you the way,' she promised, her voice wavering in her grief.

The fear in his face turned to concern and then to peace. A tremor ran through his body as his nervous system collapsed. Liz searched for his pulse but knew that there would no longer be one. She closed his eyes and wept for him.

Bethany hurried out to her side. 'An ambulance is on its way,' she said. She averted her eyes and fought back her nausea at seeing Greg's blood staining his mouth and Liz's lap.

'It's too late. God help him.' Liz looked up at her friend with pleading eyes. 'You heard me, Beth, didn't you? Three times I tried to tell him not to come, didn't I, but still he ignored me. It was his decision, not mine. I could only carry the message; I couldn't save the man...'

Bethany tried to persuade Liz to leave Greg's body, all too aware of what the press would make of the night's events. Before she could succeed, cameras flashed, turning their tragedy into front page news.

Chapter 2

Card 16:
The Lightning Struck Tower

Sudden failure in success;

ruin, collapse

Bethany handed Liz her post across the breakfast table in Chalgarth at the start of a long hot August Monday. Besides the expected confirmation of the renewal of the house lease, Liz had received a letter from her brother in Cumbria.

'Good news?' Bethany asked, ripping open her own post.

'Ricky's moved into Granda's farm. He wants us to stay there after the conference, in return for their stay here. What's yours?'

'Another love letter, headed your High Street Bank: the manager and I are friends again now the divvy's come in.'

Liz laughed and poured them both more coffee. She was wearing a light floral print dress and had loosely gathered her long black hair at the nape of her neck for coolness. 'And what is the lady of leisure planning to do today?'

'As it promises to be another scorcher, I think I shall spend every minute sunbathing in the garden and pitying you having to waste the day working in town. What is the masochist inflicting upon herself today?'

'Correspondence, business meeting, business lunch, new Tarot reader assessment, writing a report for the conference; then home to finish that chart for *Helicon* before Guy does his nut - that typesetting equipment's made him worse, not better.'

'Still the professional with two fs? If that's not the appointment diary of a workaholic, I'm a Dutchman. It's time you laid off yourself, Liz.'

'After the conference, Bethany, I promise. Will you be coming next week?'

'Next Wednesday? I'm not sure yet - it'll depend upon the weather. Which is precisely what you should be saying too. Time?'

Liz glanced at her watch and stood up. 'Time for me to dash.' She left her toast and coffee to drive herself to work.

Bethany sighed and fondly watched her leave. Though she

knew hard work was Liz's way of coping with her separation from Alec, Bethany could not accept that it might help her friend because she herself had only perceived work to be an affliction, not a cure. As the weeks had turned to months, she had continued to stay at Chalgarth, trying to protect Liz from herself. She waved her off to work and strolled outside in her sundress to enjoy the day.

Liz arrived at Neptune House early as usual and had opened all her weekend post before Terry turned in at nine. Liz had never quite got around to changing her secretary after the disastrous night at Plover's, and true to her word Terry had not let her personal feelings intrude on their professional relationship since. Terry's skill and experience with P.S.I. were proving invaluable to Liz as they finalised preparations for P.S.I.'s twenty-first annual conference and coming of age celebrations. With her efficient help Liz cleared the day's correspondence before ten o'clock, leaving the whole morning free for her meeting with the Swiss delegates Hermann Muller and Bernie Tobler.

Liz took the delegates on a tour of P.S.I. Chelsea and Neptune House before they held their business meeting. Bernie had been a founder member of P.S.I., one of the few who had not been involved in the less legitimate side of the society's past, and spent the morning reeling off anecdotes about P.S.I. with such affable wit that he kept Liz spellbound. So little business got done that Liz had to extend their lunchtime to finish off the most important matters.

She consequently arrived late at Charles' office for the Tarot reading and received a just scolding from him for keeping the novice diviner waiting. He took her along the corridor to the small plain windowless assessment room which his research section used for most of its psychic tests. As they walked in, Toni Sullivan looked up nervously from her seat at the bare table. Her face fell when she realised who the subject was for her assessment reading.

'So you're the poor unfortunate Charles has found for me, Toni,' Liz joked with a smile, projecting reassuring thoughts to calm the highly strung student. 'Remember, I'm only here because

Charles thinks it's time I had my cards read; and you're only here for an assessment of your talent, not your technique. So don't worry about your presentation or what I might think. Just tell us as best you can what the Tarot cards tell you.'

Toni nodded nervously and asked Liz to sit down opposite her at the table. Charles settled on a chair in the corner to take notes from the side-lines. Toni handed Liz the twenty-two Major Arcana cards which she had separated from the pack and asked her what she wanted to ask the cards.

'I'd like to know how the 21st Annual Conference will go next week,' Liz said as she shuffled the cards, knowing from experience that it was much easier to answer a specific question with the Tarot than to give a general reading.

She handed the shuffled cards back and Toni dealt out ten cards from the top of the deck face down in a familiar pattern. As she interpreted the spread, Toni turned over each card in sequence and explained its position and meaning. Her voice was even more staccato than normal under assessment.

'At present, the Sun of success: everything looks happy, the conference looks like it'll go well. Your obstacle is, the Devil: someone's trying to stop you from holding the conference, or prevent it from running smoothly. Your goal is worldly; no, I mean you've got the card the World so you must want to reach the world, through the conference. In the past foundation you've got the Lovers; a difficult choice between love and ambition. Past events, the Priestess; secrets and physical abstinence - as we all know, you left your husband...'

'Walked away from wealth to pursue ambitious idealism - hardly worldly,' Liz reflected, drawing Charles' attention. Her need to justify herself warned him that her motives might be more worldly than they appeared.

'Future influences,' Toni continued, 'the Moon: there'll be deceptions and underhandedness to do with the conference. And this card describes you: the Pope upside-down; which means you teach religion but you've got your wires crossed: you're a hypocrite. I'm sorry.'

'No matter: if that's what the cards tell you, that's what you must say,' Liz reassured. 'What is the next card?'

'Future events: the Fool, which stands for God in the Tarot - oh, that's on the medallion round your neck!'

Liz nodded and fingered the medallion. 'Alec's last present to me. It reminds me that if I want to be wise, I must often appear a fool in other people's eyes.'

'It means something different here - I think God's going to step in and do something, perhaps remove the Devil's blocks. Inner emotions in the future, the Hermit: you'll step out of life for a while to think. Final result - oh, no! The Lightning Struck Tower. Oh, Liz, what's going to happen?'

'What does the last card mean?' Liz asked in a hard, flat voice.

'That in success you'll have sudden collapse; cos what you built isn't founded on good things at all, but on the suppression of God...' Toni broke off, staring at her with wide round eyes and an expression of apologetic dismay.

'Perhaps an evil spirit is playing around with the cards, Toni. Let's try a second spread to see if things change,' Liz suggested.

Toni nodded and threaded the Major Arcana cards back into the Minor Arcana pack. After Liz had shuffled the full 78 card pack, Toni laid the top fifteen cards in three rows covering the past, present and future. The spread extended the tale of woe further, dominated by the grinning Devil as the centre card dictating the surrounding pattern. It showed Liz's past decision to leave Alec because of his insensitivity, her present hypocrisy linked with others' deceptions and the parting of friends; and future ruin, tears, loss and the end of a way of living.

Toni finished the reading with a seven-card spread which briefly summed up the salient points of the two spreads before. She looked at Liz in embarrassed concern, not knowing what to say.

'Remember, Toni, the purpose of a Tarot reading is to show

the querant where he or she is going wrong, so that he can remedy his present errors, avert the future danger and return to the divine path. What is your advice to me, after a reading like that?'

'To be honest, Liz; I would say, take a good look at yourself: work out what you're doing that's not what you're saying; though heaven knows where you're going wrong. Whatever it is, that's what the Devil's going to use against you. He'll make it worse so God has to step in and stop you; and it's going to start in the next few days, so you'd better think quick.'

Liz thanked Toni for the reading and Charles arranged to speak to the student later about the assessment. Once Toni had left the room, Charles sat down in her vacated chair at the table and looked at Liz with visible concern.

'Your opinion of the reading?' he enquired.

'The past is accurate, which would imply that the present and the future are too. She's got the feel of the cards enough to be adept despite her lack of experience, and with practice...'

'Your personal view, Liz, not your professional one.'

'My personal view is personal!' she snapped, but relented to explain, 'It will take me time to weigh up her words. I've talked about hypocrisy too much recently to ignore a warning that I myself might be a hypocrite too. Do you have a pack of cards? I'd like to check the reading.'

Charles handed her a spare new pack from a drawer in the table. She broke the seal and shuffled the cards with expert thoroughness before dealing a third of the pack out in a large complicated spread. For some time, she silently studied the pattern, only her grave face telling Charles she was reading much the same message yet again.

'What is the main theme of all these?' he asked at length.

'That I will be thrown out of P.S.I. by people I trusted as friends; and that my hypocrisy is born of pride and worldliness...' She leapt up in protest at the prospect she foresaw. 'No! It's not true: it can't be - not after what I've been through already!'

'But the cards don't lie,' Charles reminded her, unmoved by her outburst.

'They can do. Sometimes, if the querant is living in the past, the cards reflect that, placing some of the past in the present, and all the present in the future. I know I'm a bit rusty on the quirks, but it's quite possible that's what's happened here. See, here it's describing the way I deposed Jon Keast at last year's conference; and here's Alec's secrets, and the parting: it's all here.'

Charles considered the possibility and shook his head. 'I admit I do not know your personal circumstances last year as well as you do, Liz, nor do I have your experience in the art of interpreting the Tarot; but do you not think you are trying to bend these readings to suit yourself? I cannot forget that something like this happened to M. Keast before you deposed him. He made the mistake of ignoring that the change needed is within, not on the surface.'

Liz gathered the cards together and stood up to leave.

'Are you saying that I am a hypocrite, Charles?'

'No: that is too strong. But I do think you should reconsider some of the things you say, in the light of some of the things you once said.'

She nodded and crossed to the door but turned back to say, 'Charles, a lot of difficult things have happened to me in the past year. Are you objecting to the changes that had to be?'

He sighed and shook his head, disappointed to hear her again justifying herself unasked. Her point made, Liz left the assessment room to return to her work.

As she walked down the corridor towards her office, a sheet of paper fell off the notice board outside Terry's door. When she stopped to pick the paper up and pin it back on the board, she realised she could hear Terry talking to her sister Bella, their low voices only audible because the door had drifted slightly ajar.

'No, I just called by on the way back to the club: you know what the grapevine is like here,' Bella said, and added a sharp comment which Liz did not catch.

'Back in town?' Terry demanded in alarm.

Bella gave a brief inaudible reply.

'Did you see him?'

'No, it was my night off. Barclay forgot to mention it till this morning. He turned up on Thursday night with his son and a guy called Robert Travers.'

'Hell! Don't breathe a word of this to Liz - she's enough on her plate as it is.'

'Don't you worry! I'm only tipping you off before the tomcat starts spraying round your door again. See you Sunday at Mother's.'

Bella left Terry's office, throwing Liz an amiable greeting as she walked past on her way out. Liz strolled into Terry's office and stopped at her desk to look through her out-tray for an urgent typescript.

'The Tarot reading did not go well, Terry, at least, not for me. What did your sister have to say for herself?'

'Nothing much,' Terry said in that unnaturally high voice which betrayed her lies. 'She thinks an old flame of mine's turned up again. And yes, the text for the pamphlet has gone to P.S.I. Chelsea. I got a member to play special delivery boy after you said it should've been there last week.'

Liz thanked her and walked on through to her own office. As she sat down at her desk, she wondered whether she knew who Terry's returning old flame might be.

2 : 2

Two days later Pete Corrie marched into Terry's office demanding to know whether Liz was there. Before the secretary could answer, he asked her how she could work with everything on Tottenham Court Road roaring through her open window, ordered a coffee with two sugars for himself, and marched on through into

Liz's office. Liz took care not to appear moved by his dramatic entrance and casually discarded a letter into her pending tray.

'Why I should get a request for a spiritualist to give a talk to a W.I. meeting, I don't know. Mary Sebastian should oblige - she usually does. What can I do for you, Pete?'

He cast a sheet of paper in front of her on her desk. 'Does this mean anything to you?'

She looked at the circular diagram on the page in amazement, scarcely noticing Terry bring in two coffees and leave again. 'Why, yes, Pete: it's a...'

'Don't tell me - it's a chart you drew for a magazine.'

'Correct. But how d'you know that, and how could you possibly have got hold it? I only finished the article last night; and I delivered it to the Print Workshop this morning - as usual I was late with the copy.'

'I dreamt it!'

Liz choked on her coffee and looked up at him to continue.

'Yes, interpreter of dreams: here's a good one for you. I dreamt I was in the Hall of Fate, a room so vast I couldn't see the walls. I was sitting at a round table in the centre of a circular mosaic. Twelve black lines radiated out from my feet. Someone said, "Read the cards," and there in front of me was a Tarot pack. "But I can't," I said. That didn't seem to matter, so I dealt two cards which became windows onto the world. One showed a farmhouse near a lake, and the other this office. Then they changed: the farmhouse became card eleven, the Enchantress, and this office became card fifteen, the Devil. "What does this mean?" I asked. The voice said, "Go to the one whose eyes must be opened; she who can see." Then the table vanished, and the mosaic wheeled about me anticlockwise, getting smaller and smaller. So like Alice, I threw the Tarot pack up in the air. The cards drifted down like petals. When they touched the ground, they all turned into card sixteen, the Lightning Struck Tower, and burst into flames. Then I realised I was standing in your study looking at this chart and thinking it was just like the mosaic in the Hall of Fate. And then I woke up.'

He paused for a moment to sip his coffee and studied Liz's bemused expression as she tried unsuccessfully to engage the correct mental vision to interpret the dream.

'I hadn't intended telling you about it as anything but a curio,' he added; 'But then I mentioned it in passing to Charles this morning - we have a standing joke about my not being psychic for overdue typescripts. He went a little grey about the gills and asked me if I knew you used to interpret dreams professionally. Then he sent me here to see you. So, what does it mean?'

Liz tried to back out of his challenge, but he would not let her. Reluctantly she attempted to explain the dream with logic rather than insight.

'You seem to regard your life from two angles, Pete: on the one side, home and serenity with Sue and your family; on the other side, your work where you often feel constrained by the blocks and prejudices of your more secular colleagues and members. At times your faith makes you question your fate, and then you come here to talk things out with me. But you know yourself that you already hold the key to the peace you desire in your own hands. If you throw it away, you'll watch it die with regret, for memories of past friendships are cold, empty companions.'

Pete considered her interpretation. His instincts told him it was wrong because it did not satisfy the proportions of his dream. 'That is all true, Liz,' he conceded reluctantly; 'But are your eyes opened? For the voice said they must be.'

'Do you think my eyes are shut?' she challenged, not willing to admit that while interpreting his dream she knew for certain they were.

The phone rang before he could answer. Terry reminded Liz that the time had already gone twelve and she had promised to see the joiner in the theatre before lunch to discuss the conference seating he was constructing. Pete apologised for holding Liz back and left to return to Charles' office.

Liz and Terry arrived in the basement theatre a few minutes later to find it deserted. From the projection room Tim informed them the carpenter had gone to lunch because his stomach could not wait any longer. Liz acknowledged the message with a wave and walked across the stage to inspect the half-finished semi-circular conference table.

'It's looking good,' Terry commented, following her across.

'The two-tier table was by far the best idea,' Liz agreed, and sat down at one of the places.

'What else did Pete's dream mean?' Terry enquired as she sat cautiously down beside her on the unsteady table top. On seeing Liz's startled expression she quickly added, 'I overheard accidentally. Pete had left the door open.'

'What else should it mean?' Liz asked sharply, not pleased to learn her secretary had been listening in, and not convinced by her facile excuse.

Terry saw her displeasure and stepped down from the table to prevent her nearness upsetting her further. 'The Enchantress used to represent you in Tarot readings; the Devil your enemies. Couldn't the dream mean that Pete is the only one who can help you deal with the people who want to do you down?'

'What people, Terry?' Liz shivered as the temperature seemed to drop suddenly. 'And where does that place you?'

'You know where I stand, Liz.' She caught hold of her arm, about to beseech her not to mistrust her again, when a footfall made her stop. They both looked up, expecting to see the carpenter. Instead, they saw Jonathan Keast.

He had stopped to watch them from the door through which he had left P.S.I. twelve months earlier: a distant, lonely figure; handsome, well-dressed, fascinating, deadly. For a split-second Liz's eyes caught his: the malice he projected made her recoil with instinctive fear. Beside her Terry froze, not knowing how to act in face of the open hostility between the woman who fascinated her and the man she realised once again she loved.

'Good afternoon, Miss Kirkland, Miss Carter,' Keast stated with such precise diction that the greeting sounded like a curse.

'Jon, what are you doing here?' Terry asked in her falsetto voice.

'Didn't you tell your secretary about our last meeting here either?' he taunted Liz with a reminder of how her silence had helped him turn her husband against her.

'Terry knows well enough how a bad penny always turns up again, without my having to tell her, Mr Keast,' Liz replied. She sensed he was not alone in the building, but because of her alarm was unable to estimate the power of the force with him.

He perceived her fear from across the stage and was pleased to discover how successful his strategies had been in undermining the faith that had made her great. To magnify her fear, he selected the weapon of suspense.

'I shall see you in the Chairman's office at two o'clock, Miss Kirkland.'

He turned and left. Liz shook herself out of the almost hypnotic trance his appearance had caused. Though dismayed and alarmed by him, she was not yet defeated.

'Tim, get after him. He's only a visitor here,' she ordered.

Tim waved from the projection room window and disappeared.

'Liz, it's lunchtime - he could go anywhere in the building, see anything he wants; and that might not be too good for you,' Terry warned.

'If Keast wanted to find smut, he would have gathered it long before he found us in the theatre to stage his return. Doesn't he love to make things look good!'

'Liz, this isn't a play! That man's in deadly earnest - he'll destroy you if he can.'

'Who will?' Pete Corrie asked from the back of the auditorium. The door swung shut behind him as he hurried down the steps to join Liz and Terry on the stage.

'Jon Keast,' Liz answered. 'He just left us through stage door right. Any messages for me to pass on? We meet again at two.'

'That explains the typescript issue I just had a phone call about. I didn't think you had recalled it.'

'What typescript?'

'The final conference programme. It wouldn't be beyond Keast to have it removed to save a print run because he expects to chair the conference himself. So if you know what's best for you, you'll sit tight in the Chairman's office to make sure he doesn't take it over, and you'll have him thrown out of Neptune House before he does the same to you.'

The theatre speaker system kicked into life. 'Sorry, Liz,' Tim announced, 'He gave me the slip - just vanished.'

Liz acknowledged Tim with a wave to the projection room and left the theatre with Pete to take the lift, Terry tagging along behind.

'I'll warn Charles and get back to P.S.I. Chelsea before anything happens there,' Pete said, getting out of the lift on the third floor. The atmosphere in the lift felt strained after he had gone.

'Jon's changed, hasn't he,' Terry said, struggling to fill the silence.

'Has he? I didn't notice in the heat of the moment.'

'You've changed too, Liz. You never used to worry about seeing him, but you're worried now.'

Liz considered the observation and realised how much her position there meant to her. 'Yes, I am,' she admitted: 'I've got far more to lose now; and a lot less to save me.'

2 : 3

Jonathan Keast arrived at the Chairman's office to find Liz staring through the window at the view she would lose if she gambled unwisely. She turned and invited him to take a seat, playing the regal role of host despite his intimidating presence in her domain. He sat opposite her at the desk and assessed her with cold eyes calculated to unsettle her further.

He had planned to take control of the conversation from the outset, but was disconcerted by Liz's appearance. Gone was the immaculately painted power dresser he had loved to hate over the past twelve months. Out of Alec Graham's influence, she had discarded the Graham ostentation while keeping her porcelain beauty and style. She looked natural and dainty in a floral and black print dress with short sleeves and a modest princess cut neckline partly covered by her long black curls.

'Before we begin, Mr Keast, I'd like to point out I am still married to my husband so there is no need to address me by my maiden name,' she stated.

'I shall bear that in mind,' he acknowledged in a manner which warned he noted it for far more than the way to address her. He sensed her own conviction of the total collapse of her marriage but was not convinced himself because of Dr Graham's strange conversation with him just before the New Year. He had accordingly taken steps to ensure Alec Graham was out of the country while he moved in on P.S.I.

'I have come to restate the challenge I made when we last met. You are free to accept or refuse as you think fit. If you refuse, I shall expect your resignation forthwith.'

'Then the answer is obvious: I must accept.'

'The conditions of the challenge you have just accepted are that the better man must prove conclusively that he is the more suitable person to hold this office, and his proof will include the majority vote of P.S.I. The loser will relinquish everything.'

His manner told Liz he had repeatedly rehearsed this scene in his mind over the past months before arriving there. He was using the words as a wall to prevent him seeing anything but the image he had constructed of her. She sensed she could only influence the conversation if she threw him off script with something unexpected.

'You have a lot riding on an open cheque like that, Mr Keast. Don't be so sure I won't take it when I win!'

Her challenge only confirmed to him the weakness of her worldly self-deceit.

'You will not win, Miss Kirkland. But if you were to resign at any time before the election, I would certainly offer you another position in the society, working with me. I'm sure a lot could be achieved that way.' He surprised himself with the offer even as he made it: her survival had not been part of his plans before. Her indignant reply stopped him having to consider acting on the offer.

'What, you think I would work for a man who stops at nothing to get what he desires? How can I possibly lose when you left behind you such a woeful train of victims and corpses?'

'Very simply. You have fallen far short of the professionalism required here, as your slander demonstrates so ably. I have been following your progress over the last twelve months. I have evidence at every level of your ineptitude. We hardly need to look further than the events surrounding the death of Sir Kenneth Bywater - a knight of the realm gunned down in the street by your handsome young "bodyguard" who died in your arms before an audience of newsmen outside the most fashionable night-club in town. The good name of P.S.I. brought into disrepute by the very person who should be its best ambassador!'

'I hardly asked the man to go that far,' she objected, her loyalty to her estranged husband preventing further explanation.

'And what of Sir Kenneth's moles? You accepted eight of his people as members, and didn't even notice their agitation splitting the society in two over your fanatical idealism. And while all this was going on, you blindly make policy decisions with no reference whatsoever to the members, even through their delegates. Such as your decision to take on more staff despite failing to advance the society in any material way to finance such an expansion. How do you reply? Or do you admit that everything I have said is true?'

'What, am I on trial here, Mr Keast?' she demanded in affront, but made the mistake of trying to answer his accusations. 'It is true that I accepted more of Bywater's men than you did, but I had started a membership drive: I accepted more genuine members as well so I doubt if my percentage is as high - and at least I didn't come to a cosy little business arrangement with Bywater about it. The increase in members made it necessary to take on another membership secretary to process applications and handle circulation lists, and her wages are more than covered by the increase in revenue from subscriptions. Admittedly, I didn't sell any industrial secrets or give some elderly member a heart attack after persuading him to leave everything to P.S.I. in his will. But it was a material advancement to this society when the four branches of the American Psychic Association affiliated after learning about P.S.I. from the news coverage of the Bywater affair. And I have always made what reference I can to the delegates and members when circumstances allowed. I based all my decisions upon good advice and sound reasoning: don't discredit them just because the decisions were mine.'

'So you do admit responsibility for leaving P.S.I. defenceless against any outside force wishing to silence its voice or absorb it into their own organisation.'

'Most definitely not!' she denied emphatically, but again hesitated to refute his claim with evidence that would betray Alec over Graplax. Her practical proof of her loyalty to her estranged husband angered Keast, who was astonished to think that Dr Graham could afford to throw away such devotion. Liz mistook his expression of displeasure for disbelief.

'I dealt with all the opposition as it arose: no-one has a reason to attack P.S.I. now.'

'There are many people with a personal grudge against P.S.I. through the society's past policies, many of them people with the influence to muzzle the authorities while they silence you. And before you is a man with several reasons for taking over again.'

He underlined his point with a pistol, a Remington 95 derringer. At first, she stared in disbelief at the muzzle facing her across the desktop. Then, thinking because he had not cocked the trigger that he was only trying to intimidate her, she gave him a condescending schoolmarm smile.

'Put your gun away, Jon. You have not been offered violence here and while you are my guest, I would ask that you act in a like manner.'

He could scarcely credit how totally she had misread her situation. 'The tables have turned, Miss Kirkland. No longer are you the host, but yourself the guest.'

She reached for the phone to call for help but he caught her hand and held her back. The touch of her velvet skin shattered the wall of hatred he had erected, flooding the ruins in a tide of lust. She looked up at him, aware of his sudden change, and their eyes met. Her body wakened in response to him and she blushed. Unable to tear her gaze from the depths of his deep dark eyes, she faltered beneath his mocking smile.

'All your officers are unavailable, Miss Kirkland. You can contact no-one, though of course you are welcome to try. In three minutes, my associates have taken over your entire hierarchy. You have been deposed.'

He released her hand. She immediately tried to disprove his claim by phoning round the offices, but got no answer from every extension she tried. Even the switchboard was not responding, nor could she get an outside line on the chairman's private phone. She replaced the receiver, taking care to control her rising indignation, and looked across at Keast.

'You appear to have thought of everything. Except the fact that the members of this society have not yet elected you back into office. Has your desire for revenge blinded you to their obvious reaction to such a sudden return?'

'I have not been blinded, and they have not been forgotten.

That is why you are about to leave with me.'

She shook her head, obstinate rather than defiant because the role of heroine was so much harder to play than to be. 'No, my place is still here, with the society.'

'I advise you to comply, young woman. You mean little enough to me - anger me and I shall not spare you.'

He cocked the pistol. She conceded defeat and picked up her handbag. He took it from her and checked its contents for a weapon. Finding none, he took her car keys and handed the bag back to her. She put on her lightweight linen blazer and opened the door. As they left the office, he slipped the revolver into the jacket pocket on his right hip where its threat would not be seen by a casual onlooker.

Terry was sitting at her desk as Liz entered. She gave Liz a nervous smile and nodded across to the window where Hendrik Gerber was standing in the bright sunshine. Liz acknowledged him with a strained smile. He responded with a polite comment. Keast handed him her car keys and ordered her to move on.

Liz gripped Terry's hand in a silent farewell. Their eyes met. She saw her own fear reflected in Terry's eyes and realised the secretary had not intended such an invasion to happen, instrumental though she must have been in its arrangement.

'Miss Kirkland,' Keast warned impatiently.

Liz obediently let go and walked out into the silent corridors of Neptune House. Keast directed her to the quadrangle carpark where his midnight blue Rolls stood by her white Oldsmobile. His chauffeur opened the back door for them. Liz thought she had seen the chauffeur's porcine eyes before but did not recognise his bearded bohemian features. He closed the door on her with a mocking smile and drove them away into the crowded London streets.

Liz gazed apprehensively through the window at the people on the pavements. Her fear sapped her concentration and turned their faces into a flurry of petals streaming past her plush cage. The image reminded her of Pete Corrie's dream, where falling Tarot cards had turned from petals to the Lightning Struck Tower. The last of her spirit evaporated to realise just how wrong she had been.

Keast watched her as the chauffeur drove them north through the suburbs, distracted by her presence which was short circuiting the hatred he had nurtured for her over recent months. When she turned her head, her green eyes looked feline in the shadows. Pressed into the corner furthest away from him, she reminded him of a feral kitten he had once found abandoned on a bombsite waste-ground when he was a boy; facing up to him, helpless yet defiant. His expression softened. Her eyes narrowed uncertainly and she turned away. In the end the kitten had died.

'I read your articles in *Helicon* with interest,' he said unexpectedly.

She turned to look at him, hoping from his attempt at conversation that she might find a non-violent way out of his control.

'You managed to find your way through the language barrier,' she replied, referring to the youth-speak idiom imposed by Guy's editorial control.

'My son provided something of a translation, Apparently, its language style has earned it quite a cult following in student circles.'

'Oh. Will it be the target of your next hostile takeover bid?'

He laughed at her barbed comment. 'No, this one will be enough. You know, I had expected a co-ordinated counterforce today, after your assurances last year. I found quite the reverse.'

'I was as prepared as I would ever be.'

'What, countering the advances of the secretary you should have transferred at least, if not dismissed.'

'I think you misread the situation,' she said tactically, having learned that defending her actions to him was unwise.

'Indeed? Then what were you trying to avoid in the theatre today?'

Liz looked sharply at him, sensing Terry's betrayal about her frequent visits to the theatre. To stop further reference to her relationship with Terry, she made the calculated confession, 'I was thinking about two Tarot readings and a dream Pete Corrie had.'

'Corrie took over the management of P.S.I. Chelsea, didn't he? What was his dream about?'

'A chart I designed for *Helicon*, linking the signs of the Zodiac with the symbols of the Tarot.'

'You choose to misuse your precious tools for divination in mathematical parlour games?'

'It's far more than a game. It can help clarify large spreads where, say, three people other than the querant are mentioned. It also relates different star sign types to each other more visually. For instance, you and I are psychic opposites, so I should expect you to do the metaphysical opposite to what I would do in a given situation.'

The Rolls turned off the road between tall ornate wrought-iron gates into a walled park, glided past a white gatehouse and drove on towards a large Georgian red brick mansion of elegant proportions and opulent propriety set in extensive lawns. Its composed red and white facade seemed to Liz the perfect front to hide Jon Keast's evil lifestyle.

'And what do you think I will do now?' he asked, taunting her with her last statement.

She turned her face away to hide the apprehension his question had raised as she imagined some of the many possibilities. When she did not answer him, he spoke again.

'What was the rest of Corrie's dream? You did not tell it all.' His question warned Liz he must have listened to her and Terry in the theatre before he had made his presence known.

'It was nothing. I interpreted it to fit in with his life. Terry interpreted it differently, that's all.'

The car drew up outside the portico porch. The broad white front door opened as they alighted, held wide by a handsome young man with well-styled chestnut hair. He smiled conspiratorially at Keast and stepped back to let Liz enter. She stopped a few feet inside the spacious wood-panelled hall to gaze in awe at her surroundings; admiring the impressionist originals on the walls, the craftsmanship of the woodwork, the impressive staircase, the antique grandfather clock, and the unusual black ceramic floor tiles with their distinctive amber circled three cherry motif.

'What a beautiful house, Mr Keast.'

'I think so. Though it's not as impressive as the manor your husband was about to give you the day you threw his jewellery back in his face and left him. But none of this was inherited: I started off like you, with nothing, and I earned every penny of it myself.'

'Aye, every penny from helpless drug addicts like Kevin Graham who should have shared Alec's inheritance!'

The young man sniggering at her self-righteous indignation. 'Is that what he told you?' he asked.

'My son Nicholas,' Keast introduced offhandedly. 'Yes, you turned your back on a mansion, to rent a small thirties detached in some middle-class suburb, all for the sake of what - ideals? Yes, opposites indeed! And you repeatedly ignored the advice of the man you claimed you loved to dismiss your secretary, even after she admitted her feelings for you, and despite her obvious betrayal of you. Do you love tragedy so much that you court disaster?'

'Of course not! And the rest is no business of yours.'

Keast laughed scornfully. 'You're not the only one to dine at Plover's.'

Liz blushed at his inference and walked away as if to look at one of the paintings. She felt the need to justify her handling of the secretary, but was reluctant to defend herself in front of the supercilious young man who laughed at her every reply. At length she said, 'I believe everyone deserves a second chance.'

As she spoke, the chauffeur strolled through the front door, cap under arm. His arrogant gait was the one clue Liz had needed to identify his familiar ruthless porcine eyes despite the unfamiliar unkempt hair and beard.

'Sandy Angus!' she gasped, stepping back in alarm.

'No, Robert Travers,' he replied with a mocking nod.

She turned back to Keast in dismay. He looked her straight in the eyes, tired of fencing with her.

'Take her, Nicholas,' he ordered, and abruptly marched out through the front door. Sandy Angus followed.

Nicholas shut the door after them and laughed openly, unable to contain his amusement any longer. Liz shot him a frosty glare.

'I have clearly offended him for some mysterious reason; but who wound you up?' she asked sarcastically.

'You both did,' he answered mildly. 'Don't worry about offending Father, Mrs Elizabeth Graham nee Kirkland: anything you said or did would offend him at the moment.'

'So glad you find our duel so entertaining Where must you take me?'

'I am under instructions to take you for a drive in the country. As my father provides me with the car, we shall comply.'

With a roguish smile, Nicholas escorted Liz out to his open-topped yellow MG Convertible sports car. After she had strapped herself in he warned, 'We have the choice of doing this the easy way: that's where you don't try to escape and we have a pleasant drive in the sunshine with the soft top down, until I bring you back here at eight o'clock or so. Or there's the hard way where you try to jump out at some point, but before you've undone your seatbelt, I've jabbed you with one of Hendrik Gerber's concoctions. This I can assure you has a kick like a mule, causes unconsciousness in thirty seconds, and leaves you with a three-day hangover.'

'Then the easy mystery tour it is.'

Nicholas drove her out into the sun-struck Hertfordshire countryside around St Albans. Despite the strained situation, he was an entertaining companion with a facile college wit and soon dispelled the cloud over their association with his light-hearted banter. Liz forgot her thoughts of escape and enjoyed the drive as much as he appeared to. She almost regretted it when the shadows lengthened and he turned his powerful car back for home.

Until then they had tacitly avoided talking about anything of a personal nature. But now Liz ventured, 'So what does your father really think of me?'

'He likes you a lot. And less of the cynical laughter! It's true - I've caught him sitting ogling your file for hours at a time.'

'Aye, plotting revenge!'

Nicholas smiled reflectively. He was very taken by Liz's air of vulnerable beauty and wished that she and his father could stop hiding their mutual attraction behind their business rivalry and begin the affair they were both fighting against.

'Why aren't you doing anything about our deposing you, Liz? Nothing's happened. Why aren't you fighting back?'

'Nicholas, your father kidnapped me at gunpoint today. You're still holding me against my will, however pleasant the drive has been. How can I fight back against that? You are your father's son, and to fight against him is to gamble with death.'

'You won't get anywhere if you've already convinced yourself you'll lose.'

Nicholas turned the car off the road through the tall gateway into his father's estate.

'Desperation can give an edge to resistance. All the things I took for granted recently, I'm starting to appreciate again. I've got an awful lot to lose now, and no Alec to save me.'

'I thought material things meant nothing to you. That's how Father described you last year.'

His comment struck Liz more deeply than he expected. He saw how easily his father would defeat her this time and wanted to give her at least a sporting chance. The MG drew up between his father's Rolls and Liz's Oldsmobile outside the Georgian house. Before she could alight, he turned to her to finish making his point.

'Liz, was the past year that hard, and your belief that small, that you've forgotten everything you used to live by?'

'It isn't that, Nicholas: it's my work. Don't let him take that away - it's all I have left.'

'You aren't worried about your work, Liz: you're worried about your life. You've made a mistake; but what's far worse, though you know it's a mistake, you're still living by it!'

Before she could reply Bob Travers appeared and sharply opened the passenger door for her to alight, concerned at what might be keeping the young couple in the car. He had discarded the chauffeur uniform for the bohemian clothes of an untidy artist but still had not lost his air of malevolence. Nicholas hustled Liz past him into the house. Travers shut the front door behind them and fetched Keast from a room leading off the hall.

As Keast came out of the room, Liz noticed its walls were painted black. She thought uneasily about the symbol of the ancient circled bunch-of-cherries on the black tiles beneath her feet. Keast played on her obvious disquiet by walking closely round her, his mien suggesting that he knew everything going on in her head. Her tension became palpable. He stopped in front of her with an air of proprietorship. She spoke to deflect his attention from the wayward arousal in her body with his proximity.

'Why isn't Sandy Angus taking up her Majesty's invitation? Could it be to do with the change of name and looks?' she asked.

'Bob Travers, do you mean, Miss Kirkland? Both the Angus twins are dead: Sandy in that crash outside Neptune House a year ago, and Douggie in a gas explosion at his home in February, shortly after the case against him was dropped through lack of evidence.'

'Dropped? When I saw him try to gun Alec down? How did you keep Alec quiet? And why wasn't I involved?'

'A certain item from Dr Graham's past, which you told me about last year.'

'You mean, you blackmailed Alec with information you stole from me under duress?' she gasped, blanching at the implications.

He smiled slightly, enjoying his control over her. 'Let us say your husband and I came to a mutually beneficial arrangement.'

'When was this?' she demanded in disbelief.

'Sometime between Christmas and the New Year.'

She stepped back in shock to realise how Keast had deliberately manipulated people and events to destroy her marriage. Suddenly she saw how through all the year past he had been controlling her like a hooked fish on a long line, allowing her the illusion of freedom until that moment when she had run her distance and he was finally drawing her into his net.

'So you're the one who told Alec about our last meeting a year ago,' she accused in a low, venomous voice. 'And you're the one at the bottom of everything else. By God, you sicken me.'

'Then you will be pleased to hear that you are free to go.'

He held out her car keys to her by their fob. She reached across to take them but had second thoughts and asked him what the catch was. He feigned innocence.

'Come on, Jon,' she insisted: 'There must be a catch somewhere - defective brakes, perhaps? You went to great trouble to keep me out of Neptune House this afternoon, but now you let me go free. What's happened in the last five hours that has made me of so little importance now?'

'Nothing has happened, Miss Kirkland. If something had, you would be staying longer,' he replied.

He tired of maintaining his self-control while making her dance for him and threw her car keys down at her feet to hide his desire for her behind feigned contempt. He turned on his heel and walked across to the room with black walls but turned back in the doorway to watch her pick up the keys.

'You need not bother going to Neptune House tomorrow,' he warned.

'Why not?' she demanded sharply.

He made her wait before finally answering, 'You will find out tonight, when you get home.'

With dramatic aplomb he stalked off into the black room and shut the door behind him. Liz hastily made her escape before he could change his mind.

2 : 4

Liz drove some distance before she came across a familiar landmark to help her find her way. As her route home would take her only a mile away from Neptune House, she called there to find out what had happened at P.S.I.'s headquarters during her enforced absence. Her keys no longer fitted the locks on the main doors. Worried, she cut across town to P.S.I. Chelsea and found the locks there had been changed too.

She drove on south with racing thoughts and arrived home to find nine cars parked near Chalgarth, forcing her to leave the Oldsmobile several doors away. As she walked back to the house, she heard loud dance music coming from her lounge windows. She glanced at her watch. The time was just past ten o'clock. She walked though her open front door to find the house crowded with people partying, all of them from P.S.I.

'Welcome home, Liz,' greeted a member standing near the door, glass in hand: 'How did your meeting go?'

She nodded with a false smile and picked her way between the revellers to the dining room where Bethany's loud voice was broadcasting an obscene joke. She let her deliver the punch line with a raucous laugh before she made her presence known.

'Liz! Glad you got back so soon,' Bethany greeted with drunken excess. 'Did you know today precisely twenty-one years ago P.S.I. was born? P.S.I. is twenty-one today. Happy birthday P.S.I.!'

Liz gave Bethany a fond sad smile for the comical figure she had become again with a bottle of wine inside her. She was disappointed to find how soon after her absence Bethany had organised a party to support her lapse into drinking.

'Who told you that, Bethany?' she asked.

'Jon did. Everyone in the Discussion Group's here. You've been a dark horse about the election, haven't you?'

'Drink, Liz? This is meant to be a party,' Terry interrupted in her falsetto voice to save Bethany from a faux pas. She waved the tray of punch she was carrying.

'Thank you, Terry, but no: I shall find my own,' Liz replied, unable to keep her displeasure out of her voice.

As she walked on to the kitchen, she left a trail of dampened spirits. Several members moved to leave, realising the surprise party had not been such a good idea. Liz piled up a tray with party food to make up for not having eaten since breakfast, added a glass of fruit juice, and carried her supper through the already dwindling throng to the study. She sat at her desk with her back to the closed door and the invasion to give herself time to conceal her disappointment should anyone come in looking for her.

A few minutes later student member Toni Sullivan and accountant Martin Kingsley slipped in, shutting the door behind them. Liz steeled herself and turned to acknowledge the only people in the whole gathering who felt able to face her.

'What happened this afternoon?' she asked.

'Can't you guess?' Martin bitterly declared: 'Those people out there betrayed you, Liz, to keep in with that bastard who kidnapped you this...'

'No, Martin: it wasn't quite like that,' Toni interrupted: 'They were simply too frightened, to admit to his face that they do still support you, Liz.'

'Stop trying to make it sound nice, Toni! He conned them! They really believe he and Liz are friends now, celebrating twenty-one years of P.S.I. together, with some light-hearted fun and frolics and an election thrown in for good measure.'

'Has violence been offered by anyone on either side this afternoon?' Liz asked, gesturing to them to sit in the two shabby but comfortable armchairs placed by her study window.

'No,' Toni said as they settled.

'Only when he marched you out of Neptune House at gunpoint,' Martin corrected; 'Not that I saw the gun from my office window: I've just seen enough gangster movies to know what it means when someone walks that way.'

'What little there was, was all implied violence, you see: just the hint, never the action,' Toni added.

'Then Keast is about to get back in. P.S.I. only threw him out because his drug team got too violent. People who've known him since P.S.I. started, like Bernie Tobler, will see the change and think he's the man they used to know again, that his men only resorted to violence to protect themselves from my husband's extreme pursuit of vengeance. And according to him, most of those associates are now dead.'

'Then I'll tell them what I saw today,' Martin offered.

'No, don't damage your position any more than necessary. We can't always choose terms, so don't actively support me during the election: there is no fortune to be found eating dust with the leader of the minority party.'

'Perhaps not, but there is glory. I betrayed you once, Liz. Now I can make up for that and pay back your favour forgiving me.'

'Thanks, Martin, for keeping your promise. But Toni, why do you join us? The way I ignored your Tarot reading gives you more reason than anyone to side with Keast.'

'No fear! Can't stand him - he likes his women to crawl, like...' She faltered, not wanting to betray Liz's closest friends before they could tell her of their change of loyalty themselves.

'Who is still on my side?'

'Charles for definite,' Martin said: 'There was quite a scene when he refused Keast entry into his section until you'd given him permission.'

'He had to give in: Keast said you were a guest in his house,' Toni continued. 'Tim's on your side one hundred percent, because you helped him get clean. He's threatening to jinx everything in the theatre by playing up on the control board. He knows the real difference between you and Keast - life and living death.'

'Then there's Pete Corrie, though he's trying to appear impartial: he's in a good position for getting you back and he doesn't want to lose it.'

'And Mary Sebastian - she gave me a kindly lecture: "Toni, dear, it's a crime not to bring home the crux of a Tarot reading".'

'And her side-kick Bill, what's his name, Wilson: he said, "Keasts are all very well in business, but I draw the line at them invading our temperamental other world".'

'And that's about all,' Toni concluded. Her heart went out to Liz because of the two significant names not on the list.

'Then perhaps I should resign.'

'No!' Toni protested: 'We'll help you fight Keast - we can't let him walk all over you without some form of protest. Don't give up before you know what your chances really are.'

'Unfortunately, we face a consensus of opinion. In P.S.I. if the majority of members want something, that is what they get.'

'Even when they've been hoodwinked into wanting something that's bad?' Martin protested.

'That's as irrelevant to the election of P.S.I.'s chairman as it would be to the election of the government. If Keast gets more votes than me tomorrow, he should rightfully take my place.'

'But he's already taken it, and we haven't elected him yet! So he's no right to boss us around. You should go right back into that office tomorrow and shove him right back out!'

'I would, Toni, but he's no gentleman in politics, so I must fight some other way. I thank you both for your support, and I'll welcome any help you think fit to give, as long as it is without risk to yourselves.'

'You can count on us.'

They shook hands. Toni and Martin left together in his car, the last guests to leave Chalgarth after the abandoned party. Liz returned her tray to the kitchen to find the house in silence and the detritus of the party cleared away. Only Bethany remained, sitting in the lounge with a magazine open in her lap and a half-empty bottle of wine beside her on the coffee table.

'Everyone gone so soon, Bethany?'

Guiltily, she closed the magazine as though Liz had caught her doing something wrong. She refilled her wineglass, drained its contents and refilled it again. It saddened Liz to see the influence for destruction Keast had already had on her.

'I thought you'd given up drinking alcohol for today, Beth.'

'No need. I can handle it now,' Bethany answered, her gestures too grand for her words to convince.

'Then what's troubling you, Beth, that you're sinking the rest of that bottle to run away from it?'

'Nothing's troubling me! So leave me alone, won't you!'

'Just let me know the score, Beth. I won't be angry, even if it's you and Jon...'

'Christ, Liz! Leave me alone!'

She picked up the bottle of wine and fled from the room in tears. Liz stared after her but did not follow. Her mind recalled her day, from its happy start to its dour ending. While it was no longer enough for her to have got safely home after fearing Keast would not release her, at least she did not need to take the drugs she had forsworn in the compulsive way Bethany now drank alcohol. That night she slept, trusting that somehow, she would find her way through to the far side of the night.

2 : 5

Liz woke late next morning to find her alarm had been tampered with, her car had been immobilised, and Bethany had gone. Annoyed at the way Bethany had sabotaged her plans to fight back, she called a mechanic to replace the leads missing from the limousine's engine, and tried to phone Terry at P.S.I. to warn her she would be late into the office.

The P.S.I. receptionist answered her call, heard her voice and cut her off. Liz realised how skilfully Keast was drawing his net in around her and disengaged her anger to fight back rationally. She redialled Neptune House and disguised her voice to sound like Bethany's as she asked for Terry's extension by number. This time her call was put through.

'Chairman's secretary,' Terry answered promptly.

'Good morning, Terry. Sorry to say I've slept in - I'll be a bit late. What's happening in Neptune House?'

'Hi, love,' she replied, trying to conceal her caller's identity. 'Sorry, I'm busy all afternoon in a meeting so I won't be able to lunch with you...'

A scuffle on the telephone line interrupted her as the receiver changed hands.

'Travers here, Miss Kirkland. The longer you want to stay alive, the further you'll put between yourself and Neptune House before two thirty today.'

'And the election I heard mentioned at the party last night? It'll take a lot more than idle threats to get me running, Sandy Angus.'

'Good: then I can look forward to some sport tonight. And the name's Travers, Mrs Graham.' He cut off the call.

His unequivocal threat made plain Keast's manipulation of P.S.I. as a series of moves to place Liz in a corner of his choosing. She needed help, but could think of only two people powerful enough to save her from Keast: her husband and his brother. She felt loath to ask Philip for help after that traumatic night at Plovers in February because of the price he might charge. And would Alec even listen to her: would his hatred of Keast be stronger than his hurt pride? Telling herself the worst he could do was say no, she dialled the phone number of Alec's Cheshire estate.

'Leigh Manor,' announced a mature female voice after twenty rings.

'Can I speak to Dr Graham, please?' Liz asked awkwardly.

'I'm sorry, Dr Graham is out of the country at present.'

'I know I said I wouldn't phone Alec again, but please, can I talk to him for just a moment. It's very urgent.'

'I would get him for you if I could, Miss, but honestly, he is abroad. If it's very important, I can leave a message at his contact number asking him to phone back as soon as possible, but that might not be for three days.'

'That could be too late, but can you at least try? And give him this message: if Keast takes back P.S.I.'s chair this afternoon I fear for my life - he and Sandy Angus have threatened as much. And ask Alec what this symbol means, like a bunch of three cherries in an open circle. I saw it in Keast's house.'

The woman read the bizarre message back to check that she had recorded its details correctly and asked who was calling.

'Why, I'm Alec's wife, Elizabeth Graham,' Liz said, startled, wondering what other women phoned her husband with similar strange messages.

She closed the call fearing she would find herself with no earthly help at all. To boost her flagging spirits, she dressed aggressively for the election in a favourite from her Briarbank days, a crimson silk shirt dress, belted at the waist. The dress felt good against her skin and emphasised the curves of her slender figure. As she expected to need to hide her emotions that afternoon, she also put on more elaborate make-up than she had worn of late.

Liz finally arrived at Neptune House shortly before two o'clock. She parked her repaired Oldsmobile next to Keast's Rolls which was occupying the Chairman's parking space, and entered the office block by the carpark door. The reception foyer was crowded with members and delegates socialising before the election. Liz wove her way through the groups to the desk and informed the receptionist of her arrival. She sensed many eyes were watching her and caught several as she turned back into the crowd.

'You've managed to get here, then, Liz,' remarked Jo Simon,

the slim thirty-year-old British delegate.

'Of course, Jo: I could hardly miss this tournament,' she replied with a sociable smile. 'But if this is an election, what about the Americans, and all the other members who won't be able to get here at such short notice to vote?'

'They contacted all the delegates yesterday. The Americans should arrive here just on time, in about half an hour. The election will be decided by the delegates and vice delegates to avoid problems getting enough members here for a vote. As their elected representatives we can be trusted to present their views in emergency situations like this.'

Liz looked into Jo's tanned face and knew that she had already lost one of the thirty-six votes to be cast. 'What are my odds, Jo?' she asked quietly.

'In years with P.S.I., twenty to one. Good luck, Liz: you'll need it.'

Liz turned away and saw Keast cutting towards her through the crowd. She gave him a regal smile for the benefit of those around and commented about the weather. He escorted her to a lift which Terry was holding open for them. The secretary greeted Liz with an unnatural grimace of a smile which she maintained long after the lift doors had shut and the two rivals had discarded their facades. In the close confines of the ascending lift the tension between them became supercharged.

'Had you waited at home, Nicholas would have collected you, Mrs Graham: I sent him for you not long ago,' Keast stated, gratified to see from her early arrival and her appearance that his tactics had brought out her fighting spirit.

'Aye? No doubt so that I would arrive like the American delegation, only just on time,' Liz returned sharply. 'Do I get an agenda?'

Terry handed her a clipboard with an especially large, almost mocking smile.

'Martin Kingsley will explain the procedure to you: he

volunteered to represent you.' Keast's tone suggested that to volunteer for such a dubious role was foolhardiness verging on insanity.

The lift doors opened onto Travers and the fourth floor.

'Bob will escort you to your office, Mrs Graham: for old times' sake I have put you where you don't belong,' Keast said.

'Why, is it easier to lie to the members that way?'

She stepped out of the lift to join Travers.

'You should've taken my advice,' he warned as he led her down the passage: 'If you'd run off this morning you'd've lived longer.'

'I shan't admit defeat until I've been defeated.'

'Your mistake. I'll be waiting right outside the door, so don't try any funny business; okay?'

Liz walked without comment into the chairman's office. Martin Kingsley stood up to welcome her and shook her hand before sitting down opposite her at her desk. They both glanced at the door to make sure it was shut before they spoke.

'It's good you got here sooner than Mr Keast planned, Liz; but we still have very little time. So though I doubt this'll be a private conversation, we'll get straight on with it. I see you've got the agenda.'

'Yes. I don't like the way Jon Keast always speaks after me. I'm on the defensive but he's placed me on the attack. Who'll count the votes?'

'Carter, Corrie and Lafayette, in the theatre straight after the votes have been cast; so it shouldn't be rigged. Hendrik Gerber is my counterpart for Mr Keast.'

'You know how things are here now, Martin. What's our best approach?'

'It's not the time to play to the crowd as the delegates hold the power. Our problem is that Mr Keast knows every last thing about you, while we've got less than nothing on him - he's hushed it all up, and none of the old timers'll betray him, just in case.'

'Perhaps I can help you there.' Liz told him the things she had discovered about Keast over the past year. As she spoke she realised how little hard evidence she held against her adversary: almost everything she had considered fact was unsubstantiated, either hearsay from Alec or based on her own experiences.

Martin asked her about her own career. She listed her achievements at P.S.I. and where she expected Gerber to challenge her. Before they could discuss her best defence, a phone call summoned them to the basement theatre. They gathered up their papers to leave. At the door Liz hesitated, a worried frown on her face. Martin asked her what was wrong.

'After the party last night, it's clearly on the cards I'm about to lose. If I don't, all well and good; but if I do, would you keep an eye out for me afterwards? Should I disappear, don't believe Jon Keast if he says I've gone to the country for a rest. I'll tell you myself if that's what I do.'

'What are you trying to say, Liz?' Martin saw her trembling hands and recalled how Keast had kidnapped her from that office only twenty-four hours earlier.

'The terms Jon dictated in his challenge yesterday were that the loser will relinquish everything, and the winner will take whatever he chooses. I accepted them because if I hadn't I would have lost P.S.I. there and then - at least it gave me a chance to win once and for all. I forgot Jon drives a hard bargain.'

'Don't worry, Liz: I'll keep everything under control for you. And I'll be giving it my best shot - we both know how long he'll keep your supporters on the payroll if he does get back in. Just remember, whatever happens this afternoon, he can't do anything to you here. So smile.'

She nodded and gave him a tentative smile of gratitude. Her smile became more regal when Bob Travers escorted them down to the basement theatre. Without thinking Liz signed herself with the rosy cross as she approached the theatre entrance. An inner peace returned to her which had been missing for some time. Serenely she took her place on stage with Martin, opposite Hendrik Gerber and Jonathan Keast, with Terry, Pete and Charles between.

They were the last to arrive. Liz acknowledged her adversaries and the adjudicators, and then briefly surveyed the packed theatre. She could see that Martin had been right to say Keast had taken the advantage by converting the delegates and giving them the deciding vote, for it left her many rank-and-file supporters with no influence on the decision. Keast's stratagem did not trouble her. She had suddenly realised how little her year of sacrifices had really meant to the members, how her only real gain had been the personal satisfaction of putting her beliefs into action, and how the only cost of ending her unrecognised suffering was to endure the one small humiliation of this public defeat. No longer did the election hold any terror for her: she smiled confidently across at Keast and was only amused by the malevolence in the smile he returned.

Pete Corrie opened the proceedings with a short introduction. Martin followed with an outline of Liz's time at P.S.I., highlighting her successes and achievements. Hendrik's corresponding review of the important milestones in Keast's career as the founder of the society, easily belittled the greatest of Liz's achievements. The question-and-answer section of the election debate followed. Martin started off less confident than he sounded, knowing Liz already needed to do a lot of catching up, but his questions made none of the impact he sought. Keast convincingly explained the integrity of his actions and his non-involvement in anything illegal. Hendrik's adept questioning of Liz efficiently destroyed her credibility in front of the crowd but failed to undermine her confidence. Even an issue he challenged her about which could only have come from Bethany's betrayal had no effect, as she had already accepted Bethany's disaffection after seeing its first effects in her compulsive drinking.

Liz used her election address to deliver an unexpectedly powerful rallying speech, quoting Plato to warn P.S.I. against tyranny, with the reminder that the most conscientious leaders rarely seek the mantle of leadership. All her former magic returned as she spoke. Picturing P.S.I.'s work as an adventurous challenge like a voyage of discovery, she asked the members whether they were brave enough to take up that challenge. The young and the young at heart applauded her when she sat back down.

Keast coolly refuted her exhortation to the sizeable youth sector with a measured speech addressed to the delegates. To belittle those naive enough to have felt inspired by her rhetoric, he asked, 'brave enough or foolish enough?' and promised he would not make P.S.I.'s work a dubious gamble but the constant step-by-step advancement of hard work to success.

The poll was taken by secret ballot. After the delegates had cast their votes, Terry and Charles did separate counts and gave their results to Pete. He checked their totals and called for silence.

'The result of this ballot of delegates and vice-delegates: Jonathan Keast, thirty-two votes; Elizabeth Graham, no votes; abstainers, four. I therefore declare that Mr Jonathan Keast, founder of P.S.I. and chairman for twenty-years, has been duly elected back into office after an absence of one year.'

Cheers and applause drowned out his last words. Keast and Hendrik shook hands, pleased with their convincing victory. Liz was momentarily stunned by the totality of her failure, but rallied her spirits to appear unmoved while still in public and turned to thank Martin for his support. Once her emotions were under control, she pulled the P.S.I. signet ring off the middle finger of her left hand and crossed the stage to hand the symbol of office back to Keast. The crowd fell silent, expecting an outburst. Instead, she shook his hand.

'Thank you for winning, Jon. You have taken a great load off my shoulders. Please accept this ring as proof that I acknowledge your return, and with it take my congratulations. I hope your next turn of office is less eventful than my year proved to be, unless it be for more future successes.'

He took the ring and watched her return to her desk with a

frown of disbelief, her glad acceptance of defeat souring the sweet taste of his success. As she gathered up her papers to leave, she realised that the theatre too was in incredulous silence and could not resist the opportunity to make one tempting little dig.

'The majority has chosen: be glad, for though popularity is not the hallmark of virtue, smile; for we shall all reap what we have sown.' With that parting shot she picked up her papers and turned for the stage door.

'Liz,' Keast called back, knowing from her gibe that she was still only an imitation of the woman he had lost to last year, good though her act had unexpectedly become.

She stopped and turned her head towards him, both of them conscious of the critical crowd watching their every move.

'Take back your ring, Liz. Keep it as a memento of a year of service which demanded and took everything you held dear.'

She walked back to his place near the front of the stage and held out her left hand for the return of the signet ring. He turned her hand over and slipped the ring on her third finger.

'You need not leave us. With your experience of P.S.I., I can easily find you a position working with me here,' he offered. His smile was for the benefit of their audience. His eyes glittered coldly.

She narrowed her eyes and mirrored his veiled malevolence. 'I was brought up to be a thinker, Mr Keast, not a beggar,' she whispered venomously, far enough away from his microphone not to be picked up. 'You have surrounded yourself once more with puppets who dance when you pull the strings. Be content with them, Chairman - I shall never crawl to you!'

She marched out of the theatre. Martin followed soon after and caught up with her as she unlocked her limousine in the quadrangle carpark.

'I don't understand it, Liz. Why did the vote go so totally against you?' he asked.

'They have lives that are dear to them,' she replied, recalling a family discussion in Alec's lounge a year ago.

Martin picked up on her inference.

'If you're worried about your own safety, you're welcome to camp out in my lounge. It's not the height of luxury, but I'm sure my flatmate won't mind. We could even go job-hunting together!'

She considered his offer as she climbed into her driving seat and closed the door, opening the window to reply.

'Thanks, Martin, but no. Tonight I need to be on my own. Then I think I'll take a holiday somewhere for a few days before I decided what to do next. I'll phone you tomorrow, let you know where I'm going. If I don't, please look out for me.'

'I will, Liz. Goodbye, and good luck. I won't forget you.'

2 : 6

Back at Chalgarth, Liz spent the rest of the afternoon brooding over her defeat. Though she struggled to be objective, she found it all too easy to listen to the whispers of self-pity. In an attempt to change her mood, she sat on the sofa listening to gentle folk music and trying to meditate on the flowing lines of a small sculpture displayed in an illuminated niche in the teak wall unit.

At first, she only noticed subliminally the bottle of champagne standing on the shelf near the sculpture. The temptation to step out of her failure for a few hours in the contrived oblivion of alcohol was becoming almost overwhelming before she consciously saw the bottle and leapt up to break its spell. Realising someone had deliberately placed the bottle there to tempt her at her lowest ebb, she grasped it by its neck and threw it through the open lounge window, determinedly smashing it on the path outside.

The action purged her thoughts of failure and guilt, for she could not be a complete failure while she could still deal with such temptation so positively. She mixed herself a soft cocktail of orange juice and lemonade to satisfy her salivating mouth and sat back down on the sofa to think more positively about her situation, throwing out after the bottle all her self-pity and despair.

Her own struggle helped her to forgive Bethany her betrayal in joining Keast, for her friend had only failed to resist the temptation to drink, to which she too had nearly succumbed. For a moment she questioned her tendency to forgive, but knew she had to do so for the peace of mind on which her sobriety depended. Martin's loyalty and Greg's total commitment showed how her mercy had been justified. She perceived how her attempts to live out her faith in her work had made her a misfit in P.S.I. And as the first rays of sunset beamed into the music-filled lounge, she realised that her words of thanks to Keast for winning the election had been quite true. She had felt upset only because her pride had been hurt in losing to him so completely.

The click of a switch brought gentle yellow lamplight to dispel the shadows in the darkening corners of the lounge. Liz turned off the tape playing on the stereo music centre beside her.

'Hello, Liz,' Terry said, her deep voice trembling.

Liz greeted her with reserve, wondering how she had come by a key and uncertain of her intentions. Though Terry might think she had come to help, she was Keast's ally now, not hers.

'Jon said you'd be sitting like this, that I should come around and apologise. Mind if I have a drink?'

'If you know where to find one,' Liz said sharply, bristling to discover who had placed such temptation in her home, obvious thought it should have been to her.

'Last night's leftovers,' Terry said with a laugh as she retrieved a bottle of sherry from the sideboard and poured herself a large measure. She saluted Liz with the glass, took a sip of her drink and sat nervously on the edge of an armchair.

'I'm sorry it had to happen like this, Liz. All things end sometime, so please don't think badly of me. I really didn't want to hurt you, but I couldn't speak to warn you.'

'Forget it, Terry. If you think you'll be happier with Jon than working with me, then don't feel guilty - you must be true to yourself. I got along quite happily without P.S.I. before, so I can again now.'

'But Liz, I don't know if I will be happier with him. He's cruel, he doesn't care; he'll have any woman who takes his fancy. He'll cheer me up, then do me down; he never listens, not like you listen. But still I have to be there, waiting for the rare time he wants me. Oh, Liz, I don't love him: I hate him; but I need him desperately.'

She sighed and sipped her sherry. 'You brought a lot to me, Liz. You opened things in my mind that I never knew were there. So I had to come back to warn you, because of what you meant to me. You must leave here.'

'You're right, Terry; I must. But not tonight: I need to be alone here for a while, to think things out.'

'No, Liz: you must go! Get in your car and drive off somewhere; anywhere, before he gets here. Get away before he comes for you.'

Her urgency made Liz see through her warning to the reason for her visit, and the hunters waiting outside for the chase to begin.

'No, Terry: I've played enough of Keast's games for one day.'

'But he hasn't had enough of you,' she bitterly replied.

They heard a front door key turning in the latch. Terry hastily set down her glass by the onyx ashtray on the coffee table and stood up. Liz sipped her fruit juice cocktail and listened to the footsteps crossing the parquet floor in the hall; four people in all, though only Bethany and Keast walked into the lounge. Bethany had linked her arm through his, but when she saw Liz's face she felt uncertain enough to disengage from him and move away to the window out of her gaze.

'Jon, you have made your killing. Must you have my friends make such fools of themselves over you in their efforts to betray me?' Liz asked him, pleading for them rather than for herself.

He shot her a look of such intense hatred that she shrank back in her seat as he approached, her knuckles white around her tumbler.

'The killing has not yet been made, Miss Kirkland,' he threatened.

Her free hand darted across the coffee table in search of a weapon. As her fingers touched the onyx ashtray, he caught her wrist with his left hand and pulled her arm away.

'You hypocrite! You Jezebel! You whore!' he snarled and struck her face.

His unexpected blow threw her back across the sofa. Her glass shattered against a leg of the coffee table, its contents spilling over the amber carpet and her crimson dress. Bethany gaped in horror, sickened to watch a scene like the many she had endured with her father, being played out now between her lover and her friend.

Keast ordered Terry and Bethany to move the coffee table aside. They promptly obeyed. When Bethany returned to pick up the broken glass, he impatiently waved her away. Liz slowly straightened herself up and tried to wrest her aching grip from his grasp. He fixed her green eyes with his intimidating glare and tightened his fingers. She strove to resist the hypnotic effect of his cobra-like gaze before he paralysed her with her own fear.

'So you will never crawl for me.'

She struggled to free her arm before he forced her to break her word. He sharply pulled her wrist across on the rebound and dragged her off the sofa onto her knees. She resisted his force and tried to get to her feet. He struck her down onto the floor, twisting her arm painfully behind her, and pulled her back up by her wrist onto her knees.

'Now crawl!'

'Never!'

She jerked her aching arm out of his grasp and tried again to stand, but stumbled. Before she regained her balance, he struck her again. She fell heavily to the ground and lay for a moment where she had landed on the broken glass, shocked, dazed and winded.

When the mist in her perception cleared, she rolled over again onto her knees in one last instinctive attempt to stand. He struck her viciously once more. She sank to the floor, semiconscious, with blood from a glass cut trickling down her left jaw and across her neck.

Keast called Nicholas and Bob Travers in from the hall to pick her up. She hung limply between them, her head lolling on her chest. Keast caught his fingers through her black air and pulled her head back up. She looked at him through unfocused eyes from the far recesses of her mind.

'You disappoint me, Miss Kirkland, giving up so easily.'

Her eyes glazed and her head fell forward. Keast emptied the contents of Terry's glass in her face. She started back into awareness with the cold splash of the volatile alcohol, her perception of light painfully acute and her ears singing.

'Can't fight a defenceless woman on your own,' she slurred.

He struck her bleeding cheek backhandedly for her impertinence, his signet ring digging into her flesh. 'You'd rather stay on the floor?'

He turned away, impatient with his victim because she could no longer respond, and ordered Travers and Nicholas to take her out to his car. After they had left, he turned back to Terry and Bethany. His expression warned them to expect no less should they betray him as they had betrayed her.

'I shall see you both tomorrow,' he ordered, and left.

Bethany watched him from the study window as he got into the back of his midnight-blue Rolls with Liz. Travers drove them away. After Keast had gone the silence in the house felt oppressive. Terry awkwardly offered Bethany a drink, but she refused. The assault they had witnessed had sickened Bethany all the more because she knew she had contributed significantly to her friend's debasement by betraying Liz to Keast when she had betrayed herself to drink. This time, instead of reaching for oblivion in the glass and the bottle, she reached for sobriety and the phone.

'The Antiquarian Bookshop,' Harry Simms quickly answered

'Uncle Harry, it's Bethany here. I've had a slip...'

Terry wrested the receiver from her grip. 'Turncoat! Whose side are you on now?' she demanded.

'I don't know, Terry,' Bethany cried: 'I'm just trying to do something about me. Please, give me back that phone.'

2 : 7

Father Jay Kingston was about to sit down with a mug of tea after refereeing a hectic youth club meeting when his front doorbell rang. In the porch stood a young man clad in T-shirt and jeans with his back to the door. The long-haired priest opened the door thinking one of the club helpers had returned for a forgotten book, to find his mistake when the young man turned around.

'Why, you aren't Roy! You're one of Dr Graham's young men, aren't you - er, Sam? You'd better come in,' Father Jay invited, and ushered him into the lounge. 'I thought you'd all moved away to the country.'

'Cheshire,' Sam agreed. 'Dr Graham's kept Briarbank on for when 'e's uptown on business. 'E's in Greece at the moment. 'E's sent me 'ere to warn you 'e'll be phoning at nine thirty.'

'From Greece? What on earth about?'

'This phone message 'e got today.'

Sam handed Father Jay a tape cassette. The priest poured another mug of tea for his visitor and sat down to listen. The recording played back the conversation between Liz and Alec's housekeeper that afternoon. By the end of it he understood Alec's concern.

'Did Mr Keast get elected back in this afternoon?'

Sam nodded gravely.

'Then if Lisbeth's life is in danger, why have you not gone to the police?'

'Dr Graham'll explain all that - I've only come to make sure you're 'ere to take the call.'

Father Jay nodded and replayed the tape, trying to assess Liz's underlying mental state from her voice, recalling her recent less regular attendance at chapel functions. The housekeeper's lack of reaction to the message struck him: he wondered why she had not identified Liz as Alec's wife. He tried to draw the symbol Liz described but the image he produced only looked like a motif used in one-armed bandits.

The doorbell rang again. With an apology to Sam he went out to answer, shutting the lounge door firmly behind him. The door drifted open again as he ushered Harry Simms into the hall.

'Can't stop long, Father, but I felt I had to call by in passing,' Harry said: 'I think Liz Graham's in some kind of trouble.'

The priest was startled to hear Liz's name again so soon. 'Harry, I think you should come through to the lounge,' he began.

'No, I can't stop - I'm on my way to collect Angela for a twelve-step call. Bethany's had a slip, and she's feeling very guilty now she's sobering up.'

'Oh, no; and she was doing so well. Is it Lisbeth she's feeling guilty about?'

Harry nodded. 'I'm not too sure of the details - it was such a strange call. Someone took the phone off her as she got through to me, called her a traitor and asked her whose side she was on. Bethany said, "I don't know, Terry: I'm just trying to do something about me," and pleaded to have the phone back. And I thought, what's Liz Graham's secretary doing fighting like that with Liz's best friend. I think they'd forgotten about me: they got pretty heated, and Bethany's voice can be particularly penetrating. "How d'you think I feel?" she said: "That little scene's just for starters - God knows what he'll do to Liz when he gets her home." I listened more closely then. The man's name is something like Jon Keith. Do you know him?'

'Oh, yes: I know of him. Don't worry: I'll get help to her,

Harry. You and Angela go and help Bethany.'

As the priest closed the front door behind Harry Simms, his mantle clock chimed nine thirty and his telephone rang. He answered the call in Sam's presence in the lounge. As expected, Alec Graham was on the line.

'Good evening, Father Kingston: Dr Graham calling from Patras in Greece.'

'Hello, Alec,' Father Jay returned, disdaining his formality. 'I understand you'll want to be brief; so I'll just say I've heard the tape, and Sam's here with me now waiting for your next instructions. What's been happening?'

Alec tried to answer with the tale he had contrived but found all his excuses empty before the man of God.

'The truth is, Father Jeremy, I have been outwitted. Do you know anything about Jonathan Keast?'

'A bit. Lisbeth sent me his victims to reclaim from addiction. A dangerous man, from all I've heard. How has he outwitted you?'

'He convinced me through his business moves, that he wouldn't try to take P.S.I. back until next week, at the 21st conference. So when I was called away to some work here in Patras I was confident I'd be back in London in good time. Circumstances have proved me wrong. I got Liz's message this lunchtime and tried to fly back at once, only to find I've somehow become entangled in a mountain of Greek red tape. It will delay my departure at least until tomorrow; and she is helpless.'

'You're not by any chance saying you knew Lisbeth might be in danger?' the priest asked in concern.

'Not exactly. I thought our separation had deceived Keast; that when he came back to retake control of P.S.I. next week. I would step in and end his games once and for all. But I was wrong to think he was only interested in Liz because she was my wife and because she controlled P.S.I. Keast deceived me. He tricked me out of the country and embroiled me in red tape here, so that he can take both P.S.I. and Liz without any opposition, a week early.'

'You what?' Father Jay asked, horrified to think Alec had used his estranged wife as bait. 'Then it's time you did something to help her, like telling your man to call in the police. I've just heard Keast's taken her to his house, and it's not a social visit.'

'The police would be no use, Father: they would only fail as I've always failed. The symbol she described is the key. It explains the reason he holds her in such fascination.'

'The three cherries in a circle?'

'*Like* three cherries in an open circle. You would call it three reverse sixes in a broken circle, the footprint of the king of demons Purzson.'

Father Jay crossed himself. 'The number of the Beast, Revelation 13,' he gasped: 'Now I understand - I will make preparations to leave at once.'

'Sam will drive you there. I have instructed him to give you any help you need. Good luck, Father. Only you can save her now.'

'No, Alec; I may try, but only God can save her now.'

2 : 8

Liz stood up to look at her bruised face in the large gilt-framed mirror over the ornate white marble fireplace in front of her. She wondered why Keast had made such a vicious and unprovoked attack on her. Then she remembered Bethany's tales of her father's assaults and knew there did not have to be a reason.

After tidying her appearance as best she could, she explored the room, Keast's private library. It was elegantly proportioned and lined with overfilled bookshelves. In the centre of the room stood a leather-topped mahogany pedestal desk lit by an anglepoise lamp. On either side of the desk stood high-backed leather armchairs. The broad oak door was locked. Heavy amber curtains across the opposite wall covered French windows which were also locked. She moved on to look at the bookshelves and picked out an old volume that looked eerily familiar.

The key turned in the door and Keast entered. He crossed to an elegant antique escritoire between two packed bookshelves and set down a small silver tray holding a pitcher of fruit punch and two glasses.

'Ah, I see you're investigating my collection, Liz. That section contains every publication ever produced by P.S.I. Chelsea; completely up to date too, despite my absence. I was surprised you didn't use the chance to get yourself into print while you could. The thoughts of Chairman Liz would have been quite appropriate, considering your efforts in *Helicon*. Drink?'

His change of manner confused her. She stared at him in astonishment as he poured out two glasses of fruit punch, hardly believing that he was now joking with her after his assault at Chalgarth. He turned with the glasses in hand and saw the wariness in her face. Then he saw the book in her hand.

'You're holding the prize codex in my collection, the original grimoire describing the King of Demons, Purzson and his demonic authority.'

She opened the book and saw that its contents were the same as the hand-written copy grimoire Harry Simms had sold her in February. The pages fell open naturally at the page describing the rite of conjuring the King of Demons and the stark warning *Do not pray to Purzson.* She strove against the unexpected temptation and snapped the book shut to dismiss it.

'Liz, why should we fight still? Come and sit down. The battle is done - it's time to call a truce,' he said, and held out a glass.

'Why ask me to accept your drink? You forced your violence on me without my accepting it.'

'It's more than a glass of fruit juice I offer.'

He set the drinks down on the desk and leaned back against the desktop, scanning the psychic plane for her underlying attitude to defeat beneath the defiance of her mask. Despite her resistance, she replaced the book on the shelf and crossed the room to sit down by him in the leather armchair. The little victory encouraged him.

'What is your view of yourself now?'

She sensed he was trying to make her feel her vulnerability and bluffed, 'The same as ever: just another rider on the Wheel of Fortune - one day up, another day down.'

'Not a fallen queen; a cast off friend, a discarded lover, a pauper?' he asked, using truth in the sense of the Hanged Man, card 12, as a weapon to destroy: 'You cannot deny you have no money, no work, no home, no husband, no friends - you're a nothing!'

She turned her head turned away to hide her expression as his words hit home despite her attempt to rise above them.

'But aye, I must be something, or I wouldn't be here.'

He picked up a glass and held it out to her.

'Let me remedy your situation. I have a proposition to put to you. Take the glass.'

She reached out uncertainly but with second thoughts drew back her hand. 'What proposition can you be scheming now, after the way you treated me at Chalgarth?'

He placed the glass against her left hand and firmly folded her fingers around its sides. Forced to hold the glass, she looked up at him and waited to hear what else he would forcefully invite her to accept.

'The conditions of our challenge did include, as you told Kingsley, the winner of the election taking whatever he chooses. After my victory, however, I resolved to show you leniency. I did attempt to say this at the election, but your disappointment at losing made you misinterpret my intentions. My immediate reaction was anger; but while we drove back here from Chalgarth, it occurred to me that perhaps I should have explained myself more before letting my displeasure gain the upper hand.'

He paused to let his words take effect. Though her blank expression suggested his oratory had not impressed her, she took a sip from the glass in her hand. Encouraged by this second positive sign, he continued his persuasion.

'This is the house of Purzson. I am Purzson's host in this world. I need a consort worthy of Purzson, and you are that woman. I offer you companionship, a fine home, whatever you desire materially, a career in P.S.I. or the contacts for you to distinguish yourself in any other career you might choose - or the time to do nothing if you prefer. I can give you everything you could possibly want; if you say yes.'

For a moment Liz could not believe her ears, his offer so astounded her. Rapidly she analysed the proposition from a dozen different angles. She knew for certain that she could not trust his sincerity but feared that if she refused his offer, he would force her acquiescence. And to accept was so tempting: to dive into the opulent ocean of his material bounty now that she had lost everything, and to give him her wayward body which still responding to his presence like a flower opening in the sunshine, to pretend that tomorrow with its reckoning would never come. But Liz had experienced too many cold grey bitter dawns of remorse after the excesses of the night before in her past and did not want to eat that dust again.

She finished her drink, crossed the room to place the glass on the tray and replied from where she stood beside the escritoire.

'Are you asking me to worship a false god?'

'No, I invite you to be my consort.'

'How long would that last? You've already claimed Terry back. She knows you are a philanderer, but she's willing to wait for the rare occasion you don't have another woman and pull on her strings. Then you flaunted yourself with Bethany, in front of her, scorning the one woman who really does care for you. Now you're asking me to take their place. Do you think the role of courtesan suits me? Perhaps you do want me now, but isn't that only because you're having to fight? The moment I say "yes" you'll be off to find a new conquest.'

'No, Liz; it's not like that.'

He took her arm and coaxed her back to sit in the leather

armchair, giving her his untouched glass:

'My desire for you is far above any passing attraction I have felt for other women. Yes, you've changed from the idealist I met last year, which enabled me to conquer you, but you are still apart from all the rest, and you are still in part the conqueror. So agree to my proposal and become my consort.'

'No, I can't, Jon. I still love Alec. I will not willingly be unfaithful to him.'

'But where is your husband; now, when you need him? He's sunning himself in Patras with some Greek girl from Philip King's vineyards. Think - when was the last time you saw this man you love? When did he last caress your face and claim your body with his? I am here now, Liz. Are you going to waste the rest of your life waiting for a yesterday?'

'If I must, yes. I vowed before God on my wedding day that I would be faithful to Alec, unconditionally. It doesn't matter what he might do; I don't intend breaking that vow by committing adultery. And I certainly don't intend prostituting myself to the servant of an arch-demon for a place to live and a meal ticket. However little I may still have, I still serve the one true living God, and God's son Jesus Christ.'

The adamance of her refusal stung him. He scowled fiercely, angered that this slight dishevelled young woman whom he had defeated so convincingly, still refused to give him what he desired. He wrested the half-full glass from her hand, tempted to empty the contents of that in her face too.

'No, you do not have much, Mrs Graham, but soon you shall have even less,' he threatened, his eyes flashing. He crossed to the escritoire to place the glass on the silver tray and turned back, a different man entirely in mood: merciless, arrogant, emotionally unreachable. 'Do you understand me, girl?' He strode back to face her. 'The winner takes all: anything he desires. What I do not get by agreement I will take by force.'

She pressed back from him in the armchair. He reached out

and undid the collar button of her crimson silk dress. As his hand moved down to the next button, she pushed him away. He caught hold of her raised wrist and held her arm up in a vice-like grip.

'Stop lying to me,' he scowled.

He undid the second button with his free hand. She grabbed his wrist in alarm and leapt to her feet, pushing back the chair.

'Lie to you? When I fall low enough to lie to you, you'll be able to buy my soul for a couple of pence!'

'If you don't give in to me now, I'll take your soul for nothing.'

'Only God and the Devil can take souls. I will never crawl to you!'

He locked her in his arms and forced his mouth against hers, his ardour inflamed by his anger and her defiance. He expected her to capitulate after a token resistance, but she still struggled desperately against him. His right hand dropped to grasp her breast. She freed her left hand and clawed ineffectively at his arm to pull him off. Then her hand darted up and gripped his throat. He struck her bruised face to stop her choking grip and threw her off. She stumbled, shaken by his blow, and steadied herself against a bookshelf.

'Where are your scruples about violence now, you hypocrite? Did they leave with your popularity?' he scorned.

'What, don't I have the right to defend myself against animals?'

He stepped towards her. She picked up the first thing that came to hand and threw it at him to keep him at bay but missed. A square-cut glass ash tray thudded forcefully into the amber curtains, smashing a windowpane behind before it dropped to the floor. Keast paused in the centre of the room, warily watching her hand as she chose the Purzson grimoire for her next missile.

'Don't you dare come near me, you monster!' she cried, raising the heavy volume ready to throw.

'Put that book down!' he ordered in quite a different tone.

She glanced at the cover to see why his attitude was more absolute and realised she held his precious Purzson grimoire.

He moved closer. She defiantly lifted the book high again.

'I warned you, don't you come near me,' she threatened, and took two cautious side-steps towards the door.

He returned to the desk and unlocked the top drawer to take out his Remington pistol. 'Put that book down,' he coldly repeated, underlining his order by aiming the muzzle of the gun directly at her through the dazzling white light of the anglepoise lamp.

She averted her blinded eyes and lowered the book a little, but raised it again in a gesture of resistance as he moved back in front of the desk.

'You will place that book on the desk, by the lamp.'

She defiantly lifted the grimoire higher and pressed back against the bookcase, shutting her mind to the consequences. He fired into the bookshelf above her. She screamed and froze in horror at the report, her ears singing. With wide fear-filled eyes she turned to place the grimoire back on the bookshelf.

'On the desk,' he insisted.

She obeyed at last, her head hung in defeat. As she stood by him and gently set the book down on the green leather desktop, her body trembled visibly. He picked up the gold chain round her neck to tear off the cross she wore and so remove the last symbol of her strength, but found in his hand only a medallion of the Divine Fool. Knowing what little protection that symbol would afford, he let it drop.

He pressed the muzzle of the gun against her ribs and ordered her to kneel. She resisted: and stood her ground in the desperate hope that something, anything would happen before he forced her to grovel. After a short pause he cocked the pistol.

She spun round and caught the muzzle in her left hand, deflecting it upwards. The gun went off, embedding a bullet in the ceiling. Plaster showered down over the floor. The sudden report made her start back against the desk.

He pulled the muzzle from her hand and pressed the gun to her heart, cocking it once more. His right hand pressed down on her shoulder. Slowly, begrudgingly she sank to her knees. With her spirit at last all but broken, he relaxed back in the leather armchair and ordered her to undress.

'No,' she refused, her head jerking slowly from side to side, her green eyes plaintive in a silent plea for him to reconsider.

'You want me to assist you?' he threatened, tiring of her beseeching looks. His hardened expression warned her not to stall any more. She faltered at his impatience and quickly undid the remaining buttons, kneeling well down in the shadow cast by the desk to hide herself. He pulled the dress from her: crimson silk fluttered to rest against a leg of the escritoire.

'Stand up, turn around,' he ordered, forcing her to parade herself before him so that he could admire her slender body. She turned, shivering violently in fear and shame.

He pocketed the gun and caught her up in his arms, trapping her semi-naked body against the solid desk, his dark clothes rough against her soft pale skin. She struggled desperately to resist him but was not strong enough to stop him pinning her down against the cold leather of the unyielding desktop.

She screamed as he pressed down and entered her. He played on her resistance, still hoping for the response that would damn her as he satisfied his own consuming lust. She lay helplessly beneath him, mutely holding on to the hope that even this assault would eventually end. By the time he lunged in the final throes of passion her emotions had become numbed and she only dimly perceived his intentionally delayed orgasm. He rested his full weight on her body for a few moments, crushing her against the hard desktop. Then he left her and stepped back to straighten his clothes, gazing scornfully on her abused body. Having mastered her, the only emotion he felt for her was contempt.

'You cannot afford to resist me, Elizabeth Graham. Last year you were like a child, and that is how I treated you. This year you are a woman. Had you complied with me, my life would have been yours. Defy me, and your life is mine.'

He unlocked the door and left the room. Liz rolled onto her side and dropped off the desk onto the floor, sobbing with relief that the assault was over.

2 : 9

Sam discussed tactics with Father Jay as they travelled north across the city in Sam's green Ford Capri. He had seen aerial photographs of Keast's estate and original plans of the Georgian house at its centre, but had little up-to-date information about the place. Neither he nor Dr Graham had been inside because of Keast's security precautions along the perimeter wall and electronic gates.

'Only Mrs Graham's been granted the dodgy honour of an invitation inside. Our first problem's 'ow to get in. I don't advise climbing the wall - Keast don't bother about 'ow much gets left.'

'Don't worry, Sam: God will open the gates for us,' Father Jay promised. He had prepared for this as for any emergency by handing the event over to God's control, enlisting the support of the chapel's prayer chain, and taking his visits portmanteau, the contents of which this time included a large heavy brass four-barred, three-circled cosmic cross. He added, 'I would warn you though, not to expect things to go smoothly when we arrive at Mr Keast's house.'

'Things never do when Keast's involved,' Sam returned with one of his half-smiles. He expected the night to be a disaster when all he had for back-up was a gaunt, unkempt priest.

They reached Keast's estate a few minutes before half-past eleven and parked near the gate in the shadow of the seven-foot high stone perimeter wall. The summer night had turned unusually dark and oppressive around them, as if a thunderstorm were brewing overhead. A sultry breeze turned the leaves on the mature chestnut trees growing both sides of the wall.

'Yes, this is a strong centre of negative energy, a place of great evil,' Father Jay said. 'Sam, if you have any irrational fears you mustn't go in there, for that negative power will turn your fears on yourself to destroy you.'

'No sweat: the only thing I'm scared of is my Mum when I've 'ad a skinful, which ain't too often in my line of work,' Sam answered wryly, determined not to let the priest enter Keast's estate unaccompanied. 'Keast won't be there alone - 'is team'll be knocking about too. The ones to watch is Sandy Angus, a right nasty knife man who calls 'imself Bob Travers now; 'Endrik Gerber who don't seem too bad till you realise 'e's the chemist who makes the drugs they flogged; and Jon Keast 'imself, who I'd've bumped off a long time ago only 'e gets away each time. If they're dancing tonight 'e'll've sent the rest packing till tomorrow and the only other one at 'ome'll be 'is son Nicholas who's been brought up to believe that's the way to do business. If not, we'll meet a lot more opposition, but Mrs Graham'll be safe enough. Only you and I both know that's not the way it is, is it?'

Father Jay nodded. 'They're already calling up the demon: his power is growing stronger every minute.'

'Then God 'ad better 'urry up and open them gates, 'adn't 'e.'

'Faith tonight, not cynicism please, Sam.'

They left the car and moved through the trees to the gateway, but pressed against the wall when a car turned off the road ahead of them. It skidded to a halt on the shingle in front of the tall wrought-iron gates. A gatekeeper came out of the lodge inside the gates, shielding his eyes from the glare of the car's headlights. A passenger emerged from the car and offered the keeper an identity card and an envelope through the bars.

'My name is Charles Lafayette, of P.S.I. Britain. Mr Keast asked me to fetch this letter of authorisation over to him personally from Neptune House as soon as it was completed,' the visitor said.

The gatekeeper checked the ID card and envelope, gave Charles a friendly wave, and went back inside the lodge to open the electronic gates. The gates had barely parted enough before the car shot through them. An older car quickly followed, turning off the road and racing in immediately after. Alarmed, the guard pressed the switch to close the gates.

Sam dragged Father Jay through the entrance before the gates shut, and ran on into the lodge to stop the gatekeeper sounding the alarm. The gatekeeper turned at the sound of feet on the step. Sam smashed an upper cut across his jaw, felling him. He bundled his unconscious body into a cupboard and locked the door. Then he reset the gate controls and went back outside to see who else had arrived.

Four P.S.I. members had gathered round Father Jay on the drive: Charles, Pete Corrie, Toni Sullivan and Tim Jackson, names all recognised by the priest to be Liz's supporters at P.S.I.

'I am Father Jeremy Kingston,' he said. 'Dr Graham sent me here to help his bodyguard rescue his wife. You are also here to save Lisbeth?'

Charles relaxed and shook his hand with a relieved smile. 'We meet at last, Father Jay: I have heard much about you. Yes, we too are here for Liz.'

'Her friend Bethany phoned me,' Pete explained: 'She said Keast had snatched Liz from Chalgarth and brought her here. Martin Kingsley had already warned us to expect trouble - I left him to phone round for more help while I brought everyone I could find right away. Others will follow on behind.'

'Then we must leave the gates shut,' Father Jay ordered. He saw Pete's sour expression and added, 'Don't look so ill-suited, Mr Corrie - it's Satanists we're dealing with here, and the demons will use anyone against us who's not strong enough in faith to resist. We can't risk any unexpected disturbance.'

'So you'd better obey the padre,' Sam threatened with quiet menace.

'Father Jay does know what he's doing, even if it doesn't sound right,' Tim tried to reassure Pete: 'He helped me get better, and that's against all the odds.'

'You must hide your cars now: we'll proceed from here on foot,' Father Jay ordered.

'But we'll waste valuable time!' Pete objected: 'Every second could count! We have to drive in and bust them before anything else can happen to Liz.'

'Mr Corrie, we must avoid alerting the people in that house to our presence at all costs. It will be hard enough for us to breach Satan's stronghold without them directing the full power of their malevolence on us too,' the priest warned.

Pete looked thoughtfully at him. Recognising his greater spiritual strength, he backed down and went to move his car into some bushes out of sight of the gate. Tim climbed back into his car to follow suit. Father Jay flagged him down.

'Tim, I'd like you to stay here at the gate while the rest of us go in. Keep an eye on the gatekeeper when he comes round and tell any other members who turn up why I want them to hold back.'

Tim nodded, disappointed that he would not be a part of the spearhead force, but accepting the power of the dragon was still too close for him to risk deliberately advancing into the centre of the evil there. He parked his car out of sight near Pete's and watched from the gatehouse as the others walked away on foot into the night.

Father Jay warned his party of the possible effects of the evil they would meet the closer they came to its heart, and showed them how to sign themselves with the circled rosy cross for protection, an action prayer they all recognised Liz having used in the past. His reassurances became less comforting as they left the lights of the gatehouse behind and their eyes adjusted to the darkness of the stormy night. Soon the only light to help them was the dim orange reflection of sodium streetlights against the clouds in the southern sky. In the blackness ahead, strange imaginings distracted them from their intent. Father Jay's reassurances helped them to counter these and press on in their quest.

They ascended a slight bluff in the grounds and finally made out the large house ahead of them as an unlit silhouette barely discernible against the deep dirty-grey sky. Their doubts increased: Charles felt certain they had arrived too late, while Sam feared he had underestimated the strength of their opposition, and Pete was convinced that Keast had already taken Liz and flown. Toni pushed through a more fundamental illusion of walking through crowds of unseen creepy creatures. Father Jay was reliving the hallucinations of withdrawal, but he could identify their cause and did not fear them this time: he was more concerned for his companions who had not been through such experiences before.

Heartened by his encouragement and unshakeable faith, they pressed on towards the house, their footsteps noiseless on the damp grass as they crossed the extensive lawns in the masking darkness.

2 : 10

Nicholas entered the library to find Liz shivering half-naked on the floor by the leather-topped mahogany desk. He dropped a white garment beside her.

'Here, put this on.'

He crossed to the escritoire to pour out more drinks. When he turned back, she had donned the long white robe and was sitting huddled in the hard leather armchair. He handed her a glass and sat near her on the edge of the desk.

'How do you feel?' he asked, thinking how small and vulnerable she looked, pressed into a corner of the large chair.

She did not answer. Her mind screamed an unvoiced torrent of protest, as if she were shouting the words at him: hurt, angry, ashamed, defiled, abused; but somehow they stayed trapped inside. In the wake of the torrent she recalled the ghosts of past abuses from the year before her recovery days, when she had willingly chosen to debase herself to feed her addictions. She hoped that because she had come safely through those, she would survive this too.

'Why fight, Liz? My father is much stronger than you. He'll get what he wants no matter what you try to stop him.'

'Stop him?' she spat, but faltered, realising she no longer had the willpower to fight. She sighed and rested her head on her left hand.

The scent of incense and flowers drifted in on the air. Nicholas recognised the heavy sweetness of the distinctive perfume to be the herald of a specific sacrificial rite and offered Liz a chance to save herself.

'How well d'you think you can get on with my father?'

She clenched her fists and disjointedly shook her head, failing to see beyond the horror of the past ordeal to what still lay ahead. He watched a tear snake slowly down her bruised cheek and realised how divorced he was from her suffering. Her helplessness tempted him to exploit her purely for the pleasure of being able to do so, though it was a risk he would not take with his father's special prize. Liz did not identify the passing evil in his thoughts for the atmosphere of evil pervading the rest of the house. She felt her own increasing intoxication in concern.

'Is there alcohol in this drink?'

'No, we had no need to weaken your defences that way.'

'Then you did use other ways - some drug again?' She realised she was trying to rationalise her defeat by them, and glanced aside even as she spoke, disconcerted by the walls which were undulating.

'So you don't think you can agree to my father's proposal?'

'What, become his tart? What d'you think I am? After what that bastard's done, I don't just hate him, I...'

She broke off, distracted by the carpet which rippled like a field of dry grass in a gentle breeze.

'Has it occurred to you that he asserted his dominance to win you over, Liz? For you do seem to take a masochistic pleasure in running headlong into the most dangerous situations.'

'What, is it masochistic to stand up for one's beliefs?'

'There you go, twisting things again! Liz, don't you understand? You are a problem to my father. You're like a thorn in his flesh he's got to deal with; and the choice is stark: either you stay here as his willing partner; or you say no once more and die.'

'But I have to say no: to commit adultery is a cardinal sin.'

'So is committing suicide.'

'Aye? And who's twisting things now?'

The atmosphere turned cold. They looked up and saw Keast standing in the doorway. He wore a long black robe bordered with a silver braid of symbols which included the motif of three cherries in an open circle. Further along the braid Liz recognised the satanic motif of a broken cross in an open circle. She backed fearfully into the furthest corner of her chair. Nicholas shook his head to warn his father of his failure to persuade her despite his earlier confidence.

Keast nodded and fixed his gaze on her. An unearthly power flowed through his deep. dark eyes. It caught her and held her, projecting into her subconscious the depth of her defeat. His face transformed into a spectral mask of impartial malice, like the expressions she had seen on the faces of the less evolved spirits on the far side of the psychic door. These already flocked around them both to witness her destruction at his hand. The room swayed around her like a reflection of itself distorting in the ripples of a pond. His eyes alone were constant: he ordered, and she could do nothing but obey.

At his bidding, she left the lounge and crossed the hall to enter the room with black walls. As she walked, her footsteps seemed to stick to the tacky sludge-covered floor. She stopped in the doorway, overwhelmed by the power of evil emanating from the room, which was lit by two black candles. The candles stood in two brandy-filled goblets on a stone altar covered with a silver cloth.

Between the goblets stood a small brazier and crucible, tended by two dark shrouded figures. The altar and its acolytes were standing on the far side of a patterned silver circle incorporated in the floor tiles.

Keast took hold of her arms and forced her to enter the room with him. She shied in his grip and desperately searched her memory for words of protection. '*Yea, though I walk through the valley of the shadow of death,*' she muttered, but could not recall the words that followed on. As she entered the silver circle, the two acolytes stepped back to stand behind her, taking care to keep inside the circle.

Keast took his place at the altar and shrouded his face with the hood of his black robe. Around him Liz could see a gathering crowd of mocking demons and wondered whether demons were flocking around her too. The altar shimmered, and the air filled with the heavy sweet smell of the incense burning in the crucible.

The three men recited a monotonous chant. Keast threw powder into the crucible three times, causing green flames to flare and spit. Sulphurous smoke sharpened the air and cleared the mind. Afterwards Liz noticed the walls no longer rippled and the demons were no longer visible.

The chanting stopped. The atmosphere tensed. The two acolytes grasped Liz firmly, circling her waist and forcing her hands forwards with the palms uppermost. Keast turned from the altar to face her. In his left hand he held a glowing branding iron. Liz struggled against her captors, but they only held her the more rigidly. The white-hot metal bit into her right forearm. She screamed and bucked, conscious at first only of the searing pain. To her horror, Keast turned back to face her with the white-hot iron again. She fought desperately to break the rigid hold of her captors but was helpless in their arms. The glowing iron bit into her left forearm. She screamed and bucked in pain, her nostrils flared with the acrid smell of her own seared flesh. The two acolytes released her: she fell to her knees, unable to ease the heat of the burns.

Keast turned away to put down the branding iron, but turned back to look at Liz again, unsure whether he wanted to go through with the rite. Her vulnerability had unsettled him again, as it had done before when he had planned to kill her. He crouched down on one knee and gently rested his left hand on her neck.

'You still have time to save yourself.'

She dropped her head. 'I shall never crawl to you.'

'Do you not understand?'

His fingers entwined in her hair and gently pulled to raise her head. Their eyes met across six inches of darkness. She shrugged free from his hold but continued to stare at him.

'I shall never crawl...'

'Save yourself, you fool! No-one else will save you now!'

He clutched her arms to implore her. She cried out in pain and pulled her burnt wrists free. As she doubled up, sobbing on the floor, he stood back, angered by her helpless resistance.

The silver goblets exploded into flame as the spent candles guttered into the brandy, casting a smoky yellow light across the silver tablecloth and Liz's white robe. An eerie moaning filled the room, and the temperature dropped to an unearthly coldness.

'Oh God, please help me,' Liz softly cried.

Keast turned from the altar to mock her prayer.

'There are no angels here, Elizabeth Kirkland, though demons may oblige you if you care to step out of the circle,' he said, knowing she would not commit so lethal a folly.

He turned back to the altar and chanted an incantation over the crucible, casting a dark powder into it three times which created a heavy black pungent smoke. Then he stepped back with his arms extended and looked up at the air behind the altar. The moaning ceased. The room filled with an ominous silence.

A strange green light appeared to emanate from the wall, filling the room with such an overpowering sense of pure evil that Liz fell back against the worshipping acolytes in terror. 'Oh my God, please help me!' she beseeched, her palms pressed together.

Keast laughed and turned to face her, a silver ritual dagger clasped between his upheld hands. She screamed and tried to back away. The two acolytes gripped her and forced her to present her unprotected chest to him. The green light glinted on the sharp blade poised to take her life.

'God forgive me, and save my soul,' she screamed, as the knife swooped down.

The door crashed open. A heavy brass cosmic cross flew across the room and knocked Keast's hands and the dagger aside. The evil discharged instantly with a crack of lightning as the cross landed in the centre of the silver circle. The expending force flung the demon worshippers across the room. The silver dagger thudded home, impaled in an acolyte.

Liz looked up, scarcely believing she was still alive. In the doorway stood Father Jay, a silhouette against the light from the hall. She ran to his arms, crying tears of gratitude and relief.

2 : 11

Sam dragged Keast back into the library before he could shed his long black robe. He pinned him firmly down on a hard-backed chair, determined not to let him escape this time the way he had so many times before. Pete was already there, piecing together the story told by the scattered clothing, hungry to confront the demonist with every scrap of evidence he could find of his foul deeds.

In his determination to catch Keast, Sam had let the other demon worshippers escape. Nicholas had already vanished, even though he had not taken part in the aborted rite. Charles had tried to catch one of the acolytes as he passed through the doorway, only to be left clutching Hendrik Gerber's empty robe. He chased off after him into the corridors of the large house.

The other acolyte lay in a pool of blood, the silver ritual dagger protruding from his chest. Father Jay crouched beside him and pushed back his hood to check for a pulse in his neck. Liz gasped, recognising Sandy Angus. The priest shook his head and covered the dead man's face.

Toni put her arm round Liz's shoulders, sensing she was in shock and worried that the fatality would set her back even further. When Father Jay asked them to join the others in the library, she objected on Liz's behalf.

'Is that necessary?'

'Sadly, it is. We have to hear Keast's defence. Only Lisbeth can tell us if he's trying to fool us with yet more lies.'

Charles followed them into the library, reporting his failure to catch Gerber. Keast heard his report and held his head a little higher. With Nicholas and Hendrik still at large, he was confident he too would soon be free, despite the presence of the man of God who had breached his stronghold.

'What in heaven's name have you been up to, Keast?' Pete demanded. He leaned against the mahogany desk to glare at him and added, 'Or should I say in hell's name, Chairman?'

Keast regarded him with fiery eyes but said nothing, which inflamed Pete's self-righteous indignation all the more.

'Come on, Keast: are you going to tell me yourself, or do I have to throttle it out of you?'

'Pete, hasn't there been enough violence already for one night?' Charles protested gently.

'If he won't understand any other language, I have to speak to him in one he can!'

Pete crossed the room to face Keast, standing so close he could see the pattern of the irises in his dark brown eyes. Sam adjusted his grip on Keast's arms. Though Alec's orders constrained him to obey Father Jay and the priest's request to avoid unnecessary violence, Pete was not. Without warning Pete lashed out, his sudden blow throwing Keast's head sharply to one side. Keast straightened himself and glared at Pete with venomous intent.

'Pete, do you have to?' Liz cried, struggling against Toni's concerned restraint. Her eyes strayed desperately towards the open French windows, longing for escape.

Pete swung round on her in astonishment. 'What do you mean, Liz? I'm only doing this for you!' He turned back to Keast. 'How d'you like a taste of your own medicine, Chairman? Though no-one could descend quite as low as you! If you've laid one finger on Liz tonight, by God I'll make you feel better off dead for it!' He raised his arm to strike him again, enraged further when he still did not flinch before him.

'Stop, Pete!' commanded Father Jay, sensing Pete's intolerance was a product of the evil atmosphere pervading the house. 'How can you possibly hope to redeem Mr Keast while you fight using his tactics?'

Pete snarled at the priest with contempt for any thought of reforming such an evil man, and lunged forward to throttle the captive, egged on by Sam to do what he could not. Charles and Father Jay leapt across to pull Pete off but had to fight against his obsessive anger. At length they restrained him forcibly in the leather armchair. He struggled frantically against them, shouting, 'Sadist! Pervert! Satanist!' until Charles slapped his face to shock him out of his mad rage. Pete collapsed back into the chair, suddenly deflated after the discharge of his extreme emotions.

Keast turned his head to regard Liz with cruel, unforgiving eyes. 'Welcome home, Mrs Graham!' he sneered.

She stared at him and went pale. With a sickened cry, she pulled free from Toni's hold and ran sobbing out through the French windows.

Her unexpected flight startled the others, delaying their response. Toni was the first to chase after her. Sam resolved his conflict between obeying orders to save Liz and continuing to hold Keast by giving his captive a rabbit punch to keep him quiet and ordering Pete to take over guard duty.

Sam ran outside after the two women. He caught up with Toni

as she stopped to rest, winded and gasping for air at a corner of the house. Her hopeless gaze drew his eyes to the cars lined up by the porch. The yellow MG sports car started up and raced away with blazing lights down the shingle drive.

'Liz?' he asked.

Toni nodded between gasps. A thud made her turn to look back. Instead of Sam, she saw Hendrik Gerber. Sam lay at his feet, felled with a blow from the butt of his Webley revolver. Toni screamed and stumbled back into the arms of Nicholas, who had been lurking in the terrace shadows to catch her.

'What now?' he asked Hendrik, his eyes following his stolen car.

'Let it go, Nicholas: your father's more important,' Hendrik replied. He quickly outlined a plan, which Nicholas readily agreed to because it gave him the star part.

Hendrik took struggling Toni from Nicholas and dragged her back towards the library's French windows. Nicholas bundled Sam's unconscious body into the boot of his father's Rolls and went back into the house by the front door to enter the library from the hall.

Nicholas threw back the library door and strolled in, a Beretta 75 pistol in his right hand. Pete, Charles and Father Jay looked up in surprise, taken aback and off guard. Keast smiled wryly at his son as Pete released him, and reflectively rubbed the back of his neck. Nicholas nodded to his father and took three steps into the room to address the intruders.

'Your friend Mrs Graham has left in my car. You will now let us escort you off the premises after her, or we shall be forced to hand you over to the police and have you charged for breaking and entering.'

'You would dare hand us over to the police when the evidence of your crimes lies all around?' Pete demanded.

Keast smiled as he warned, 'You have lost your principal witness, Mr Corrie, and I have a lot of friends in the police.'

'And if we still refuse?' Father Jay enquired, thinking the dead acolyte would be a difficult thing to cover up, even with friends in the police.

Hendrik Gerber forced Toni in through the French windows, his revolver held to her head. Father Jay waved his hands to acknowledge his disadvantage.

'Can Miss Sullivan confirm Mrs Graham got away?' he asked.

Toni nodded. When Gerber shook her to answer more fully, she said, 'She drove off in a sports car.'

'Then Mr Corrie, Mr Lafayette and I will accept your offer of an escort off the estate, with Miss Sullivan and Mr Buxton,' Father Jay conceded.

The priest departed the premises with all who had accompanied him there, satisfied that he had at least achieved his objective in rescuing Liz. He felt concerned though, that two of the three demon worshippers responsible for her ordeal still survived at large to continue their evil, with a new third member already waiting in the wings to take over the dead Sandy Angus' place.

Chapter 3

Card 20: Judgement

The truth shall make you free;

release

Sam phoned Dr Alec Graham from Briarbank in the early hours of the morning, after he had got back with Father Jay from Keast's estate. Alec was not pleased to hear his report. The priest took over the phone call, not wanting Alec to hear about Keast's abuse of his estranged wife until he was present to soften the blow, but Alec automatically suspected the worst. He asked Father Jay and Sam to do what they could to find Liz to ensure her future safety, and promised to return to London with Theo as soon as Goldie and Philip had persuaded the Greek authorities to let him leave the country.

Next day Pete and Charles reported the night's events to the members of P.S.I. Their reaction was one of shock. The delegates held an emergency debate and formally elected Elizabeth Graham back into office to put Jonathan Keast legally out. They charged Pete and Charles to deputise for Liz in her absence, to trace her and to notify her of her reinstatement, giving her until the first of November to decide whether she would accept the position and resume office at Neptune House.

Bethany returned to Chalgarth after the emergency conference to collect the last of her belongings before moving back to her apartment. Overwhelmed by poignant memories of her six months' stay there with Liz, Bethany asked herself yet again how she had allowed herself to be taken over by Keast's power for that one day and through it to betray her friend so disastrously. As guilt threatened to overwhelm her, she sat down at the telephone in the study to call Uncle Harry but stopped when she noticed heavy indentations on the clean top sheet of a notepad beside the phone. She found a pencil and lightly shaded over the sheet to highlight the indented writing. The revealed note listed the times and connections for two early morning trains from Euston to Whitehaven with a change at Carlisle. Bethany's heart leapt to have found out where Liz had gone, the one place she should have known her friend would run to after such traumatic experiences: the refuge of her brother's Lakeland farm.

Bethany searched the house to see what Liz had taken with her. Missing were a few clothes including a pair of jeans and a jumper; a rucksack and the ten books Liz treasured most. Everything else, including her bank stationery and her car she had left behind. She had burnt the white robe in the lounge fireplace with a pile of her business and personal correspondence and had filled the dustbin with other possessions, including her intact photograph album. The evidence told Bethany Liz had left her old way of life for good.

Bethany sat back down at the study worktable and wept with guilt. After her tears had subsided, she picked up the phone beside her to call for help. She tried Harry Simms' number first but got no reply. Father Jay answered her second call almost at once.

He had been getting ready to go to Briarbank for dinner with Alec on his return, but stopped what he was doing when he heard Bethany's distress. For fifteen minutes he patiently listened as she confided all her guilt and indecision. When she finally flagged and paused, expecting him to console her, he scolded her instead.

'Bethany, do you enjoy feeling guilty, or are you making yourself a good excuse to go out and have another drink? So you slipped, yes; but that was yesterday, not today: there's nothing you can do about it. So you made a mistake - you failed to see through an evil man when he tricked you into betraying your best friend; but did any of the rest of us do any better against that man, that embodiment of the Devil? If you must do something about your guilt, write Liz a letter apologising for your mistakes. If you post it to her care of her parents, I'm sure they'll be able to pass it on. Then get on with the task of getting better again. Lisbeth forgave that Martin boy before: she'll forgive you too.'

'Father, would you write to her first for me? She's gone to her brother's farm, and from the look of things she's gone for good - she'd only tear up a letter from me.'

'You know for certain she is there?'

'I found details of the trains to Whitehaven on a notepad by her phone. She'd taken the top copy, but I deciphered the dents in the page underneath.'

'Who else have you told?'

'No-one, Father - I've only just found out myself.'

'Praise the Lord! Listen well, Bethany, for her sake and for your own: destroy the evidence you found and don't breathe a word of it to anyone else, or you could betray her straight back into Mr Keast's hands. If anyone asks you where she is, refer them to me. If we want her back, there must be no pestering - we must leave her to get over her shock and respond herself.'

'Okay. What should I do about Chalgarth? She's just extended the lease.'

'Keep it on and keep an eye on it for her. She only needs time to recover, to let her mind heal. She will be back, I'm sure.'

Father Jay felt less confident than he sounded though as he finished the call. From Liz's sharing in the past, he knew about Blakeley End, the farm which had been the Kirkland family home, once lost to strangers for several years but repurchased by Liz's brother Ricky when the opportunity came. Liz had often referred to the farm as a childhood refuge; but now the priest feared it was to be her hermitage, a place where she could turn her back on life and choose never to return to the real world again. He resolved to encourage as many people as possible to write her letters of support for him to pass on, to ensure that despite her flight she could not hide away completely from her past.

He drove over to Briarbank and arrived only a few minutes after Alec and Theo had got home from the airport. As Sam admitted Father Jay into the hall, Alec came out of the study to greet him, a visibly tired and anxious man.

'I'm very grateful to you for coming, Father Jeremy, especially at such short notice.'

'I'd have come even without the bribe of dinner, Alec, but it does help,' Father Jay joked.

Alec offered him an aperitif in the lounge which he politely refused. The priest sat in an armchair, his opening levity gone.

'Has Lisbeth contacted you yet?'

'Nothing; even though Sam says she definitely recognised him, so she must know of my part in her rescue. I do know she's safe - her parents reassured me of that when I phoned them; but that is all they would tell me. Do you have any idea where she might be?'

'I do; but don't expect me to tell you after the trick you played on her. I suggest you write her a letter and I'll send it on. If she answers you, all well and good; but if she doesn't, well it's only to be expected.'

'Why, what's your price?'

Father Jay shot him a look of fiery reprimand. 'My price is her safety and well-being, which is what yours should have been, Dr Graham.'

'I'm sorry!' Alec apologised sharply. He crossed to the window, turning his face away to look at the garden, hiding his expression from the priest while he tried to bring his emotions under control. Suddenly he turned back. 'Why didn't you stop her? How could you have let her run off into the night like that? What went wrong?'

'It wasn't as simple as that.'

Alec saw his sincerity of expression and nodded to accept his defence. 'Nothing ever is when Jonathan Keast is involved,' he admitted. 'That's why I asked you to step in - I thought you of all people would be able to better him.'

'Alec, last night may not have gone as you wanted, but it was most certainly a success. We saved your wife from being sacrificed to the arch-demon Purzson by three Satanists, because you sent me there. She fled the moment she got the chance only because of the ordeal they had put her though beforehand.'

Alec looked sharply across at him. 'So they did assault her sexually?'

The priest's expression became impenetrable. 'We don't know that happened.'

Alec interpreted his lack of denial as proof and went white with rage. 'Why, I'll murder him!'

He strode across the lounge to leave at once to carry out his threat. Father Jay leapt up and barred the doorway to stop him.

'Alec, you'll do no such thing! You're not dealing with an ordinary man. If you make yourself dangerous to Keast, whatever your advantages, he will destroy you. Your wife was the one he was after this time, and your wife was the one he got; but don't think you won't fall like she did - that demonist hatched this plot eight months ago or more, and you fell right into it.'

'What, you're going to let him walk around scot-free after what he's done? To do it all over again to Liz, or to some other innocent, unsuspecting woman?'

'Of course not; but as you yourself had realised, there's only one way to better a demonist, and that's through faith. You can't defeat Keast with treachery or violence because that's trying to beat the Devil at his own game. Of course you've never managed to outwit him! But your wife did; until you threw her away. If you hadn't meddled, she would've had Keast helpless by now. Instead, her faith was so weakened he almost destroyed her.'

'What, you are blaming me? For what Jonathan Keast did to Liz?' Alec strode back into the centre of the lounge, emphatically shaking his head. 'Oh, no! We may have argued so much that she felt forced into leaving me; but in no way did I undermine her beliefs, strange though many of them are. I even offered to link Graplax with P.S.I. to stop Keast trying to stage a comeback; but would she listen? Criticise me for being outwitted by Keast if you must, but you can't blame me for Liz's weakness of faith.'

'When you betrayed the trust she placed in you? When you pretended you didn't want her anymore, in your ruthless desire for revenge. Alec, marital love should be the closest earthly experience people can get to the fullness of God's spiritual love for us. You turned it into a battlefield with no hostages taken. So tell me now, do you really love your wife?'

'Of course I do.'

'There's no *of course* about it. And even if you do love her, after everything that's happened, do you want her back?'

'Father, why are you torturing me with these questions now? You know I do.'

'No, I don't; nor does she. So if the answers to those questions are both yes, I suggest after dinner we go to your study and you write your wife a letter telling her so, while I admire your collection of old pots.'

Alec looked at Father Jay with such alarm that the priest felt moved by compassion for this emotionally fettered man.

'I'm not asking you to make a confession, Alec, though that would probably help, just a short simple letter telling her you love her, you miss her, and you want her to come home. Forget her scorn the last time you made such an appeal. The circumstances are different: your letter would be a great comfort to her at this time.'

Father Jay hoped, as they went through to the dining to eat, that he had distracted Alec's thoughts from revenge with the more immediate problem of persuading Liz to come home. Before they had finished the hors d'oeuvres, Alec proved him wrong.

'You were saying only faith outwits devil worshippers, Father. Then how do you suggest I deal with Jonathan Keast?'

'I don't, Alec: try to let this man go - *vengeance is mine, sayeth the Lord*. Pray for his recovery, as the chapel's prayer powerhouse is praying for him. His contract with Purzson must be coming to an end, and he will seek direction.'

'Surely you don't believe that Faustian legend in this day and age!'

'It's not so much a matter of what you or I believe, Alec: only a desperate man would sacrifice the one he loves to his idol.'

Alec mistook the priest's statement to be another criticism of his own recent conduct and was about to take offence, but a second look at his guileless expression told him that Father Jay had simply been stating a fact about Keast. Suddenly he understood the claim Liz had once made that he and Keast were very similar. The thought of being the same as Keast shocked him enough to make him want to change.

After dinner, he followed Father Jay's advice and wrote to Liz. He sealed the letter in a pale blue envelope and handed it to the priest to forward, confident that as soon as Liz read his letter she would forgive him and come home.

3 : 2

The second Sunday in October, Bethany was driving past Briarbank when she noticed Philip King standing in the drive. She reversed her car back to the house hoping he would speak to her, for local gossip was speculating about the future of Briarbank and its owner, and it was a most desirable property. As Bethany strolled in through the open gateway, Philip greeted her with a friendly wave and a welcoming smile.

'What are you doing here, Mr King? I though Dr Graham was in the process of selling Briarbank,' Bethany remarked.

Philip laughed at the directness of the copper-haired woman whose spirit and appearance he had long admired, but for her occasional heavy drinking. It was no chance that he had been standing in the garden when she drove past, at the time she always headed home after Sunday lunch with her parents at Ainhurst.

'No, Alec's keeping the place on, for when we have to come to London on business,' he replied. 'But why so formal, Miss Broome? Did I somehow offend you the last time we met? If you have time to come in for a cup of tea, I shall give you an unreserved apology.'

'Thank you: I'd love that. The tea, I mean, not the apology - I never know whether to take you seriously or not.'

'Good: I love to keep a beautiful woman intrigued. Come in and sample some of Mrs B's excellent fudge cake.'

Bethany let Philip escort her inside, flattered by his attention despite knowing he turned on the same charm for any available woman between the ages of seventeen and seventy. The panelled hall's unchanged appearance brought back her memories as she waited while her host asked the housekeeper to serve them tea.

'Wistful?' Philip remarked on his return, making her start. He showed her into the lounge.

'I was thinking about Liz. Has she contacted Alec yet?'

His face became more reflective as he sat with her on the sofa.

'No, I'm afraid she hasn't. Have you heard anything?'

'So far as I know Liz hasn't written to anyone, not even to P.S.I. No-one's seen her since she fled from Jon Keast's estate in Nicholas Keast's car. I did hear the car was found a few days later in the carpark at Hyde Park Corner, but Liz? She's vanished. Only Father Jay seems to know where she might be, and he's not telling.'

'Then why is it I still keep thinking you have an idea?'

Bethany blushed. The timely arrival of the tea trolley spared her loyalty. Philip waited for the housekeeper to leave again before he challenged her further. Bethany hastily spoke first.

'You were quite right, Philip: I haven't forgiven you yet.'

He placed their cups of tea beside the plates of sandwiches, scones and fudge cake on the coffee table in front of the sofa, and sat back down beside Bethany before he answered her.

'I was? And what was my heinous crime?'

'The way you propositioned Liz at Plover's the night Greg Vincent and Sir Kenneth Bywater died.'

'Ah, that.' Philip assumed a suitable look of remorse. 'I don't expect you to believe this, but the truth is, Alec asked me to do that. I know people consider me to be unprincipled, but in reality I would never have dreamt of doing such a caddish thing myself.'

Bethany laughed cynically at his defence, yet did not like him any the less for his flippant placing of the blame on someone else.

'You're quite right, Philip - I don't believe you. Alec's far too possessive to want to keep it in the family to that extent, however much he came to loathe her.'

'True; but that wasn't his motive. I see it's time for confidences with the *confiture*.'

Philip paused dramatically and finished his scone before continuing, to increase Bethany's curiosity. She waited in suspense, her tea and sandwiches forgotten on the coffee table.

'Alec set a trap to catch Jonathan Keast. The bait he used was Liz, because the reptile is so fascinated by her. Before Alec herded the scapegoat out into the wilderness, he wanted to be sure Liz would be faithful no matter what happened - hence the catalogue of unpleasant events that night. And don't think I condoned any of this - Alec presented it to me as a virtual *fait accompli*: all I'm trying to do is ensure some benefit does eventually come from his idiotic plan. I did everything I could to persuade Liz to leave Plover's with me that night. Had she shown even the slightest sign of weakening, I could have persuaded Alec to give up the whole foolish idea. But she just wouldn't listen.'

'Philip, are you claiming Alec set Liz up so that he could get Keast? That he was responsible for letting that drug pusher rape her and almost murder her...' Bethany paled and faltered as she realised the full implication of the timing of events between February and August. 'Oh, my God!' she gasped: 'Why did the silly fool have to marry such a stupid, thoughtless, self-centred ass! His plan went wrong, didn't it.'

Philip nodded. 'Yes, just as I warned him it would. And now, two months later, Liz is still hiding somewhere, completely unprotected; openly vulnerable to Keast's next attack should he discover her hiding place before we do. Father Kingston refuses to tell us where he sends her letters for the understandable fear that Alec might play yet another trick on her; and approaching her parents is like trying to storm the Bastille: the one thing her family is good at is silence. Not like ours: if one of us is injured we all feel the hurt. How are you getting on with your family these days? Given the brandy decanter back?'

'Yes - even my father's trying to give it up since he's seen the change in me. Things have gone a lot better since I stopped measuring my parents against what I wanted them to be; and started seeing us all for what we really are.'

'That helps. So you've got over the slip Keast made you make?'

'I can't blame Mr Keast for that mistake. Only my weakness made me drink that night I fell under his influence - he didn't force my mouth open and pour the wine down my throat. Is it really true, what you just said, that if he finds out where Liz is living before you do, he will attack her again?'

'What do you think?'

Philip paused to refill their cups, giving Bethany time to consider his question. Because she saw Keast to be a wealthy and debauched man whose depravity came from a jaded palate after years of never refusing himself anything, there was only one answer. She shuddered to think that Keast had once deceived her into his arms, and looked up at Philip, seeing him in comparison like some golden modern-day chivalrous knight. As he sat back down beside her, she smiled unsurely at him. His eyes twinkled conspiratorially with the smile he returned to encourage her.

'If that's the case, then I should tell you, shouldn't I,' she said. 'I misled you. I do know where Liz is - I've known since the day she left. I didn't say anything because Father Jay told me not to tell anyone, for my own safety as well as hers.'

'A sensible precaution to take - I'm sure no-one else beside me guessed. Is she still in London?' Philip prompted with bated breath.

'No. She's staying on her brother Ricky's farm in Cumberland.'

'At Blakeley End? Surely not. That was one of the first places we checked.'

'True: she's not at the farm itself - she'll be living in the crag bothie, a shepherd's hut halfway up the hill behind the farm. I stayed there once with her: camping in a stone tent - no plumbing, no electric: just two rooms, a fireplace and a roof; and the nearest road a mile away across country. The place drove me nuts, and I only stayed a week; but she loves it. The locals always said that land's in her blood: she could hide away there for the rest of her life and be content.'

'I don't recall seeing anything like that up there. Could you point it out to me on a map?'

'It's too small to be on a map, and you wouldn't see it because it's camouflaged - it was built beside a cliff. That used to give me nightmares, even though the rocks would've had to fall sideways to go through the roof: it just felt too close to be safe. Liz called the bothie an overgrown bield, a sort of lookout shelter dating back to the stone age. She said there were lots of them in that region and you could signal from valley to valley from them, but I thought she was letting her imagination go a bit too far.'

'Alec did too - I can remember us all discussing them once. He was quite put out when I agreed with Liz - I've seen similar buildings in other countries, including my homeland, Greece. Even Mother was surprised at that: she tends to think of me as being cynical all the way through.'

'And Goldie is always right!' Bethany sympathised, laughing. 'How is she, by the way? I owe her an apology for not looking after Liz as well as I ought.'

'Mother is well, if a little bored: she's staying with Alec at Leigh Manor at present, counting poachers and admiring country churches, which is very restful but not the most stimulating of holidays. When she suggested Alec's chapel would be the perfect setting for me to marry my second cousin Dominica whom she knows I detest, I fled here to escape the Te Deum of her incessant nagging - if I'm not careful, my bachelor days shall soon be over. Would you consider accompanying me on a last fling doing the town before Mother finally ties me down?'

'I would love to do the town with you, Philip, as it seems all your girlfriends left the city when they heard you were coming,' Bethany laughed, knowing to expect nothing from his invitation beyond a casual relationship and a few good times. 'If you're very good, you might get a Stanley Broome sculpture for your back garden too. As long as you respect my desire not to drink.'

'Certainly I will. I should sue Alec for slander: he has everyone convinced I respect nothing and no-one, and that is not the case at all.'

Bethany looked at Philip with a reflective smile.

'Yes, I do believe you. In my experience, the guilty often accuse others of the crime they're guilty of themselves. Pity Alec - he must envy you.'

'Not half as much as Dominica will envy you. Where shall we start tonight?'

3 : 3

Bethany called in to Terry's office for coffee as usual on the morning of the last Friday in October. Since Liz's departure she had become more involved in the work of P.S.I. as if to atone for the damage she had done in August.

Terry was convinced that Liz had decided never to come back and said so yet again once they had exhausted the latest gossip. 'There's less than a week left now; and not even a letter, or a phone call: not even a postcard.'

'What I don't understand is the attraction Cumberland has over the joys of living in London; even if her family does come from there,' Bethany said.

Terry struggled to hide her surprise at Bethany's unexpected slip. 'That's only because you're a town mouse, Bethany,' she said, hoping she might get her to give more away. 'Neither of us know what it's like to have real roots in the country and dependable family support.'

'But that's just it! Her brother hardly gave her dependable family support in the past, and I don't know that he improved when he married Sophie. The Kirkland family's always been in a sort of cold war, like each of them is in their own state of siege. Maybe that's what comes of living out in the wilds. What will happen next week if she doesn't turn up on Wednesday?'

'A vacancy will be declared, and we'll invite nominations from the delegates to elect an alternative chairman into office. But it wouldn't be the same, however capable the new person may be. Liz made a lot of changes here in twelve short months, but we're all coming to see they were changes for the good, unwelcome though some of them were at the time. She's badly missed here.'

Bethany finished her coffee and returned to Charles' section on the third floor. As soon as she had gone, Terry locked herself in the chairman's office to contact Jonathan Keast by phone. She soon found him at his city office. His greeting when she introduced herself suggested he had been expecting her call.

'Jon, I must see you tonight: it's very important.'

'I already have an engagement this evening.'

'Then cancel it, please: by Wednesday it'll be too late.'

He calculated her comment to be a guarded reference to Liz Graham and hoped she was about to betray her to him again.

'Meet me tonight at Plover's, at eleven thirty,' he instructed, and put the receiver down on her gratitude. Then he checked his diary for the week in case he needed to make an unexpected business trip.

Terry dressed for the evening reunion in the elaborate style she had always created for Jon in the before Liz days. As she painted her face, she wished it was still that time in her life, that simple, straightforward time when her father was still alive and she was still content with Jon. Liz had made her see the flaws in Jon and become dissatisfied with him; but Jon was still about town whereas Liz was not; and the information she had learnt from Bethany would make him available to her again. If she played her hand right, she might even persuade him to bring Liz back to her too. She checked her coat in at Plover's precisely on time, ready to play the scene ahead for all she was worth.

Keast was waiting for her at a balcony table, half concealed by a decorative maroon curtain round the balcony booth. He had been watching the occupants of a balcony table opposite, also half hidden by a decorative curtain, whom he was trying to identify. Barclay Plover escorted Terry to his table and introduced her to alert him to her presence. His tired face became more animated as he rose to greet her and complimented her on her appearance.

He had ordered a bottle of vintage champagne, as had been their habit two years before. Terry could see though that he was not the same: the characteristic fire in his eyes had been replaced with a more introspective intensity. She chattered away brightly to bring him out of his pensiveness, but his thoughtful gaze kept returning to the half-hidden balcony table on the far side of the dance floor. Prompted by her, he talked offhandedly about his latest acquisitions: a print co-operative he had taken over for damages after it had libelled him, and more business property deals in the Midlands. She became more and more concerned.

'Jon, are you feeling all right?' she asked at length.

'Yes, Teresa. It just seems I can't go anywhere at the moment without being followed. But where is Dr Graham if that is Philip King over there?'

Her eyes followed his across to the far balcony table where Philip King was sitting with a female companion whose features were indistinguishable from their viewpoint. Jon turned to look at Terry and remembered how Liz had once described her as the one woman who really cared for him. Her concern was obvious. For the first time in many years, he ventured to risk admitting his vulnerability.

'My ascendancy is coming to an end, Teresa. Others will start to gain the advantage over me. I know, because the presence of that man tells me so.'

'Jon, this isn't like you at all! You must be sickening from something.'

Her response warned him she loved her image of him, not the man he really was. He had long understood honesty destroyed emotional relationships based on fantasy alone, and shook his head deciding not to tell her the rest.

Bella finished the last song of her second set and left the stage to her customary applause. She arrived at their table shortly after to shatter their rapport with a few ill-chosen words. Terry greeted her with strained familiarity, anticipating her reaction.

'"Hello, Bella"?' the singer sneered. 'Don't come the innocent with me, T.C. If this meeting's work I'm a Dutch uncle.'

'But Bella, you've got it wrong.'

'You don't get cow eyes like that wrong, T.C. To think I believed you two days ago, sobbing your heart out threatening suicide because you'd betrayed Liz to him and you couldn't live with the guilt!'

'Miss Santon, your sister is only here to find a way to persuade Mrs Graham to come back, before her time runs out on Wednesday.'

'Stuff and nonsense! She just wants to run rings round you all again, and a bed for the night!'

Bella flounced dramatically off backstage. Terry gulped down her glass of champagne in embarrassment, forgetting her intention to drink only in moderation. Jon promptly refilled her glass and then glanced across at the balcony table opposite. Philip King was watching him more openly.

'Was Bella accurate, Teresa?'

She gave a wry laugh. 'Would that she were!'

Their eyes met. She wondered whether she would ever be more than his occasional sleeping partner. Fearing she was far more intoxicated than she had wanted at that stage, she tried to appeal to his vulnerable side, his fondness for P.S.I.

'Liz has got until Wednesday, Jon, but I know she won't come back unless someone makes her change her mind. P.S.I. needs her desperately. We've all tried our best without her, but it's just not enough. Pete and Charles have their own work to do without her job too, and no-one has much confidence in me anymore. It's like everyone's afraid in case they make things worse; and the members sense the lack of leadership: club activities are down to nil except for Toni Sullivan's struggling discussion group; and now the Los Angeles group has withdrawn its affiliation. If only Liz were back, everything would be fine. That's why I had to see you. I know your name isn't good in P.S.I. anymore, but you've always kept an interest in the society. Can't you do something for us now?'

He knew she was acting but could not see through it to her motive. It mocked him for his earlier intention to confide in her.

'That is not your only reason, is it?' he coaxed, his eyes compelling her to tell him the truth.

Tears crept down her cheeks. 'Must I tell you what you already know? I'd do anything to bring Liz back, to hear her forgive me.'

He freshened her glass, untouched by her tears.

'So you've come to me, after all I've done to her? Don't you realise what she must think of me now?'

She dropped her head to dab her eyes with a corner of a paper handkerchief.

'What else have I got to lose? You could always make me believe black's white when you want to, and I'm the only one. Surely you can do that with her too.'

'Not if she's convinced she's better off now than she was before. She is one of the few people I could not always persuade. I only succeeded when she herself was in doubt. She suffered much during her year at P.S.I. She fled from pain in search of peace: if she has found that, I will fail, no matter how much you believe in me.'

Terry nodded mutely and sipped her champagne as Keast continued.

'Even if Liz does come back, she will have changed. The changes in her outward appearance will reflect her inner change. She will no longer look the fashionably groomed London socialite. Would you still want her back then?'

'A lot of that was in her nature anyway. Alec and P.S.I. were the ones who changed her into the smart executive - it wasn't her own choosing. When I first met her, she wore T-shirts and jeans and things: she was no mannequin then.'

'And you betrayed her, more than once. What if she's not able to forgive you anymore?'

Forced to confront her own duplicity, Terry choked back more tears. Once again, she ran away from the sharpness of her emotions, draining her glass to blunt them in a vinous haze while she found the self-control to reply.

'I'm willing to take that gamble, Jon: how can I succeed if I don't try? If the answer's still no, I'd prefer to know the truth than live the rest of my life like this.'

She looked up at him with an anxious expression which wordlessly asked him whether he would do what she wanted. He glanced sharply across and caught her eyes. The unexpected contempt in his gaze cut through all her shamming to the small core of soul she daily prostituted in her intense emotional insecurity. She tried to move, but his eyes had arrested her.

'I will go,' he promised.

She clasped his hand in joy across the table, thanking him effusively as she passed him a slip of paper with the address he would need. He studied it thoughtfully, suspecting duplicity because of the relative ease with which he had gained the information.

'How did you come by this?'

'Bethany Broome let it slip while we were having coffee this morning, just before I phoned you. She couldn't understand why Liz is living out in the wilds of Cumberland with her brother Ricky and his wife when she never got on with them in the past.'

As soon as Terry mentioned Bethany, Keast knew the tip off was Alec Graham's ploy to lure him to his death. He looked across at Philip King, who nodded back and raised his glass. King was playing a game of double bluff, trying to make him think his companion was Bethany to warn him not to risk any involvement. Still, Alec Graham had played and lost before, and despite his own partial failure with Liz that summer, Keast still had enough confidence in the power behind him to know that if he firmly resolved to force her back, his adversary could not stop him.

'When you see Liz, please don't tell her I asked you to go.'

He looked back at Terry and laughed coldly, his laughter twisting their conversation in an unfavourable direction.

'Don't be concerned, Teresa. As you will appreciate, I have several reasons myself for going to see her.'

She glanced sharply up at him, realising in dismay that he was using her as much as she was using him. He laughed again, that cold mocking laugh which always suggested answers but never confirmed them.

'I've betrayed her to you again, haven't I.' she said huskily.

'No, Teresa. You will have Liz back with you before the end of the Discussion Group's meeting on Wednesday night. Unless she has definitely decided she will never come back. But remember, she will have changed. Don't expect her to forgive everyone merely because she has come back. Expect nothing more than her return to office. The rest will take time.'

Terry nodded and picked up her handbag to leave with him, satisfied that their barter was complete.

3 : 4

Jonathan Keast left his house that Saturday morning long before Terry awoke. He planned to visit Cumbria the following Tuesday because Halloween was an auspicious date for his cult.

Before then, he needed to get a lot done. He sent two men from his Manchester office to the Lake District to scout out the lay of the land around Liz Graham's hiding place and find out what measures Dr Graham was taking to protect her. Over the weekend, he concluded business at his London office for the next few days. On Monday night he met Hendrik Gerber during a stop-over at Manchester en route north.

Philip King followed him closely all the way to Manchester despite his attempts to elude him. There his luck changed overnight, for the next morning he gave Philip the slip with relative ease by leaving the city at five o'clock in a rented saloon car while his shadow kept a watch on his Rolls.

By eight o'clock on Tuesday morning Keast and Hendrik were two miles from the Lakeland village of Upper Beckby, rendezvousing with the two scouts at a sandstone quarry on the western edge of the Beckby valley. From their vantage point above the quarry face, they had a clear view of Blakeley End through their binoculars. The farm nestled in a fold of the fells to the south, about half a mile from the village and a mile from the lake. The scouts pointed out a small stone building about a mile from the main farmstead, built into a dry-stone wall below a craggy outcrop halfway up the fell.

'That's where she's living; but she'll not be back now before dusk - she's out on the fell-tops with her brother and his sheepdogs,' reported the elder scout. 'With the risk of fog and the boglands up there, the locals wouldn't advise a stranger to the area following them this time of year.'

Keast scanned the fell-tops with his binoculars, looking for Liz and seeing only sheep. Lower down the slopes he spotted a man settling into position on the crag overlooking the bothie. He pointed him out to Hendrik. The scouts pointed out other sentry posts: ten combat-clad men in all.

'Dr Graham is using reinforcements,' Hendrik said.

'They only watch the windows: we may still enter by the

doors,' Keast observed.

They discussed tactics. The younger scout would set out with Hendrik from the village, approaching the bothie along a public bridleway and footpath through the fields to the fell wall. Keast and the other scout would approach from the opposite direction, driving to Blakeley End Farm in a borrowed green forestry Land Rover, then cutting across the upland pasture to a larch wood covering part of the fellside to the wall. To help them pass unnoticed, the scouts put on two dark green forestry uniforms left in the Land Rover, while Hendrick wore hiking gear. By noon the two parties would take the craggy outcrop with the bothie in a pincer move and stay in position there until Liz's return.

'Just like the old days, eh, Hendrik, when we first started the run together,' Keast commented as they scanned the terrain one last time before going into action.

'Except that was for profit; and we are a lot older now,' Hendrik replied. He lowered his binoculars and warned, 'Jon, your obsession with that woman will be the death of us both.'

'Not yet, Hendrik,' Keast reassured without foundation.

Hendrik and his companion roused no suspicion as they walked into the village of Upper Beckby and left again by the bridleway towards the fell. Keast concealed himself in the back of the forestry Land Rover while the scout drove him the first stage of his journey. As he expected, a man stopped their vehicle when it turned onto the Blakeley End farm track.

'Have you seen a loose 'ound?' Sam Buxton asked the driver, his clothes and accent betraying him as an off-comer.

'Nay, but I'll keep a lookout for yan,' the scout replied, broadening his northern accent without fear of being questioned by the Londoner.

Sam thanked him and slapped the Land Rover's side as he drove off along the track. About half a mile further on, the Land Rover arrived at the farm gate and parked in the yard. Keast and the scout alighted. Sophie Kirkland strolled out of the house to speak to them, a basket of washed nappies in her arms. She was a well-built young woman, dressed in dungarees and a hand-knitted jumper, who looked more than capable of taking care of herself.

'Good morning, gentlemen: you're bright and early,' she greeted with a friendly smile, but her eyes were quick to notice Keast's overcoat and shoes were of a far superior quality to the clothes the local forestry workers wore.

The scout sensed her suspicion and said, 'Mr Rawling's over from Area Office, looking into the effects of acid rain.'

'Really? And in what way can I help you? My husband says it's because we don't lime the fields anymore,' Sophie replied.

'I'd like to check the trees in your larch wood,' Keast said: 'I know we should get written permission in advance, but formal applications take time, and I only want to have a quick look while I'm in the area.'

'Go ahead,' Sophie agreed. 'But you'd better watch you don't get taken for a rabbit while you're up there – we've had a lot of hunters round here these last few days.'

She pointed the two men towards the path to the larch wood and crossed the yard to peg out her washing. Half an hour later, as she pegged out a second bundle, two gunshots echoed across the fellside. She looked up toward the sound of the shots, along the fell wall beyond the outcrop. Seeing nothing untoward, she went back inside, presuming a hunter had shot something for the pot.

Five fields away, Hendrik stepped back into a hedgerow for a few moments to recover after an unexpected encounter. As the scout with him had clambered over a fence, he had stumbled into the range of one of Alec's sentries who had shot at him without warning. Hendrik returned his fire automatically before diving for cover. When he emerged cautiously again a few moments later he found the two other men both lay dead, the younger man in combat gear sprawling across the body of the older man in forestry green. Hendrick headed on alone across the field towards the fell wall.

In the larch wood a couple of miles away, two sentries in

combat gear speculated together about the shots and their colleagues stationed across the fellside. While they talked, Keast and his forestry green companion approached unnoticed from behind. Keast garrotted one sentry, who dropped to the ground spurting jugular blood. The scout grappled with the other sentry. As they wrestled, they missed their footing and tumbled down the steep needle-covered slope into the boulder-strewn beck at the bottom. The forestry scout struggled to his feet, gasping with the coldness of the water, and hauled himself with difficulty onto the rocky bank, his right leg badly strained. The combat sentry did not move, unconscious in the water after striking his head on a rock.

Keast scrambled down the slope after them. When he saw the forester scout's injuries, he sent him back to the forestry Land Rover as he was no longer fit for the task ahead. Once the forestry green scout had hobbled out of sight down the beck-side path, Keast crouched on the side of the bank and held the combat-clad sentry's face under water until bubbles stopped coming from his mouth. Keast climbed back out of the valley and walked on up through the wood towards the dry-stone fell wall.

Over a mile away, Hendrik scaled the fell wall and climbed further up the fellside, intending to drop down the slope onto the summit of the outcrop from above and surprise the sentry stationed there, Alec Graham's driver Theo. Oblivious to the spectacular view of the dramatic Lakeland valley, Theo was watching a flight of startled rooks above the larch wood when Hendrik struck. As Theo turned toward his footfall, Hendrik leapt down on top of him, knocking him across the flat summit to the craggy edge. They grappled fiercely above the fifty-foot drop, each struggling to push the other over without following him. Theo's training and relative youth soon told: despite Hendrik's skill, each time they rolled back towards the edge of the cliff, Hendrik was the one about to fall.

Theo held him at the cliff top and head-butted his stomach to throw him over. Hendrik kneed him sharply at the same time. The crumbling slate edge gave way beneath them. They slid over the cliff together, locked in combat. With a desperate twist, Theo forced Hendrik beneath him as they crashed down onto the rocks below. Stunned by the shock of the impact, Theo lay on top of Hendrick for several moments before attempting to move. The pains he felt proved to be just bruising and a broken arm. He hid Hendrik's smashed body between the boulders, concealed from the blind side wall of the bothie by a buttress of the crag.

Theo radioed for a replacement and alerted Alec to the surprise attack as he walked off down the fell, cradling his broken arm gingerly in his coat sleeve. He followed the dry-stone wall towards Bridge Farm and crossed the fields to Upper Beckby to seek help.

Keast had seen the start of the fight on the crag from the shelter of the larch wood, but a buttress of rock stopped him from seeing the outcome after the two men had fallen over the edge. He waited for some time, hiding among the trees until he was certain the fight was over, before he risked continuing his advance. He cautiously scaled the dry-stone fell wall and then used it to cover his traverse across the fellside moor, creeping in its shadow with his head well below the coping stones, his senses constantly alert for danger.

At length he achieved his objective and reached the crag bothie without being seen. For a few moments he stood between the window and the door of the small single-storey building, a gun ready in his hand, but heard no sound from within. He tried knocking on the door but got no response. Encouraged, he tried the handle and let the door swing open. Nothing happened: no shots rang out, no-one sprang out at him. Unchallenged, he walked inside.

His first impression was of neatness and austerity. The bothie was a building of basics and necessities alone: two rooms with a shared chimney, no plumbing, no electricity, and bare stone walls. The small living room was simply furnished with a scrubbed wooden table and a stool by the window, and a wooden rocking chair on a rag mat over the uneven flagstones by the hearth. To one side of the chimney breast some crude shelves supported a few pieces of crockery, several books including a loose-leaf file, and a few plain provisions. On the windowsill stood a trimmed paraffin lamp and a turnip jack-o'-lantern, surrounded by apples. In the black-leaded grate a fire had been laid ready to kindle, and by the hearth stood a covered ewer of water and a blackened kettle. A sturdy wooden door led off to a small bedroom which had been simply furnished with bits and pieces picked up for next to nothing.

In comparison with what Liz had left behind, her new home was a hovel; but it was clean and cared for, and Keast could understand why she had chosen to hide there. The dramatic view from the windows across the valley was superb, and the walls radiated peace and tranquillity.

Keast took down the file from the shelf and settled in the rocking chair to see what Liz had kept in it. The pages contained a record of her changing attitudes and feelings since retiring to her hermitage, as she came to terms with the past she had left behind. He read on, wondering whether he wanted to persuade her to return to the world she now shunned, while her writings gave him all the information he needed to succeed.

3 : 5

Keast heard Liz arrive back at the bothie with her brother Ricky as dusk fell. They paused on the path outside the living room window and arranged to meet again at dawn to search for more missing sheep. Against the misty grey evening light, Keast saw how similar they looked in build: slight and wiry and dark, almost Romany; but their forefathers had not been travellers as often supposed of Liz: they were descendants of exiled Celts whose pre-Christian beliefs were the source of her psychic talents and abilities. Taller, broad-faced Ricky thanked her for her help and strode off down the fellside, whistling to his sheepdogs to follow.

Before she came inside, Keast concealed himself in the bedroom.

When Liz raised the latch and pushed the door open, she knew at once that someone had entered and disturbed the tranquillity of her home. Having sensed injury and death on the fellside earlier, she assumed the hunters shooting on the fell that afternoon had sheltered in the bothie for a while to escape the biting wind. She left the door open to see her way to the windowsill in the last of the twilight, and struck a match to light the paraffin lamp and the jack-o'-lantern. Leaving the lantern among the apples on the broad stone windowsill to ward off the roving Halloween spirits, she placed the paraffin lamp on the table, and closed the curtains and the door. She set a match to the fire and took off her anorak, her knitted hat and her wet Cumberland clogs.

'Good evening, Liz,' Keast said, walking through the bedroom doorway.

She leapt round in horror, calling on God and signing herself with the rosy cross for protection. Her hand reached for a poker to defend herself.

'Keast! What are you doing here?'

'I've come to talk with you.'

He closed the bedroom door behind him and stood inside the front door, blocking her escape.

'Well, you can just walk right out again, can't you!'

'I don't usually travel three hundred and fifty miles at great risk to myself, merely to talk to someone,' he quietly countered.

'What, you expect a civil answer from me, after you scar me for life?' She thrust her left wrist towards him. 'That isn't the only place you marked me, Keast - it's all burnt just as deeply into my mind.'

'Please let me offer my sincere apologies, Liz. I made a mistake.' His persuasive tone sounded false and manipulative.

'A bloody big mistake! Or do you bugger up people's lives every day? I guess you do - you're rich enough!'

She turned aside to bank up the kindled fire with logs and

place the kettle on a hob over the flames, her hands trembling. The tasks helped her hide face as she fought with the torrent of emotions flooding her mind. Anger, revenge, hatred and grief cascaded in a kaleidoscope of self-pity, challenging her recent meditations about the need for forgiveness. Alone in her hillside retreat, it had been easy to forgive those who had hurt her, not for their sake but for her own, to stifle the resentments that would otherwise lead her to drink again. Now, faced with the object of her greatest resentment, she struggled to live by the truth she had accepted, but knew she had to rise to the challenge of this toughest test.

'You've changed a great deal, Liz, since we first met,' he said, controlling his own emotions to coax her beyond her first reaction.

She stood up to face him again. 'Aye, I have, Keast, much thanks to you. I'm now older, wiser, more experienced, more disillusioned. So I'm busy forgetting there was ever a place called P.S.I. and a place called London; a person called Bethany, a person called Alec, and a person called Terry. And I would be busy forgetting you too, only you keep coming back for more! So get out, will you? I didn't invite you here. Go away and leave me so I can go back to forgetting you too!'

'If that's what you really want, then of course I will go, and leave the recluse to her hermitage. Before I go, may I ask you a few questions? Some things have been puzzling me since August which I would like to understand. Afterwards, I promise we will never meet again. Unless you choose to see me.'

Liz gazed distractedly into the fire, torn between her mistrust of him and the reasonable sound of his request.

'After all you've done, I should send you packing now, for I know I can't trust you. But a few questions shouldn't amount to much, and I hope I can bind you to a promise.'

'You can.'

'Then you'll have to wait while I do a few things first.'

She turned her back on him to complete some household

chores with slow, methodical absorption. It gave her time to control the spectres of the past now haunting her: the memories of his systematic destruction of her life that summer, and all the sordid prostitutions she had committed in the days before her recovery eight years before.

Keast had expected her emotional turmoil now charging the atmosphere. As he watched her timeless movements, he realised how bound up his own life was with speed and haste. He realised too how his attraction to her had progressed beyond infatuation and lust.

At length she settled in the rocking chair, with her Cumberland clogs balanced against the fender to dry. He sat on the hard chair by the table and sipped the tea she had given him. Only when she gave him her full attention, did he ask the first of the questions which would make her think again.

'Liz, why did you leave London, even though you had won P.S.I. back again?'

She breathed deeply before answering, as if steeling herself for a distasteful task.

'Had I? I didn't realise I had.'

'Didn't you read any of the letters sent to you?'

'No. I came here to forget all that past life. The letters brought it all back again: all the pain, the betrayals, the loneliness. So I didn't open them - I just threw them on the fire.'

'One of those letters you threw away, invited you back as Chairman of P.S.I. You have until tomorrow to return. If you had known you'd won, would you still have left for good?'

'Oh, aye. You did your bit very well. There I was one day, busily organising an annual conference; and the next day my life collapsed round me like a pack of cards. You'd already tricked my husband away from me, but I was learning to live with that. Then you stole my work, my colleagues, my friends, my reputation, and nearly my life. You broke me. I couldn't take any more; but somehow there wasn't an end to it - Pete raving, going for you, claiming he was doing it for me; and you said, "welcome home". I saw what you meant at once. That wasn't what I wanted out of life, not that endless cycle of violence. So I left to find a new home, one with a better cycle of living. This is where I belong now.'

'But you left behind so much: how can you compare? - your house, your affluence, your food, your career, your companions. How could you turn your back on all that for this lonely existence as an unpaid farm labourer in this unsanitary hovel?'

She recognised he was using insults to rouse her dissatisfaction with her new life, but felt too tired after the rigours of the day to rise to them.

'Mind that chart I did for *Helicon*, which showed how we're complete opposites? My actions in a crisis tend to be the opposite to yours, because the rewards I seek are quite different from the goals you pursue.'

'Are you claiming that this existence is more rewarding?' His voice was disbelieving: 'So much more rewarding than your former life in the capital that you wish to stay here for good?'

'Of course it is! I have time here - time to think and beautiful surroundings to think in. I'm one with nature again: I've re-joined the common psyche; I've returned to my proper place in the order of creation. It seems strange now I didn't realise sooner how far I'd strayed from that for so long. And I'm fulfilling a childhood dream now, living the life of a hermit in disciplined solitude, helping the people around me where I can, and meditating on truth.'

He saw through the mystic imagery of her words to the erroneous spirit of self-sacrifice which was helping to hold her there, identifying the weakness in her philosophy which he could exploit to persuade her back.

'What else do you meditate on? Religion? Politics? Where you went wrong?'

She slid the poker into the fire to spread the logs so that the flames would blaze up more fiercely: the bothie seemed unexpectedly cold that night.

'Aye, I've thought on my own mistakes. And I've also thought on religion, as my small library will have shown you.'

'Do you still love God?'

His questions were prying deeper than she wished to go for him. She hesitated to answer; but he fixed his eyes on her, obliging her to tell him, compelling her to face that step beyond.

'I don't know,' she confessed. 'I used to, certainly. But then I grew proud. I still respected God, of course, but when it came to trust I began to rely on my own ability more.'

'Do you still respect God now?' he asked, turning her word games back on her.

'Oh aye. I see now how all my success came from God and all my failure from the Devil. I'd forgotten that. The material world had so mesmerised me that I came to believe I was the one who'd created my good fortune and earned it. So when you came back in August I was frightened, because I didn't want to lose any of it. That desperation was precisely why I did lose it all. Now I've turned my back on the tinsel transience of the material world. Dedicating my life to selfless service is far better for me than any amount of wealth or the greatest prestige; for the further I get from the earth, the closer I get to insanity.'

'Didn't you once dedicate your life to serving not just your brother, but the world? Which is the greater task, the harder task?'

'Serving the world, of course, but it needs someone much greater than me.'

He laughed with derision at her continuing self-deception, scorning the false modesty she used to conceal motives far less noble than she claimed. She looked up at him in alarm, fearing what he might do next when he showed her such contempt again.

'Stop lying to yourself, Liz! You've just admitted that mental comfort is more important to you than physical comfort. You've also admitted you feel happier emotionally living here. Don't try to hide behind virtuous platitudes! You've ducked out! You're simply living where life is easier for you; instead of returning to P.S.I.

where the challenge of life and the importance of your work are so much greater.'

Her eyes flashed with anger to have her continuing hypocrisy pointed out to her.

'How can I go back to P.S.I.? How can I face the members after all I'd said to them? At least they didn't condemn each other for the faults they themselves were far more guilty of.'

'Liz, when will you stop being a hypocrite? Are you still too proud to apologise to P.S.I.?'

She turned away in shame from his accusation and fiddled with the fire so that he would not see how accurate his shaft had been; but he did not need to see to know. He continued to tie her up with her own words.

'You claim you respect God. Have you apologised to him yet too? For you failed him badly when you failed to resist me.'

'What, do you blame the victim for the attack now?'

'No; but one can only blame oneself for lack of faith. Indifference is a choice too, and practical atheism has sent far more people to Sheol than worshipping the Prince of Darkness has ever done. So what do you love the most now? This land, your ancestors, God, the Devil, or yourself?'

'God, of course.'

'Really? Then how will you prove it?'

He watched her expression as his last question interlocked with the rest and completed the image he had had sought to create in her mind. She hunched forward, gazing into the fire, too caught up in the rationale of guilt and redemption to answer him, her preoccupation the proof that his task of persuasion was complete. He stood up and slipped on his overcoat to leave. She was so lost in thought she did not notice he had moved until he opened the door and turned back to tell her he was leaving.

'This is the last time we shall meet, Liz. Tomorrow I shall return to London to find a new Chairman to replace you at Neptune House, before P.S.I. falls apart completely.'

She sensed that even in his farewell he was manipulating her, but could not stop his words from having their intended effect. Suddenly she did not want him to leave, because she needed time to reconsider her decision before it was too late to go back on it. The foggy black night outside the door gave her an excuse to make that time without having to ask him to stay.

'If you want to find your way off the fell in this weather, you'd better wait for me,' she said, and slipped her clogs back on her feet.

Her offer relieved him, for he did not know who might be waiting for him in the darkness outside the bothie. He took the torch she offered him but did not turn it on and let her leave the bothie first to avoid making himself an easy target. She raised up her storm lantern to light their way.

Outside, the night was cold and damp and still. The heavy fog deadened the lamplight and the sound of their footsteps, and enveloped the sloping fellside around them in a foreshortening grey curtain of silence. Liz confidently led the way along the streaming path beside the fell wall, at one with the elements. Though she felt disturbed by the aura of death overshadowing the crag, the messages from the rocks reassured her that should anything threaten her in that eerie walk, men would spring up from the very stones in her defence.

Keast followed her cautiously, using her as a shield against Alec's men who he knew would be waiting among the rocks ready to kill him as mercilessly as he had killed two of them earlier. The eerie trek brought to his mind another bleak night when he had followed a woman who had shown him the way to a darker destination. All the women he had loved had had the power to elevate and destroy; but he could not understand even now why they had used such powers so capriciously. He stopped on the path and spoke to chase them back into the past where they belonged.

'Liz, how can you live with this solitude?'

'I'm a Celt: I am one with these surroundings. There is no solitude here,' she said. She turned back to look at him and laughed as scornfully as he had so often laughed at her.

'You thought this night was yours, Jon, didn't you; but even you are frightened now. All Hallows Eve is far older than the syncretic Christianity which adopted it and spawned your bastard faith. This night is Oidhche Shamhna, Samhain, when the gates of Hades, Ynys Wair, are open to receive the dying sun. Tonight the spirits rove the earth again to torment those who once tormented them. For the next six winter months nature will sleep with the spirits in the underworld; but if you join them now, you will not return with them in the spring.'

She turned and walked on down the path, leaving her unexpected threat hanging in the air. He hurried after her, knowing not to retaliate against her bizarre tirade because she could easily extinguish the storm lantern and disappear into the night, leaving him to the fate she had threatened to bring down upon him.

They passed through the fell gate into a ploughed field and walked down a tractor track along the dyke. Liz was still absorbed in her thoughts. Her outburst at Keast had marked the opening of an emotional box in her mind which she had kept sealed a long time. She understood at last that the grey feeling she had ignored for the past six months was a sublimated loneliness from her craving to be loved. Once again, she could feel her incompleteness like a stabbing pain deep inside. She knew she could not go on any longer without making some attempt to finish or renew the relationships she had severed so abruptly when she had left London three months before.

Out of the murky darkness loomed a field gate opening onto a metalled farm track. Liz let Keast through the gate and closed it between them.

'This is where we must part company. If you follow the lonning down to the left, it will bring you out in the centre of Beckby,' she said.

His dark, brooding eyes caught hers in the flickering yellow lamplight to make sure that his last words hit home.

'Thank you, Liz; and goodbye forever. Unless you decide otherwise, we shall never meet again.'

'There's one of your questions I haven't answered yet.'

'No matter - when you have the answer you can write to me.'

'But then it might be too late. Can you defer your decision about the chairmanship a few more days?'

'No! P.S.I. has already waited long enough for you!' His refusal bore all his former arrogance. 'If you're not at the discussion in Neptune House tomorrow evening, I shall present your successor there. P.S.I. cannot be allowed to slide down any further.'

'But I don't even know if I want to go back there!' She paused as a further realisation came to her. In a low suspicious voice, she asked, 'Why do you want me back in office so badly?'

'If you choose to return, I will explain my reasons to you; after you are accepted back.'

She shuddered at his blatant attempt to manipulate her. 'I'll give you a ring tomorrow night,' she said, trying to slip through a gap in his persuasion.

'I shall wait for you in my car, outside Neptune House,' he replied, not allowing her even that concession.

He handed back her unused torch and disappeared into the foggy darkness. She turned to cut cross the fields, heading for Blakeley End to tell Ricky and Sophie of her sudden change of plans.

3 : 6

Ricky drove Liz to the station in his red Bedford pickup early next morning. She gazed at the passing countryside, hungry to take in every detail of the fine fresh autumnal morning after her sudden decision to leave. All trace of the previous night's inclement weather had gone but for some caps of snow on the fell tops. The cold white sun shone brightly down from an azure sky.

The pickup halted outside Whitehaven station. Ricky carried Liz's rucksack onto the platform while she bought a one-way ticket to London at the booking office. She joined him on the platform with the news that the train would be a few minutes late.

'Well, if you still won't reconsider staying,' Ricky said unsurely, not wanting to see her go, 'the least I can do is keep the bothie ready for you when you need a few days off out of it all.'

A station announcement almost drowned out his last words, asking him by name to go to the booking office. He apologised and hurried off, promising not to be long. Liz fondly watched him go, presuming Sophie had forgotten to give him an important message to carry out while he was in town. Then she gazed into the tunnel through which the train would approach and hoped he would be back before it arrived.

'Liz?' asked a familiar voice.

She spun round in surprise.

'Alec!'

She was shocked to see her husband standing there, only a few feet away from her; and realised all over again how much she loved him. A torrent of thoughts flooded her mind. She wanted to run and throw her arms around him, but dared not risk yet another rejection in such a public place. She knew he would have found out about the events of the summer and feared that in his fastidiousness he would think her unclean, no longer worthy to be his wife in anything but name.

He saw the mixed emotions chasing across her thin face and realised in dismay how much she had suffered through his arrogance. No longer was she the svelte mannequin of his creation, but once more the woman of mystery he had first met only twenty-one months before, with the strange depths in her large green eyes and the enigmatic look on her heart-shaped face, haloed by her long black windblown hair.

'I hardly recognised you, Liz. Did you get my letter?'

She nodded shyly. 'What are you doing here?'

'I just happened to be in the area. Why didn't you reply?'

She laughed at his excuse, knowing West Cumberland was not a place people happened to find themselves in, and felt encouraged to think he had come there especially to see her. But then she recalled Keast's visit the previous evening. Her face fell again to realise he had not come to Cumbria to see her but to catch his enemy.

'I couldn't bear to open the envelope, Alec. But I did keep your letter - it was the only one I didn't throw in the fire.'

He felt a flash of anger to hear she had not read the apology which had taken him so much effort to write, but caught his breath. Father Jay had cautioned him to bear in mind her recent suffering when he met his wife again. He set his impatience aside.

'Then I would ask you to read the letter now, Liz: it says several things I could never tell you face to face. You look set for a journey. Are you going anywhere special?'

'I'm going back to London, to resume my work with P.S.I.'

'Good: I'm about to drive back to London - I can give you a lift.'

She shook her head. 'Not yet, Alec.' Uncertainty charged her voice and her eyes.

'Then at least accept my invitation for dinner at Briarbank tomorrow night.'

She mistook his reason for the invitation and gave him a bitter retort.

'I can give you Keast sooner than that. He'll be parked outside Neptune House tonight, during the Discussion Group's meeting, waiting for me to speak to him.'

'He will what?'

Alec grasped her shoulders in horror and turned her round so that her face was in the light. She flinched. He let her go at once as though she had burnt him, taken aback by such proof of her emotional damage.

'I'm sorry, Liz. But how can you possibly know that when you've been a recluse for the past three months?'

'Jon Keast was waiting for me in the bothie, when I got home last night, as your men will no doubt have told you. They were watching him, weren't they, when I brought him down off the fell.'

'Why didn't you cry out when he turned up? We would have come to help you.'

'I didn't know you were there too! I was too scared, and fear blocks the vision. But he didn't touch me this time - he just asked a few questions.'

'And persuaded you to return south, and arranged to meet you outside Neptune House tonight!'

'I know, I can hardly credit it myself. But there's something different about him. Something fundamental has changed, like his conscience has caught up with him.'

'Liz, don't be a fool: that man's evil! Four men died so that he could see you last night, two of them by his own hand: one garrotted, one drowned. If Keast told you he was sorry, it was only a form of words to get what he really wants, because he can't get it any other way. He almost destroyed you once. Don't give him the chance again.'

'God is far more powerful than Jonathan Keast.' Liz drew out the gold medallion Alec had given her eight months previously, the Tarot symbol of God as the Divine Fool which she still wore on a chain round her neck. 'That's what I forgot before: to match his faith in Purzson with my faith in God. God willing, I shan't forget that now.'

'Liz, please don't go. I don't want you to get hurt again.'

His unexpected concern made tears spring to her eyes. She felt inspired to respond with an apology which she knew deep down was long overdue.

'Alec, it's not your fault. I'm sorry for the way I turned on you, that day at Neptune House: you came to patch things up, but I wouldn't let you. I was the one who got me hurt since then, not you.'

He could hardly speak for knowing what he should say in return but could not. He struggled to beg, 'Please, Liz, read the letter, before we say anything more...'

The tannoy announced the train was about to arrive, and the rails started singing. Alec squeezed Liz's hand and hurried off before his emotions betrayed him further. As he turned the corner, Ricky ran onto the platform and briefly caught sight of his back.

'Sorry I was so long, Liz. What a wild goose chase that was; but where they got my name from, I don't know.' Ricky swallowed to catch his breath. 'Was that man bothering you?'

'No. What makes you ask that?'

'It's probably now't; but I'm sure I've seen that coat before; in fact several times around Beckby in the last few days.'

The train pounded into the station, distracting him. Liz's heart quickened to learn Alec had been there for several days to defend her, not just for one day to catch Keast. She climbed aboard the train and leaned out of a window to wave goodbye, her black hair billowing in the breeze. They were barely halfway through their farewells when the train moved off and she was on her way.

After saying goodbye to Cumbria, Liz took out the creased and grubby pale blue envelope she had treasured so long. Alec had written her name in his neat angular script, below which Father Jay had written her address in his cursive scrawl. It reminded her of the lifestyle she had left. Father Jay had protected her from outside pressures while she had needed the time to heal in her retreat. If she went back to Alec, the priest could no longer protect her should the pressures become too great again. She tore the envelope open and unfolded the six-page letter.

Alec's handwriting told her he had felt great emotional stress while he wrote the letter. As she read on, she understood why he had told her at the station that the letter contained things he would never admit to her face. She had not dreamt that such a change in attitude was possible in him.

In his tightly emotional script, he confessed in detail his ill-conceived plan to use her as his unwitting lure to destroy Keast, from its inception the day he had met Keast in late December, to his many failures to protect her because Keast had outwitted him at every turn. He said he had a good idea how she had been treated at Keast's house that August night and apologised for placing her in such danger. He promised her he still loved her and missed her, and whatever had happened, if she came back to him, he would not make the mistake of ever letting them become separated again.

Liz stared at the letter, furious with Alec at first for his callous treatment of her. Her anger abated when she recalled his bitterness about the deaths of his brother Kevin and his father, caused by Keast's drug trafficking. While she understood Alec's motives, she could not trust he would not gamble her life again in his obsession to exact his revenge upon Keast. She knew without doubt from his comments at the station, that he too would be waiting at Neptune House that night, hungry for Keast to put one foot wrong. Despite this, and despite her uncertainty about intimacy after Keast's rape, she wanted desperately to be back with Alec, and hoped that as Alec had never been a passionate lover, he would give her the time she needed to overcome her fears.

Inspired to respond at last, she settled down with pen and paper and scribbled a lengthy reply, while her train sped across the Midlands towards London.

3 : 7

The Discussion Group attracted far more P.S.I. members than of late that Wednesday night because of a club rumour that something unexpected would happen there. About forty people gathered in the Neptune House basement theatre to discuss *Identifying Truth in Psychic Perception*. Despite Chair Toni Sullivan's attempts to prevent side-tracking, the debate quickly fell into the trap of trying to define truth. Her team of two on stage were of little help: Pete Corrie kept wandering off the subject on tangents, while Mary Sebastian seemed too preoccupied with perceiving truth to contribute much to the discussion.

In the auditorium, Liz watched from her vantage point at the back of the audience, halfway up the tiered seats. No-one had recognised her in her casual country clothes with her hair caught up in a woolly hat, like the practical styles worn by the students present. Below her in the middle of the audience, Terry sat in uncomfortable guilt, no longer confident enough in Keast to trust that Liz would return. Diagonally below her, Bethany was craning round in her seat, unashamedly curious to know who had turned up. Down in the far corner, Charles sat wondering what he should do if Liz did not turn up, with Father Jay beside him invited there in case she did. The priest was not impressed with much that was being said, but refrained from speaking in case he dominated the debate. Instead, he whispered comments to Tim sitting on his left. Tim nodded in agreement but chose not to voice his ideas and let the discussion move on.

Suddenly Mary Sebastian realised who she had been gazing at in the middle distance. She caught Bethany's eye and nodded in the direction she should look. Bethany turned and stared at Liz, astonished that she had not recognised her friend when Liz had only returned in appearance to an earlier image. Terry noticed Bethany's interest and also looked back. When she saw who Bethany and Mary had spotted and identified Liz herself, her hopeful face fell: the change which had so disguised Liz warned her she would no longer be able to string her along.

'But the religious prophets say their truths come from God,' Pete declared: 'Where do they get this idea of God from? And where do they go to hear God's voice when we can't hear it?'

Liz sensed Pete had deliberately thrown his tangential contribution into the discussion for her to take up the point. It surprised her that he had realised she was there when others more psychic had not. Having wasted enough time struggling to find the courage for the apology she knew she must make, she clutched the medallion at her throat and spoke.

'God said through the Psalmist, *Be still and know that I am God*. When we close our senses to the things of the moment and open our minds to the eternal, we can start to perceive God and understand the nature of truth.'

The familiar voice turned every head in the theatre. They were astonished to find the woman they awaited had been hiding there in plain sight, camouflaged by her altered appearance. The youth beside her cried out, 'Liz!' and shook her hand in joyous welcome. Toni invited her to join her on stage, and though she tried to refuse, the members propelled her forward. She shed her hat and anorak and stepped down to the edge of the stage to continue her address.

'Seeing with that third eye is the starting place for using our gifts of prescience. Society either idolises our gifts or dismisses them as nonsense or even as evil. But in themselves they are not evil: they are gifts from God. As we use them, we need to be aware of the source of the power and our motives in using them. If we make the mistake of thinking the power is our own and parade our ability to read the future, we follow the lead of satan. Or we can use our gifts knowing that to rely on them alone is sin: we should rather rely on God alone and to trust only in God to look after the future.'

Liz paused to order her thoughts, and felt that familiar sharp thrill of awareness that she held the attention of everyone in her audience. She reminded herself she was only there to apologise to P.S.I.

'This summer I listened to satan's deadly lies and attributed all my successes to my skill rather than to the One who bestows all blessings. Pride, complacency and conceit made me ignore the warning signs and cut me off from the faith in God which had supported me. When I became weak enough to be deposed, I failed P.S.I. as well as myself, and for that I apologise.

'I'm grateful to you all for re-electing me in my absence. I can't hold this society to that decision, because events have changed me. No longer can I be a person of compromise on matters of faith: I rediscovered the hard way that everything comes from God, and God alone. If that's what a ballot proves this society wants in its chairman, then return this ring to me and I shall be happy to take up office again; but I shall be equally satisfied if you do not. The choice is yours.'

Liz took off her P.S.I. signet ring and handed it to Pete. She turned to walk back up the tiered seats to leave. The members rose as one to bar her way, cheering and applauding her. Hands propelled her back to the stage where Charles stood in front of the debate speakers with the ring in his hand, volunteered by Pete to answer Liz's speech. The crowd quietened as she joined him.

'Mme Graham - Liz, as we all know you - by the power given us by the members and delegates, Pete and I are happy to invite you back into the office of chairman of P.S.I. The apology should be ours, for we know we all failed you in the recent past, and we have all missed you here. Please take back the ring, and with it the position. Let us all start afresh, doing what we all joined this society to do - working to advance psychic science, education and research.'

Liz took back the ring and shook on the agreement with both Charles and Pete. The members gave her a standing ovation. Toni made no attempt to bring the meeting back to order. Instead, she closed the discussion and invited everyone to go up to P.S.I. Britain's main lounge on the third floor for an impromptu party.

The celebration was chaotic and joyous, quite different from the forced gaiety of the last P.S.I. party Liz had endured at Chalgarth three months before. Once everyone had welcomed her personally, Terry drew her to one side, requesting her help to deal with urgent society business. She went with her up to the chairman's suite on the fourth floor, with Bethany determinedly tagging along to stop Terry trying any tricks before she had warned Liz about her.

As the lift doors closed on them, the atmosphere became charged with embarrassment. Bethany felt compelled to cut the silence.

'Liz, I've got to know - have you forgiven me? I know I made a complete fool of myself with Jon Keast. I was old enough to know better than to believe him; and I didn't even get thirty pieces of silver.'

The lift doors opened onto the fourth floor. Liz stepped out onto the landing and turned to answer Bethany, finding it far easier to forgive her friend's betrayal after having publicly confessed her own faults only a short while before.

'How could I not forgive you, Beth; or you, Terry. What power have either of you got to fight satan's changeling single-handed?'

Terry watched as Liz hugged Bethany, her psychic guard relaxed in her intense jealousy. Liz glanced up at her over Bethany's shoulder and faltered to see Terry's psychic image, which had become a corruption of worms. She averted her eyes in dismay, realising that the secretary was so mentally unstable she was psychically dragging death down upon herself. Liz's changing expression made Terry feel even more jealous and resentful. Bethany broke off the friendly embrace, oblivious to Liz and Terry's exchange of looks, and led Liz along the passage towards Terry's doorway and the chairman's suite.

'Glad you're back, Liz, but what took you so long?'

'The truth may be a lot easier to find than people realise, Beth, but it can still take time.'

Bethany deftly turned in the doorway to Liz's office after Liz had entered and shut Terry out, locking the door with a cheerful promise she would not keep her waiting long.

'Well, it's certainly done you good to get away,' she continued conversationally while checking the switches on the telephone. 'Yes, you look much younger, and a lot more peaceful - the way you used to look when you and Fran shared that garden flat.'

'Ah, country air works wonders, you know,' Liz returned,

guessing what her friend was about.

Bethany emphatically switched off the intercom button. Her voice dropped.

'You know you mustn't trust that woman, Liz.'

Liz nodded and dropped the venetian blinds to shut out the night.

'There's no need to arrange her dismissal: she's already dead.'

Bethany looked at her friend in alarm, her skin going cold. Liz gave her an enigmatic smile.

'Spiritually speaking, of course. What did she do?'

As Bethany replied, Liz opened her rucksack and changed into her grey Sunday dress.

'She only betrayed you again, to Keast last Friday night; and that was just the down payment! Your stylish Greek brother-in-law and I baited a trap for her that morning - I casually let slip you were in Cumberland. Before the day was out, she was in Keast's arms.'

'And four days later he was at my bothie, persuading me to come back.'

Liz sighed, dismayed that despite the promise in his letter, Alec had again set her up as a lure to catch Keast. Once again, he had failed to protect her.

'Oh, no: I've betrayed you again too, haven't I!'

'I thought you'd already got the measure of Philip King.'

'He's changed a lot since I first met him at your engagement party. How long does it take to learn Greek?'

'Longer than it takes Philip to have an affair, so don't burn your fingers again!'

Bethany gave an arch smile and crossed to the door. 'Ah, but you're not the only one to get Goldie's approval, since I gave up the retsina. Are you ready?'

Liz slipped on a pair of plain grey court shoes to compliment her demure grey jersey dress. Though her quick change had transformed her appearance, she still did not have that polished look which had been her hallmark before she had disappeared north. She nodded. Bethany unlocked the door and flounced out.

'She's all yours, Terry.'

Terry stalked warily into the chairman's office, surprised to see yet another change in Liz.

'What was all that about?' she asked.

'I think Bethany's in love again.'

But Terry knew that Bethany had been talking about her, just as she knew everyone else in the society talked about her behind her back. She fetched through some papers for signing and watched Liz closely as she read through each document before scribbling her signature where required.

'You've changed, Liz,' she said at length in a low voice.

Liz looked up from the last sheet of paper, her expression firm to keep her distance. That confirmed Terry's fears that Bethany had betrayed her. The secretary turned away in alarm, too bound up in her own imaginings to notice Liz blanch and steady herself against the desk with a premonition of danger.

'You're a lot harder, Liz: I didn't even recognise you at first. Guess I was expecting the Liz who left, not this version of you.'

'I've been living a hard life,' Liz replied, sounding distant as she tried to shake off the distracting premonition. 'It's a world of realities I mustn't forget now I'm back with P.S.I.'s false facades.'

'Why didn't you write back to us, at least tell us where you were?'

Liz signed the last document and stood up by the window. She made a chink in the venetian blind to look out at the busy evening streets. Already the sinister city was crowding in on her through the rain-washed night. She recalled the friendly village she had left behind that morning and felt a stab of regret that circumstances had forced her to put that part of her life behind her again. Discarding her regrets, she turned back to answer Terry.

'I wouldn't have recovered at all if I'd let myself listen to any of you. I didn't intend coming back.'

Terry bowed her head lower, hoping that a confession would

undo the damage Bethany had done her cause.

'I didn't think you'd come back either. That's why I asked Jon Keast to help.'

Liz looked back, startled to hear her admit her betrayal so readily. Terry gave an odd laugh and raised her head to look Liz defiantly in the eye.

'Jon's the best person I know for making a person do something they've set their heart against. I knew, if he could just talk to you for half an hour, you'd come back to me.'

She crossed to Liz's side at the window and pulled down a slat of the blind to gaze out at the night as she continued her confession, her manner more rehearsed.

'I'm scared of Jon, but I would do anything to have you back here. So on Friday I rang him. He took me out to Plover's. Bella was there - she tried to cause a scene; but he just ignored her. We sat and drank champagne and he bored me stiff talking about some magazine publisher he'd just taken over, prints the *Iron Fist*.'

'Oh, no; don't say he's bought out Guy Simms because of me.'

'Bailed out rather than bought out, I believe - he shopped the printer to the police for publishing subversive literature, then used his influence to get the charges dropped in return for the business. Not that I remember much from that night - he got me that drunk. I did ask him to go and fetch you. Then I thought, I've just betrayed Liz again, but he said I hadn't. He gave me lots of reasons why you wouldn't come back, but when I still insisted, he agreed to go anyway. And here you are.'

Liz moved away to the desk with a reflective smile. 'How much did you pay him for that?' she asked, recalling Bethany's comment about the down payment and suspecting Terry was paying on hire purchase.

'Nothing much: at least, nothing he hasn't had from me before.' She turned away from the window, her face accusing. 'And as you already know, he wasn't there for me at all - he was there for you, for himself. He's down there now, isn't he: waiting for you!'

Terry's body began to shake with increasing hysteria. Her voice rose in a mounting crescendo.

'You're desirable to him again now, Liz - you've come back here and you've said yes. He's lured you back into his trap; and like a fool, you're running straight in!'

Terry thought her wild outburst would deter her, but Liz read it quite differently. She saw through it to the forces of evil which were trying to stop her from seeing Keast once more. His faith in Purzson must be weakening and her testimony might persuade him to repent. To Liz, Terry's attack only confirmed she would be doing the right thing in going to speak to him once more.

Liz psychically sheathed herself in the blue-white light of God's truth to protect herself from Terry's onslaught. She lifted the phone and called Father Jay in the P.S.I. Britain lounge, asking him to leave the party and meet her in the entrance foyer. As she replaced the receiver and gathered her shawl to go, Terry sprang into the doorway to stop her.

'You're a fool if you try to speak to him, Liz,' she screamed. 'I promise you, this time Jon will destroy you!'

'No, Terry, he can't touch me now. So start praying, in case the one who'll be destroyed is really you.'

Terry blocked the door to stop Liz leaving the office, looming over her in fury. Undaunted, Liz manhandled her aside as she would have shifted an awkward sheep the day before and shut the door on her.

Liz strode resolutely out of the chairman's suite towards the fateful rendezvous.

3 : 8

P.S.I.'s entrance hall was in darkness when Liz stepped out of the lift. The only light shone in from the streetlamps outside the large plate glass doors. Father Jay greeted her softly from the shadows. He was standing there alone.

'I'm glad you made it back, Lisbeth; but must you really tempt the Devil so? His man is waiting over there, and not one word would I trust from him.'

Liz gazed out across the street to the electronics shop opposite. In the dark entrance to the service alley beside it, she could make out the shadowy outline of the bonnet of Keast's midnight blue Rolls.

'It wasn't his words that convinced me, Father Jay, but because someone tried to stop me from going to him. Is Alec here?'

'Yes, your husband is here. What do you expect? I told him to leave the vengeance to God, but he wouldn't listen. Even he's under the spell of Keast's evil.'

'I have a letter for Alec. Would you take it for me before I go?'

'Sorry: I've given up playing postman for you - it took too long to get a reply. You'll find your husband waiting in the shadows, just like Mr Keast, but his car's in the entrance to your carpark. I suggest you deliver your letter yourself after you've spoken to Mr Keast; though why you should put yourself in such danger, I don't know: there is no need for you to do so.'

'What, is this man not permitted to repent?'

Father Jay sighed and shook his head. 'That is not what I meant, Lisbeth: to be sure, even a demon-worshipper is worthy of spiritual guidance back to the Divine Path; but it is most unlikely he would ask. Let me go talk to him, in your stead.'

'No, Father: it was me the Devil tried to stop just now through Terry, not you. Keep watch for my secretary when I walk out there. She's very disturbed and she may try to stop me again.'

'Lisbeth, the Devil will not let him go easily.'

'Not even with my prayers for him to be saved? Jesus said, *Do good to those who hate you, bless those who curse you, pray for those who abuse you*. Beauty wept for the beast and made him human again. God made Tim better through me once - can God not make Jon Keast better through me too?'

'Yes, God can, if that is truly your motive for going to speak with him. But are you sure you're not after vengeance of a kind too?'

'I don't think so, Father. I prayed for him last night, for the first time since it happened; and all the hatred and the resentment I'd felt suddenly disappeared. I pitied him, his fear as we walked off the fell through the foggy night. I didn't have that fear, because I knew God was keeping me safe, even from him. But all he had was his conscience, the coals heaped on his head as I led him down that stony path through his enemies.'

Father Jay nodded in understanding, relieved to hear her spirit of forgiveness despite all the man had done to her.

'Then go do God's will, Lisbeth; and I shall pray for you all, while you go out and walk on water.'

'Thanks, Father. And thank you for always being there, ready to save me before.'

She gently squeezed his right hand, adjusted her black shawl over her shoulders and stepped out into the damp misty night.

A light rain fell greasily on her forehead as she crossed the pavement to the busy road. She sensed eyes watching in tense concern while she waited at the kerb for a break in the traffic and used the moment to hand the meeting ahead over to the care of her Higher Power. With renewed serenity, she crossed the street and turned down into the shadows of the service alley.

Nicholas stepped out of the driving seat of the Rolls and opened the nearside rear door for her. She peered into the car and saw Keast sitting at the far side of the rear seat, barely discernible in the twilight. She joined him inside. Nicholas shut her door and walked away, leaving her to converse with his father in private. Keast coughed to veil the operation of the central locking system.

'So, Liz, you came back to London after all.'

'Yes, Jon. I've also accepted the chair again. I know God knows how much I love Him without me having to prove a thing;

but your questions reminded me of some duties I was neglecting. So I've come back to do my duty again. Now will you answer my question?'

'Which was?' His contemptuous tone taunted her for revealing that mere curiosity had steeled her to sit alone beside him in the back seat of his car despite their common past.

'Why did you go all the way to Cumberland to speak to me?'

'I destroyed my chances of chairing P.S.I. again in August when I tried to destroy you. No-one has the courage to run the society well. Even Corrie and Lafayette together could not stop its slide downhill. You're the one the members want, no-one else. I had no intention of writing off twenty years' work when all I needed to do to save P.S.I. was find two days to visit you and persuade you to come back.'

She looked into his shadowed face, unable to equate his plausible answer with the risks he had undergone and the deaths of the four men his visit had incurred. In the darkness she could see the psychic shroud of death highlighting his silhouette. Waves of turmoil eddied around his screened thoughts, a sign she had expected. It gave her the confidence to go on.

'Jon, don't lie to me now - the shadow of the Reaper is at hand. I know you had other reasons. Tell me, before it's too late. Your confidences will be safe with me.'

Astonished to hear her inviting him to confess, he turned back to look at her earnest face, visible in the reflected light of a streetlamp. Her gullibility seemed to have no limits.

'It isn't easy for me, knowing that this is the last time we shall meet. You have entered the limelight again. Reporters will soon arrive at Neptune House to hound you about the last three months. I may stand in the wings and watch your latest performance, but you will never see me again on your stage.'

He studied her face as she looked at him through the darkness. Though her image had changed yet again, her effect had not: she still ignited his desire the way her presence had always done since the day they had first met. He strove to contain his lust, knowing that to yield to such a hunger at that moment would be fatal.

'Then you're content for me to take your place at P.S.I. for good, if that is what the members want?'

'Revenge tastes sweet but would be misguided here. And love too would be misguided, yet I cannot deny that I love you.'

Her head dropped and she twisted her fingers tightly together as she strove against the impulse to escape before she had completed her task there. He sensed her nervous reaction and looked at her eyes, willing her to look up into his while he still had the power to quieten and reassure. When her gaze met his, he spoke on.

'Try to forget the past, Liz: the past was a mistake for which I shall pay beyond the grave. I couldn't have created such an empire from nothing without spiritual help; but oh, how the Son of the Evening toys with his subjects! Once I was content with my way of life. But then you came along and changed everything. You made my soul revolt within me. I can't sleep for the torment in my mind.'

He glanced briefly away, thinking he had caught a fleeting sight of one of Alec's men outside. When nothing further moved, he turned back to gaze in Liz's eyes.

'For a while I thought to free myself from my bond. The terms to cancel my contract with the Prince of Darkness included your death. Cunning Purzson! He knows you were the one who sowed these seeds of regret in my heart - with you gone, I would return to the life you made me despise. Three months ago, I sought to kill you but failed. Your weak faith at its lowest ebb proved stronger than our triumphal power at the climax of our worship. Too late I discovered your Higher Power is stronger than mine, your way of life is a viable alternative to mine. Since then, I have lived in turmoil. But it is worth the repentance if I can win your respect.'

The flattery in his confession did not deceive Liz.

'There is a way back, Jon, but it isn't easy. You will need to do it for yourself, not just for the hope of winning me, or you will fail the moment I say no. It's not just two *Hail Mary*s, then you're free.'

'I realise that! After spending over thirty years taking from the world on my terms, I can hardly expect one prayer to make everything better. Tell me what I should do.'

'That I can't tell you. I can only tell you what happened to me.'

Liz described her own descent into hell as a youth and her miraculous release from a living death while still in the springtime of her adult life. She had shared different aspects of the same recovery story with many people standing at the crossroads of the spirit, and could recognise when her shares had changed those who heard her. Though Keast gave her message the consideration she expected, it did not seem to touch his soul.

'It is a great step,' he said at length.

'Jon, if you're only trying to evade the consequences of the end of your contract, I'll stop wasting my time here - Father Kingston will be of far greater help to you than I can be,' she warned, her left hand reaching for the door catch.

'Wait, Liz! You know your husband's men already surround us. The moment you leave this car I will be dead.'

She drew back her hand. 'Not if you are sincere in your desire to put your past life behind you and start again.'

'The Prince of Darkness is strong, Liz, far stronger than you or me. No man on earth is strong enough to withstand his power, and that is what holds onto me.'

'Aye, but God is stronger: Purzson only exists because God gives him leave to be. God will throw him down from the stronghold of your soul if you just ask. With God's protection you will walk away from here alive no matter what surrounds you.'

'Then you will go with me? - take me across to Neptune House now and arrange for me to speak to the priest who rescued you from my house?'

'Not this time, Jon. I shielded you from Alec once, last night, without realising it. I shan't shield you again.'

'But Liz, leave me here, and you leave me to certain death. Is that the help that saved you?'

'Yes, Jon, it was. I too had to take that first step of faith, to place my full trust in God for the slender hope of a second chance in life, or stay as I was and die before the new year. That's the choice you face when you finally realise what you've lived by, you're about to die by. It's your decision, Mr Keast. Goodbye.'

Liz turned the handle to open the car door but found it locked. Keast caught her right arm to hold her back. She cried out in alarm and pulled away from him, her shawl coming off in his hands.

The car's central locking system clicked and three of the doors swung open. Keast looked fearfully up at Alec over the muzzle of his revolver as Sam pulled Liz out onto the pavement and Philip leapt into the driving seat. Five silenced shots thudded into their target. Keast fell back, dead, emblazoned with the sign of the cross in bullet holes and blood.

Alec and Sam sprang back from the Rolls and slammed its doors as the engine came to life. Philip drove the car onto the main road, hoping to take away the evidence of the killing before anyone realised what had happened. Terry was too quick for him though: having seen the shooting from the entrance hall, she raced across the plaza with Father Jay in pursuit.

'Jon, come back!' she screamed.

Her escape distracted Theo who had been struggling with one arm in a sling to restrain Nicholas Keast in the shadows of the close. Nicholas broke free from his grip and sprinted across the plaza to grab Alec roughly from behind.

'What have you done with my father, you bastard?'

Theo caught up with him and smashed his plaster-cast covered arm across his head. As Nicholas dropped, stunned, to the pavement, tyres squealed further up the street. Alec and Liz looked up to see a car skid across the greasy road and plough into Terry. She tumbled across its bonnet and screamed as she fell under the wheels of a van.

'Terry!' Liz cried, and leapt forward to help her, slipping from Sam's grasp.

Alec caught her and held her back. At first, she fought against the strong imprisoning grip. Then she realised it was her husband who held her and turned to him in tears, pressing her face against his shoulder. He wrapped his arms around her in a protective embrace.

'Alec! Not Terry too,' she cried.

He looked at Sam over her shoulder and nodded a command for him to take Nicholas away before the police arrived. Theo flagged down a taxi in the slowing traffic and Sam bundled Nicholas inside, leaving the scene with him.

Liz pulled against Alec to go to the lifeless body lying in the gutter. He tried to pull her away but she insisted on seeing Terry one last time. Father Jay glanced up at them from where he knelt on the kerb beside the dead young woman.

'I'm sorry, Lisbeth. I did try to stop her - I'll be carrying the bruises for weeks.'

'It's not your fault, Father: she brought it on herself. I'd always hoped one day she'd get better too.'

'There's nothing you can do here now. I'll wait with her till the ambulance arrives. You two run along home.'

'But she's dead, Father; and the people at P.S.I. will be missing me.'

'No: go, Lisbeth - you've done enough by saying you'll come back. Leave the rest of us to it and carry on talking with your man now you've gone beyond the letters stage. Merciful heavens, it's about time you two started putting each other first instead of your own careers!'

Both Alec and Liz protested, but he ignored them and turned back to Terry. Alec led Liz away to his hidden limousine, leaving Theo with the priest. As they crossed the plaza together, Liz took an envelope out of her pocket and tore it up. Alec asked her what it was. She turned to look at him and realised that his psychic image of the sword had gone. Instead, she saw the image of a pillar.

'This was the letter I wrote back to you, Alec. It said... Well, it doesn't matter now: Keast is dead, so that's the end of it, your obsessional vendetta.'

'Yes, Liz: I've finally won.'

He had always imagined he would feel elated at this moment. Instead, his emotions were far more mixed. A part of him mourned the death of a motivation which had driven him for many years. Yet he also felt free, in a way he had never felt before; as though he had escaped from some oppressive spell and had walked out of darkness into light. Threaded through this was his guilt-tinged joy to have his wife back at his side.

He cradled her in a caring embrace which made her feel safe and appreciated. When he had settled her in the front seat of the Lincoln, he looked thoughtfully at her and gave her another hug.

'Liz, can we start all over again?'

'Just don't expect too much of me at first?'

He reached across and kissed her. She pulled back a little. He broke off and fondly cradled her head against his shoulder, sensing her unasked question.

'Don't worry, Liz. I'll wait for you,' he promised.

He kissed her forehead and released her, freeing himself to start up the Lincoln and drive her away from the heart of the nightmare city. She rested her head against his shoulder as he drove, the way she had done on another dark and rainy night more than a year before. This time, when the car stopped, he put his arm around her shoulders and felt glad she was there once more by his side.

'To Chalgarth?'

'No: I'd rather not go back there, ever again.'

He nodded and drove on south, to Briarbank and the quiet suburb Liz had left nine months before. As they parked on the shingle drive, Liz looked up at the homely lights in the windows of the Tudor-style house and wished she had never gone away.

He opened her door and helped her alight. She stood with him in the drive and held his firm hand in her trembling fingers.

'Thank you, Alec, for taking me back.'

'Thank you, Liz, for wanting to come back. And welcome home.'

THE END

www.ingramcontent.com/pod-product-compliance
Lightning Source LLC
Chambersburg PA
CBHW070450260626
47161CB00004B/1263